SURROGATE COLONY

To my first nephew,

Love you to the moon & back.

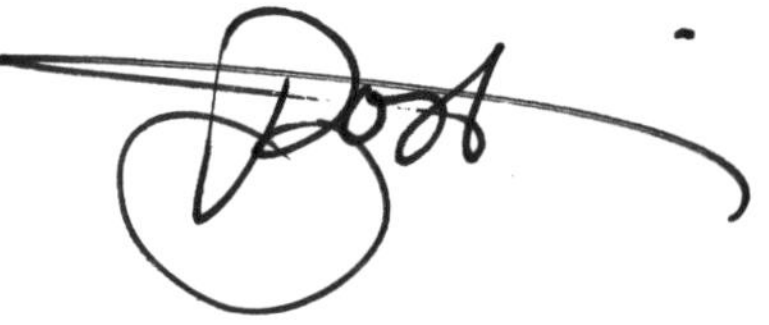

27 June 2022

To my first nephew,

Love you to the moon & back.

Dot

SURROGATE COLONY

BOSHRA RASTI

atmosphere press

Published by Atmosphere Press

Cover design by Senhor Tocas

Atmospherepress.com

For every innocent questioner,
for every faultless outcast...

Chapter 1:

Read and Hide

Crouching down, I fish the book from under my bed, *Successful Relationships*. It's a book about relationships before MicroScrep. A shot of intrigue ripples through me. They would do the unthinkable to have babies then. There were even pictures about how it was done. I shouldn't be reading it, but I can't stop.

A rapping sound startles me as I shove the book under my bed. A few seconds later, I open the door to Zach.

"You scared the Mills out of me!" I breathe a sigh of relief. A knowing smile etches itself on his face and then he looks down shyly. "Has Laura not noticed it's gone?"

Zach shakes his head. "No, but I'll need you to get through it before the ceremony."

"Do you think she'd ever try to do any of that stuff in the book with Cody?"

Zach's sister, Laura Molten, has been matched with my brother, Cody, by Harmony, the database that collects our biological and social data from birth. On our eighteenth birthday it matches us with a Perfect Matched Pair—someone who is perfect for us according to its data. Their ceremony is in a few days' time. How can someone like Cody be matched with Laura? They seem diametrically opposed.

"No! She's really regimented about taking her pills and is faithful to the system. She wouldn't question it...like someone I know." He wags his finger at me.

"You're so boring!" I pout and then my eyes narrow. "I want to try something that I read in that book."

Zach's face turns red with embarrassment. He is thinking of the unfathomable, what MicroScrep deems preposterous.

I snort a laugh. "No, silly, not that. I'm not that crazy, and you take your meds every day, or else you would've been flagged by now. Let's, what's the word...slow dance."

After some cajoling, Zach holds the small of my back securely and we sway to the sound of nothing. The book called this 'intimate.'

"Pre-MicroScrepians danced this way to instrumental music." My voice carries a twinge of longing. "They danced during weddings, something like our bonding ceremony."

Zach sighs softly. I want to think he's hoping that we'll be matched just like Laura and Cody. I wonder what was so terrible about pre-MicroScrepian music that it was outlawed? It must be better than what we have now, a deafening electronica. One can only bob to it like a lonely boat on the swells of the sea.

"Wouldn't this be so much fun to do at a ceremony," I whisper in his ear.

I smile at Zach as we move slowly around the room. "This will be just another one of our secrets. It's not so terrible if we look at it that way."

I hear the downward hover of Mother and Father's vehicle as they park. We instantly let go of each other as I scramble to grab the book and press it against his chest.

"Quick, Zach, out through the window."

Chapter 2:

The Wedding

There is a distinct moment during any Bonding Ceremony when the bride sees the groom and a connection is made. It's all artificial of course. The drugs give you enough oxytocin to sustain the nurturing bond that is characteristic of the family groups—that's the official line. I would call the bond forced at worst, and lackadaisical at best.

"She likes what she sees, Adriana," my mother whispers in my ear. "The pills have worked their magic again." She smiles, her eyes hazy with the drugs she takes regularly. They create more oxytocin, or the bonding hormone, in the blood stream.

Cody looks back at his bride, Laura, with platonic endearment. I recall him nervously taking another vial of oxytocin this afternoon, worried he wouldn't feel a bond. We've questioned the drugs before. When we were kids, we were forced to take the large tablets with gulps of cold water to bond with our parents who were given to us by Harmony.

Easy familiarity is frowned on in MicroScrep. No extremes of any sort. We would make good robots— except Cody and I, we've always bonded over our questions. Ones that we learned to hide from our mother and father.

My eyes zero in on Laura. She's altogether different—enigmatic and aloof. I shared some classes in high school with her. She was always a top student, and the teachers loved her. Her obedience to the system is probably the reason for her current position working with Harmony. It's rumored that she's a descendant of Arthur Mills, the founding father of MicroScrep, but that information isn't available. It is housed safely in Harmony. Besides, biology doesn't matter in MicroScrep, where a database is deemed a better determiner of our fate. At some point in high school, Cody and I stopped asking questions. Instead, we found solace in sharing our questions with each other about the system we were born into.

I scan Laura for viruses using the X-ray vision that all MicroScrepians are given at conception, though mine has always performed differently than my family's. I'm pretty sure it's because of my wonky eyes, one brown the other blue—the medical name I learned in childhood was heterochromia. I was obsessed with knowing about my condition when it was pointed out to me in kindergarten, that was until mother and father bought me a brown colored contact lens and insisted that I refrain from talking about my differences to anyone. My eyes aren't normal in our society, where every person is ensured by Harmony to be free of defects. I'm pretty sure that my eyes must work differently than others, although I haven't confirmed it in years.

Laura's veil flutters and is swept away by the breeze as

she walks slowly down the aisle toward Cody. Usually, weddings are only performed in the MicroScrep Registration Hall, with only two witnesses from each side of the family. The beach is an odd place to have a ceremony. The humidity might harbor bacteria or viruses, but they have taken precautions, misting the air with antibacterial spray and wiping down the seating.

MicroScrep has just allowed these types of Bonding Ceremonies, but only if all are vigilantly scanning every few minutes or so. During the great plague of 2119 CE, what was left of the population banded together under the only politician who survived, Arthur Mills. He promised the people life, hope, and cleanliness under a new country, our country, MicroScrep.

Arthur Mills launched a vaccination campaign that we still apply to this day. All MicroScrep citizens were logged into Harmony, a computer database that was originally used to track citizens in the event of a virus outbreak, but now we use it to provide Perfect Bonding Pairs and Perfect Family Matches for citizens. Cody and Laura, though, I secretly doubt whether they'll be the best of matches. I look at her with her back towards me and squint, as if I am trying to find the slightest movement out of alignment with what she's supposed to be feeling today.

I look at the small crowd gathered around. Standing beside Laura is her brother, Zach. He turns and winks at me. I am sure that we'll be assigned to each other in Harmony. I can't imagine anyone else having a better bond than we share. When I look at Zach in this light, his green eyes glow iridescently. A rush of warm memories flood me. He motions me towards him. As I approach him, an anxious thought ripples through me. What if I'm not

Zach's Perfect Bonding Match? I'm terrified of telling anyone about the feelings I have for Zach. It is unnatural to have such feelings for anyone other than your Perfect Family Match, or Perfect Bonding Pair, and Harmony has yet to assign me a position or match in society.

Father is standing in front of Laura and Zach at the flower arch. He fumbles with papers and clears his throat.

"Thanks be to the Harmony database and the great country of MicroScrep that we are all gathered here today. I remember the first time I laid eyes on Cody. The Eunuch who brought him from the off-grid Surrogacy Center laughed when he saw Cody instantly coo at us. Praised be to Harmony." Father chuckles. "That such bonding happens so naturally. Long live MicroScrep, long live Harmony."

The crowd roars with applause. Father laughs and clears his throat to find his place on the page.

"Cody's mother and I were a newly assigned Perfect Bonding Pair, and Harmony quickly found Cody to be perfectly paired for us in temperament and genetics. Not long after, we were given our dear Adriana too."

My face flushes. I didn't know he was going to mention me in his speech.

"Some families wait so long for a Surrogate to be able to birth a child for them, but we were given the opportunity quite soon after our Ceremony. I hope this is the case for Cody and Laura. I hope Harmony will assign many children to you! We hope that your bond serves MicroScrep and that you will both forever be free of disunity, viruses, and bacteria!"

The crowd claps loudly and Zach pops open a bottle of sparkling water. The fizz strays toward the sea. Cody and

Laura scan each other before the customary distanced hug.

The ceremony continues and guests filter into a reception hall, with a quartet playing classical MicroScrepian music, an electronic monotone that bothers me. While everyone scans for viruses, I wonder how much longer MicroScrep will allow for such a divergence from norm.

Cody comes home with us after the ceremony. “Mom, tell us again about what your great-grandmother said about marriages in the past?”

Mother laughs. “They were so barbaric. First, they’d kiss instead of hug. Terribly disturbing, and it would cause all sorts of microbes to move between the pair. When one was sick, the other became sick too.”

Sometimes Mother reminds me of a parrot. She’s like a MicroScrepian history book. MicroScrep is much more controlled now. After that first plague ravaged the world, a second virus, this one spread through sexual acts people used to commit to have babies, made its way through the population. It was decided that the only way to get rid of the virus was to change the culture. All were given medication to control their sexual impulses, all sexuality was deemed unclean and hazardous to the health of society. MicroScrep decided that pure love was to be revered. The family unit was to be safeguarded. The only change was the inability to have conjugal relations.

“People were so reckless and disorderly then,” Mother continues, despite the silence. “Like animals with no rule of law, no technology to keep everyone in order. And that wasn’t the worst of it. They’d do the unthinkable to have babies. Complete brutes! Venereal diseases were what caused the plagues that killed off ninety-five percent of the population of the world before MicroScrep and Harmony were established. Thank goodness for Harmony and MicroScrep for sorting all that out."

Cody yawns and nods his head. "Gross!"

Mother brushes his hair out of his face as Father weaves in and out of traffic.

"I can't wait to be a grandmother. I hope the Surrogacy Center is able to provide you with a temperate child that matches you and Laura in all the right ways soon enough." She looks lovingly at Cody and then to me. "Then you'll be able to have a home together under one roof. What a blissful existence!"

A car's horn beeps loudly beside us. Mother looks through the mirror and bursts into laughter. Laura's father, mother, Zach, and an older man—maybe in his late forties—that I don't recognize are in the car next to us.

"Who's that man sitting beside Zach?" I ask out loud.

"Oh, that's Kevin," Cody says. "He plays soccer with Zach and me. He's someone high up in the Harmony database. He's an engineer for it."

I look in the rearview mirror at my reflection, my mismatched eyes hidden with a custom, brown contact lens. You'd have to look incredibly close to notice the pixelated pattern of color, ever so slightly different than the natural brown in the other eye.

"Really?! I have a slight grievance about my eyes," I say half-jokingly. Cody turns, sticks out his tongue, and throws a tennis ball that he's found in the cup compartment at me. Mother looks back at me with a frown. "I told you not to speak about that out loud!"

I don't know how I came to have one blue and one brown eye. The scientists must have gotten it mixed up when they did my genetic testing before I was born. It's very rare that a doctor who does the Endowing gets it wrong, but freak accidents happen; we're all human, right? Maybe he was inebriated. Scientists are exempt from the alcohol ban in MicroScrep, needing something to curb the stress of their job. Perhaps absent-minded, getting the DNA peptide nucleic acid calculations wrong. Anyways, it is what it is. I've embraced my freakishness.

But still, I wonder how can you get something like that wrong when we all start out in petri dishes? Wasn't the point of the "In-Vitro for All Campaign" to not have to worry about abnormalities? Arthur Mills, the founding father of MicroScrep, had a lazy eye, I saw in one of the history books at school. Arthur Mills created MicroScrep with the help of only one hundred scientists who were caught in a gas explosion after the Cleanliness Campaign had been launched. Only seventy bodies were found, but all the scientists were immortalized in MicroScrep for their contributions. I wondered if they had abnormalities too. I have a stubborn sense that some things have been deliberately kept out of the history books. I look at my mother's oblivious smile and am sure of it.

When I commented about Arthur Mills's eye to my teacher in high school, she swiftly tutted me. "Don't ever say that again! The photographer' timing must have been wrong!" I still remember Laura scoffing at my comment. In fact, that's the only time Laura really reacted to anything I said in school, although she did have an air of ruthlessness about her.

I still have a hard time believing what the teacher and the textbooks said. What I don't understand is how people are selected for their positions in society. Like, can I have the specific algorithm please? That bugs me; there are certain people I frankly don't want to be matched with. Harmony is supposed to be all knowing, having algorithms to figure that out. I reckon the chip that is inserted in us as embryos collects that information too, as well as giving us X-ray vision. As a child and young adult, I would ask these questions, but aside from a vague answer and a reprimand, I was given nothing.

I vividly remember the principal in high school calling a meeting at school with my mother and father. Mother was nervous that day, pleading with us, "Cody and Adriana, if you don't stop asking questions at school, it can affect your position in society. Don't you want to be successful and well-regarded?" Strange that Mother worried about saving face and now Cody has been matched with Laura, who has a fine job working with Harmony.

This makes me wonder, how does MicroScrep tick? I realize I've been given a golden opportunity to find out with Laura being my sister-in-law now. She is an engineer at Harmony, but what does she do exactly? How much influence does she wield? It is wildly wrong to ask her upfront, and anyways, she isn't the kind of person you can really ask such a question to. In fact, a certain type of person only seems to get jobs at Harmony. Mother's voice rings in my ear, "curiosity killed the cat." But my favorite teacher, the late Ms. Bonito, said something to me on the eve of her untimely death that I won't ever forget. "Adriana, it is true that curiosity killed the cat, but satisfaction brought it back." Her eyes twitched with emotion as she said that to me. On her way home from school, she was killed in a car crash.

Chapter 3:

Parade

"I can't find the darn flags anywhere!" Mother is in a frenzy looking for the flags that she has stored from last year's National Day. "I am certain I left them in this storage box."

I walk over to her and help her rummage through the large storage container.

"Found it." I pull the flag out. The flag is crinkled, the colors of MicroScrep sit crumpled before us, an army green with a pure white circle in the middle.

"Cody is in the parade today. Laura got him on one of the floats that re-enact Arthur Mill's founding of MicroScrep. He's one of the sick who died because of the diseases that ran rampant before Harmony. He'll be covered by this flag, a dead, motionless lump." Mother's eyes sparkle with pride.

"That's a bit strange," I start to protest, but Mother stops me as usual.

"Adriana. Stop. Just, please, stop. It's National Day. Be

grateful that Laura was able to make him a participant. Because of this we can be part of the audience behind the plexiglass barricades. Just think of that, we will be able to watch it live!"

It is true, Mother was overjoyed when Laura helped our family get selected to be part of the limited audience that stands behind plexiglass, watching the procession. I'll give Laura that; she has been able to dazzle and win over Mother.

"I just find it strange that Laura will be acting as a veterinarian during the reenactment and not presenting her own position, as an engineer, while Cody is just a dead person covered by a flag."

Mother retorts, "How can the parade show what an engineer does? They show historical scenes, and active positions, like the jobs the Eunuchs, Surrogates and veterinarians have."

Active positions, my mother's turn of phrase rings in my ears. She's right, engineers are boring and terribly serious. Maybe it is because their jobs are monotonous, sitting in front of a computer database all day, watching, checking algorithms. Harmony does the hard work, apparently.

"Mother, do you know who's going to be a Surrogate in the parade today?"

"Yes, a girl...I forgot her name." Mother brings her hand up to her temples, trying to remember the girl's name. "Her mother sometimes meets me in the park when I go on my daily walk. Tanya, yes, I remember now. Her name is Tanya. We were chuckling about that last week. Tanya's going to be fed grapes by a boy acting as a Eunuch. Those Surrogates must live such a fine life off-grid!"

Surrogates are the most beloved in MicroScrep. They are the ones that supply Perfect Bonding Pairs with their perfect genetically matched child. There is a great amount of self-effacement that they must have and that's probably why they are chosen by Harmony. Children who are genetically stronger are larger, weakening a Surrogate when they are growing inside their wombs. Most of the time Surrogates don't survive after one birth.

Harmony's algorithms deem which egg and sperm should be used to create the best offspring. This is a Perfect Genetic Pair. Through this natural selection, stronger and more robust MicroScrepians are created to combat possible future outbreaks. The embryo from a Perfect Genetic Pair, is implanted into a Surrogate through in-vitro fertilization.

Mother is placing water into the steaming receptacle, and I wonder who the Eunuch will be at the parade, feeding Tanya the grapes.

Eunuchs live off grid and serve Surrogates, making them as comfortable as possible, so that the Surrogates can live out the rest of their lives in comfort and bliss. They are also revered greatly by people in MicroScrep. I remember reading about a religion called Christianity which venerated Virgin Mary, a woman who sacrificed her only son for the good of the world. Surrogates are our Virgin Mary, but instead of sacrificing someone else, they sacrifice themselves. The idea of religion has always been alien, but this allegory, perhaps because I am a woman, touches me deeply. I look at mother, who is frantically steaming the crinkles off the flag. Is she also sacrificing what she really wants in life to be our mother?

"So is Laura going to be managing any of the animals?"

I ask Mother.

"How should I know? It would be rude to ask about every little detail." She huffs at me in exasperation.

In MicroScrep, only veterinarians can own animals. The veterinarians train the animals to work for the benefit of MicroScrep. The bats are used for their sense of echolocation. They use it to locate citizens who go missing. From time to time, we have cases of this. It could be a little child who wanders off their compound and gets disoriented, or very rarely there have been cases of MicroScrepians who have memory blocks. Scientists haven't figured it out yet, but sometimes you get MicroScrepians who have memory glitches and forget where they were or where they're going. We are told it is a biological problem, one which is happening less often, as inferior genes are selected out by Harmony. Embryos are getting purer and purer with each generation.

Veterinarians also train dogs who can literally smell carelessness. So, they play an important factor in the re-education system in MicroScrep. Some children get careless and do not habitually scan for diseases with their X-ray vision. This poses a problem for all. Every so often, dogs sniff through the schools, identifying any child that is not conforming to the X-ray vision protocols. The strange thing is, for some reason, I have never been flagged. Perhaps it has something to do with my eyes. There were times in school where I would intentionally go days without scanning, and never once was I discovered.

I find it peculiar that historically people ate meat and lived with animals. They called them pets. I remember reading about that in a history book and thinking to myself that people must have been very foolish. Animals are unpredictable and need specific people to handle them. Also, animals harbor diseases that can jump from one species to another, given the right circumstances and proximity. What would make a human want to harbor an animal other than for control?

Cody runs down the stairs, jumping past the last several steps. "You'll hurt yourself before the parade!" Mom shouts.

"What does it matter, Mother? I am only playing a dead person."

Mother raises her eyebrows and shakes her head.

"Where are you in such a rush to be off to?"

"Well, I have a few hours before the parade. I am going to play soccer with Kevin."

Mother is absorbed in her steaming. Lifting the flag up at the corners and inspecting it for any wrinkles or creases that she might have missed.

"Don't get carried away," Mother says absentmindedly as Cody leaves.

I hear Cody's car move out of the garage. I catch a glimpse of it from the window. It hovers above the driveway, the roof top and the undercarriage light flashing red, before it speeds away. I walk back to my mother, who is rummaging around in the storage.

"Mother, can you hand me that folding chair?"

"Are you going to watch the setup of the parade?" she asks before handing it to me.

"Yeah, if I get there sooner, I'll be able to find the best place, right in the middle of the hall, behind the plexiglass."

"Good thinking," Mother says and continues, "I'll wait for your father."

I bundle the chair under my arm, sling my purse over my shoulder, and mumble a goodbye before I leave.

The setup looks fantastic. The plexiglass I sit behind is new and transparent. If I focus on the shine of it, I can see my own reflection. A few yards away people are getting into their costumes, moving to where they are meant to be on the floats that are decorated with different designs and historical scenes. I'm early, so there aren't very many people sitting in the audience yet.

Music blares over the speakers, it's an ode to Arthur Mills that continuously plays on loop. It is this year's hit. There's an electronic tempo that makes those that are setting up the floats sway to it. Their faces are a blank expression, but they are mesmerized by the lyrics, their hands working busily in time to the beat. I personally dislike music. I don't understand how anyone can be so fixated on it. The beat is monotonous, the tone is monosyllabic, and you can never carry on a decent conversation with someone when there is music playing, even if the electronic sound is turned down. I get very bored when I listen, as if whatever appeals to everyone else about it, doesn't apply to me. That's the one issue Zach and I don't agree on, MicroScrepian music. He explains it as a rush of feeling that makes his hair stand on end, but his mind isn't thinking, it is vacuous and void. I just can't get into it, and it certainly doesn't make my mind go blank. This isn't public knowledge though. I haven't told anyone about it, only Zach, but Zach is different. He's my protector; he understands me in a weird way, or at least has enough empathy to understand.

There are public health officials dressed in orange overalls, large spray tanks connected to nozzles that protrude from their backs; they walk around disinfecting everything. When one gets close to me, he nods his head in a gesture meant to rouse me from my chair. I stand up, and he sprays and wipes down my seat and the plexiglass in front of me.

A float for the parade is on the other side of the glass covered in flags. A large, golden screen engraved with a rose gold plaque reads, Harmony. Garlands of roses are strewn on its corners. A slogan is held up by two, young girls in white and green dresses. “We owe our happiness and bliss to Harmony.”

Ahead of them is a float with a holographic reenactment of horrors of life before Harmony and MicroScrep. These are the regular depictions of life before MicroScrep: people looking like monkeys in large family groups, pollution and soot everywhere, animals roaming in their homes, alcohol available at every turn, drunkards limping back to their homes and falling unconscious onto the beds they shared with their lovers, children living in broken homes after the love matches turned out to be only frivolous, short-lived emotions. They had no X-ray vision, couldn’t scan for viruses, and were vulnerable wherever they went.

I get up and walk further down to observe the other floats being set up. A tall, strong, red-haired man is shown as Arthur Mills, the founder of MicroScrep. He is standing in front of the Tower of Tears, where the roundabout of Purity is located now. The scientists, in his time, who created vaccines and the microchip for X-ray vision, were killed in an unfortunate gas explosion. Out of the rubble only seventy of the hundred scientist bodies are as of yet recovered.

I pace on, noting a MicroScrepian cultural float, decorated in white and pink flowers, representing purity. A slogan reads, "Because we have pure love, we have no disunity."

I am about to find my way back to my seat when a loud bark snaps me to attention. Several yards ahead, Laura is holding onto a leash with a large-headed dog at the end of it. I've never seen a dog with a head that massive. Laura is almost overpowered by it, as it sniffs and growls. Laura pulls back on the leash, shouting at it to shut up. Past Laura, there are several others with smaller canines on leashes, these dogs are the ones you see in schools from time to time. There are others who hold cages with bats fluttering around. I wonder again why Laura is acting as a veterinarian in the parade. The others that are handling the animals are veterinarians as I can see from the badge and the way they handle the animals. Aside from Laura's shouting, there is little skill she has with the large dog she has on leash. One of the veterinarians moves over to her and helps Laura wrap the leash tightly to control the animal better.

I notice more people filtering in and decide to go back to my chair. I scan the audience and seating for viruses. Finding my chair, I am almost ready to sit down, when a little, frail, blond girl approaches me, tapping me on the back before I take my seat. She can't be older than ten. A cloth patch covers one eye. I recognize her; she's a little girl that lives on our compound. I haven't seen her before with the patch over her eye, though.

"Oh, is this your chair?" she asks, one bright, blue eye

looking up at me.

"Yes, sorry sweetie, it is. Where are your parents? Aren't you here with them?"

"Sort of. They are in charge of the music," she says, looking down to the ground. "They won't play any of the music that I've composed," she says glumly.

"What kind of music do you create?" My curiosity piqued. I've never heard her playing music before on the compound. Come to think of it, I've never heard of a child composing music. I thought it came from an algorithm from Harmony.

"Nothing like the music played here. Father tells me to imagine what a flowing stream sounds like, or what birds must sing like, off-grid." She mumbles this quietly, and I incline my ear to listen to her whistle a tune.

Goosebumps cascade down my arms, I choke out a whisper. "That's very beautiful. You have a great talent." This is the closest to an emotional response to music I've ever had. How peculiar, I notice that beyond the little girl is Laura, who is facing me, the dog lunging and barking at us. When she notices me watching her, she turns, pulling the dog away.

The little girl smiles, her one eye fixated on my face, and without a word, she turns and skips away. I want to follow her, to make sure she gets a seat and to compliment her and her parents at the end of the parade, but something on the other side of the plexiglass grabs my attention. Kevin is walking with Cody, their backs to me. I can see that their heads are tilted towards each other as if they are exchanging private comments. This strikes me as strange, Cody seems to increasingly spend more time with Kevin, even though Kevin is far older than Cody is. I wonder what they have in common that makes them spend so much time together? They do have soccer in common, but would a sport make two people so close? Kevin places an arm around Cody's shoulder, and he gives it a pat as they part ways. Kevin wraps around the last plexiglass barricade and sits in the audience beside the little girl who whistled so sweetly.

My mind overwhelmed with all these sights and sounds around me, I now desperately want the parade to begin and be over so that I can go home. The parade will start shortly. I can hear the music amplified and the people in the parade taking their positions on, or in front, of their floats. I look around for Mother and Father and see them in the distance. I wave them over and take my seat.

A holographic projection reads, "Pre-MicroScrep Barbarians." The music starts off chaotically to match the first floats that depict the pre-MicroScrep era. An unorganized swarm of actors dance wildly with synthetic blood covering their faces. They run up towards the plexiglass, sticking out their tongues, or showing long, bloody fangs. They hoot and holler to communicate; the audience taken aback by the abruptness, some laugh and point. A flash of light brings oohs and aahs from the crowd. Everything goes black. The next float that passes is of people coughing and sputtering, some are choking. Cody's body lies covered by a flag, one of a half dozen strewn on the ground. The holographic projection reads, "The Pandemic Hits." A strong, large man depicting Arthur Mills stands back, bringing the scientists together in a circle to come up with a solution to the terrible pestilence that has hit mankind. All the while another float depicts men and women swaying, depicting the animalist urges that they did not control and what caused the pandemic to move through the population. Then finally, a float depicting the children that came of these wild pairings. Ugly, dumb and mad. Their mouths contorted into barbaric sneers.

The music becomes softer, timelier and more organized, although still electronic. A hologram of Arthur Mills projects largely to the clap of the audience. Some are in tears, pointing to their Perfect Family Matches, the grandness of his face, the redness of his hair, the symmetry of his features. A float of scientists that are busy working on a vaccine is depicted. The music becomes grander and louder, the crescendo coinciding with the hologram showing the mandatory vaccine inoculating the masses against the unseen enemy, the virus.

Holographic fireworks light up the sky. The music takes on a whimsical note, although it still beats rhythmically. My mother chuckles, clapping her hands. “Look, that’s Tanya! She’s showing life as a Surrogate! Look, the Eunuch is feeding her.”

The words, “Your sacrifices will forever be revered in MicroScrep,” is projected above the scene. I find it odd that they don’t bring a Surrogate from off-grid for the parade. I know they are meant to be kept in peace and relaxation, but wouldn’t it be nice for them to experience the appreciation of the crowd and of MicroScrep? My train of thought abruptly ends when I hear screams from the crowd. A procession of veterinarians follow the Surrogate float. The bats and the dogs bring out fear in the crowd who are furiously scanning for viruses and bacteria. Laura is at the back of the procession, the large dog struggling against her leash. As they make their way to the end, Laura loses control of the dog, and it goes straight to the last barricade, springing onto the little girl whose deafening scream reverberates through the hall. My heart is racing as I stand frozen, watching the horror unfolding a few yards away from me.

Mother grabs my hand. “Let’s get out of here!”

“No, take Dad and go home. I’ve got to help,” I yell back as I stumble forward against the crowd that is moving to exit through the back doors.

Laura also stands motionless as the audience churns in on itself, pushing, shoving and running towards the exit doors. The veterinarians run towards the sound of the girl’s screams. Kevin jumps on top of the dog who has hurled itself on the girl. He grabs its jaws and pulls hard, releasing the girl’s arm from its grip. The music has stopped, the little girl’s parents by her side. Her father has her in his arms in the next few minutes, and he is running to the nearest exit, her mother in tears behind them. I glance at Laura whose face is red and teeth clenched. She still stands at a distance, now glaring at Kevin through narrowed eyes. Kevin rolls and tumbles, trying to get the upper hand on the dog. A veterinarian sticks a needle into the dog’s side, and it immediately slumps motionless on the ground.

Later in the evening, after the events of the day, Mother thought it would be comforting to make a vegetarian casserole. The kind she makes on a stormy day, when we cannot go outside for fear of catching a cold. The sounds of her chopping, and the smell of herbs roasting make me feel slightly calmer, despite the heightened anxiety of the day. In my mind, Laura's inaction weighs heavily. Why didn't she try to run after the dog when it got away from her? Why did the dog go after the girl with a patch over her eye? Kevin was seated closer to it. The dog seemed to single her out. What bothers me the most about the whole occurrence was the look on Laura's face when Kevin was struggling with the dog. Her narrowed eyes. It was almost as if Kevin had disrupted something, as if he wasn't meant to help the little girl. The dog was more familiar with her and might have responded if she had shouted at it, but she didn't. I must keep an eye on Laura. I need to understand why she's so insensitive. Something isn't sitting right with me, and for once I'm not hungry for mother's casserole.

Chapter 4:

Animals

Several days have passed since the National Day Parade, and I cannot shake the feeling that somehow, something isn't adding up. Laura is as aloof as ever, spending the last three evenings late at work. Cody has also been absent, visiting Kevin at his home while he recovers from the dog incident. I think of what happened to the little girl during the National Day Parade. My suspicions of Laura have not subsided. Why would Laura just stand there and watch the dog she was supposed to be handling attack the little girl? *Do the girl's parents know Laura, or that she is an engineer at MicroScrep and not even supposed to be handling dogs?* I wonder.

I could bear it no longer and yesterday made a point of walking by the little girl's home in the evening, knocking on the door and introducing myself. Her parents were odd and seemed slightly on edge, almost suspicious of me coming around to ask about her. "Her arm is healing," her father reported, not getting into any other details. They did not call her down from her room; they just stood side by side as if barring me from entertaining the thought of seeing her. I wanted to ask them if they knew Laura, whether they have inquired as to why the dog managed to get away from her? Her parents just stood there with a cold look in their eyes; it made me feel like I was intruding on their home. I wanted to ask about the lovely tune she whistled to me before the parade, to break the awkward silence, but her father motioned as if he was going to close the door on me, so I turned and left feeling even more anxious than I did before going there.

After this, I watched from the window. I live up in the loft of the house, so from my vantage point I can see most of the compound. Nobody entered or left her home. No doctors. No nurses. No visitors. Every hour or so, frustrated with the inaction, I would pass her house, inclining my ear to any sound of music, but I never heard anything, let alone a tune or melody.

The days after the parade coincided with the start of my course of oxytocin and fertility injections. All females are given fertility medication to have optimal egg retrieval. Once the eggs are retrieved, the data is inputted into Harmony, and a Perfect Genetic Match is found. Then, in the MicroScrep laboratory the sperm is introduced into the egg and an embryo is formed. The embryo is then implanted into a Surrogate, who births the child off-grid.

This all happens before my eighteenth birthday which is in a few weeks. All MicroScrepians on their eighteenth birthday are given a position during a Calling Ceremony. Harmony selects what position one will hold with data collected from a person's personality traits and genetics. Most citizens are placed into Perfect Family Matches. The oxytocin is to ensure that just enough pure love is felt for their Perfect Family Match. A flush of heat overtakes me. Goodness, I hope I am paired with Zach, although I should never have these feelings to begin with. If anyone knew I felt this way about Zach, having such desires would demonstrate my lack of faith in Harmony—blaspheming is the term used in MicroScrep.

Mother says the oxytocin gives her a little kick of love whenever Father does something annoying, like forget to brush his teeth, or when he doesn't notice that morsel of food that's found its way into his beard. I notice those little moments less as I'm spending more time with my mother these days. Cody is immersed at work. He's a teacher in MicroScrep and spends a lot of his time tutoring children after hours. He always comes back home sweaty and runs to take a shower before Laura arrives.

"What are you all sweaty for?" I asked him a few days ago when I noticed that he'd get home late.

He looked at me lethargically. "You're going to get yourself in a lot of trouble with that curiosity of yours."

"You didn't answer my question!" I retorted, making a face at him.

"I was playing soccer. Any other questions, Ms. Interrogator?"

"With Kevin?" I was not letting him off the hook this easy.

"Gosh! What's with all these questions! YES!" He threw his t-shirt into the disinfection device and ran upstairs to shower.

"He isn't recovering from the dog bites?" I yelled after him.

"Obviously, but not enough to stop him from playing

soccer," he grumbled before closing the door to the bathroom.

⦸

In the evening, sometimes Laura comes over for dinner. She is a workaholic too, often staying late into the evening to finish a project, so perhaps that's why Cody spends so much time tutoring and playing soccer. If Laura doesn't come over, she stays with her family. Cody and she won't live together until they have a child assigned to them. This way they have a purpose to their union. A reason to become a family. I remember reading in *Successful Relationships*, the book Zach had stolen from Laura's library, that pre-MicroScrepians often lived together before having children. I remember being struck by disbelief and then on closer examination of my feelings for Zach, I realized that I wouldn't necessarily need a child with him to feel that our bond was complete.

The last few nights, I've been waking up at around two a.m. I've tried to relax, but my mind goes back to the poor little girl who was mauled by that terrible dog. I can't shake the sense of suspicion I have for Laura; something about her cold stare at Kevin really bothers me. The weather is getting cooler, and with it a sense of fear permeates the room. Tonight, I get up, and when I can't get back to bed, I check how much time I have left from my recreational time.

I sign into my telephone and whisper, "How much recreational time is left this week?" and it replies, "Thirty minutes, Ms. Adriana." I might as well use it before it ends at the break of dawn and resets for another week. I look outside my bedroom window and wait for my eyes to adjust to the darkness outside. From my loft, I am the only one in the whole compound who can see the derelict shed tucked in behind the hall, a recreation center on our compound.

I notice a strange figure moving from the pool area to the shed. Who would be going there this late at night? I stand on my toes, trying to see the figure who has now closed the shed door and is inside. Before I can even think straight, I have wrapped myself in a knitted shawl and am tiptoeing to the shed. I can see the glow of a phone screen from the spaces where the plywood has been haphazardly nailed together. If the door opens, I'll be exposed, so I tiptoe to the side of the building. I can hear someone talking. My goodness, it's Laura! Her whiney, nasal voice is unmistakable.

I bring my ear to the wooden façade and hear almost as clearly as if she were only a few feet away from me.

"Father, I don't want this match. I don't want to be with him. I can't stand the guy. Listen, Father, listen! I've proven myself. It's not my fault that that idiot got in the way."

Father? Laura can't be speaking to her father on the phone, it's the middle of the night! I press my ear against the façade.

Laura huffs out an exasperated sigh. "Okay, I'm listening. Yes, it's safe speaking in English, nobody is here." I peer into a small, ring-sized hole in the plywood, and notice a door in the shed leading to another section of the shed that's closed off. I see Laura's back to me, she is pacing back and forth, on what looks like a phone, but with an antenna. I duck back before she turns.

"Look, you need supports in place off-grid. I just want to be there with you..."

The person on the other end shouts, although I cannot decipher what is being said.

"Okay, yes, I know she's a freak. I doubt the drugs are working on her. In fact, I am convinced Harmony can't come up with the proper algorithms for people like her. It gives errors, every time I enter her damn name. I am going to have to take matters into my own hands. I have the amulet...yes, I know it will hurt me if it isn't real."

I can almost make out the voice on the other end, oh goodness is she nearing the door?!

"Daddy, why can't I just get rid of her?"

The voice on the other end shouts louder than ever.

"Damn Harmony. We need to program every, single, little, gene..." The person on the other end must be losing his temper because Laura's voice goes low, as if defeated.

"Yes, I'll fix the Kevin problem and then focus on her."

I hear a click and then a low growl. My face flushes with fear. I bite my lip. I've got to look back into that hole and find out what's in there. I'm just in time to see Laura open the other door and feed a large dog what looks like a human jaw. The lips are purple, and the skin is a greyish blue. I hold my breath in fear, my legs getting weak. All I can think of is home. I need to get back home. My legs feel like lead, but I manage to tiptoe out of earshot and then sprint. When I'm in my room, my mind is buzzing with fear. She was speaking into a weird-looking phone, to someone she called Daddy, who isn't here. She wants to join him, but she needs to take care of the Kevin problem and then she can focus on 'her.' A shiver runs down my spine, and I move to wrap the shawl around myself, but it isn't there. This time when my knees weaken, I am on the ground. Where is my shawl?! Did it fall off me and I didn't even notice it? My heart races, and I can hear my heartbeat in my ear. What if she found it? What if Laura finds it and realizes I was there? I wait several hours until I muster up the courage to tip toe back to the shed, but I can't find it anywhere. Exhausted and depleted, I find my way back into my bed. When I wake up, I hear Laura chatting with my mother downstairs.

I splash my face with cold water. I need to control my anxiety. The feelings I have about Laura are right: she's a ruthless, terrible person. She has no scruples about hurting people, or even murdering them. She must have let that dog off the leash. She must have let the dog get away and hurt that little girl! But why would she want the little girl to die? Was she going for Kevin? Is she even talking about the same Kevin? It must be him; she said he got in the way. How could it be? They both work for the same system. Unless...unless, she wants to get rid of him so she can have his job? But why would she want his job? My mind is a windmill of thoughts, circling around without answers, torn apart by the revelations of last night. She talked about a freak, someone who isn't susceptible to Harmony's algorithms and the medicines in MicroScrep. All I noticed that was strange about the little girl, was the talk of composing music, and the patch she had over her eye. Could the little girl be the person she is trying to get rid of? But why?

A knock at the door makes me jump. I dry my face off with my towel. Another knock at the door, this time slightly louder.

"Who's there?" I shout out.

"It's me, darling," Mother says. "Come on down for tea. Laura is here."

I take a deep breath. I need to stay calm. I need to figure out a way to warn Kevin about her. I can't let her sense my anxiety.

"All right, I'll be right down," I say, my voice taking on a more certain tone.

Downstairs I can smell apple spice tea. Mother knows that is my favorite. The smell comforts me, and I straighten my back.

Laura is sitting on an armchair. She watches me descend the stairs; her face plastered with a grin.

"Hello, Laura," I say, my voice as certain as ever.

"Adriana, how are you today? All rested up?" She squints her eyes momentarily as she brings the cup of tea to her lips and sips.

"I'm well, thank you." I am adamant not to answer her question about rest.

Mother stands up and turns towards the kitchen. "I'll be right back; do I have a treat for you two. I've made rhubarb pie."

Laura crouches down and rummages around in her purse as I sit down on the sofa, opposite Laura and beside where mother is sitting.

"I think this is yours," she says. Her eyes squint like a snake about to recoil and strike. She extends the knit shawl that I lost last night.

My heart skips a beat, as I get up and take it from her. "Yes, that is mine." I swiftly snatch the shawl from her. She recoils again. In my mind, there's only one thought I am certain about: I will not let her do whatever evil she has planned with Kevin, or the little girl, or with me.

Mother breaks the awkward tension in the room with her rhubarb pie and her obliviousness.

"Oh, it smells divine, if I must say so myself," she says, prancing in the room jovially.

"I am sure it is the most delightful pie in all of MicroScrep!" Laura praises.

"Praise to Harmony for creating such a wonderful mother who bakes the most delicious pies!" I say in veiled mockery.

Mother is oblivious to this, but I sense Laura understands my cynicism and recognizes I won't go down without a fight.

When Laura leaves, I feel a sense of lightness, a sense of relief. I stood up to her. She knows I know. She knows that I have something on her. This sense, though, is only momentary. I soon realize that I can't fight her on my own. I need someone else to know what's happening, what I've witnessed, so that if I am defeated, they will be able to pick up where I left off.

I can't tell Mother or Father, they are too patriotic, and too averse to my curiosity. The furthest I will get with them is a reprimand for following her into the shed. I can almost see their reaction: shock, reprimand, denial. They'd deny that I saw anything. They'd make it up to be a nightmare, that it is a figment of my imagination, something that I'd need to forget, to label as a surreal vision in the night.

Perhaps Cody; he's the person I can speak most naturally to. He's my brother, but he is also her Perfect Bonding Pair. He has been spending an awful lot of time with Kevin, though. Laura did say in the shed that she wanted to take care of Kevin, but she didn't only say Kevin.

She said she'd fix the Kevin problem and then work on her—who is she referring too? This is bigger than Kevin, so getting him involved at this point might not expose the situation for what it is, if she is even speaking about Cody and Zach's soccer friend.

Zach—that's it, Zach! He's been my protector since childhood. He's the person who I can confide in. He knows me and will believe what I have to say. I think of him and my heart skips, but if he doesn't believe in me, then I'll know that my feelings for him are only fantasy. If he truly loves me, he'll stand up for me. He'll believe me. True, he is Laura's brother, but I feel that they haven't had such a strong bond lately. He once even suggested that he doesn't know why Harmony chose them to be siblings. He said he felt she had some darkness in her personality. I didn't see it then, but I saw it last night. Yes, I will tell Zach. He's due to come over today. I'll pull him aside and speak to him about what happened.

Chapter 5:

Flashes of light

"You know Zach's coming over and wants to go for a swim in the compound pool," Cody says as I jab myself in the stomach with a cocktail of hormones. Egg extraction happens in three days. I was hoping that Zach would come over sooner so that I could pull him aside and tell him about the parade and about what I saw in the shed.

"Ouch." A warm sting accompanies the alcohol swab on the injection site. "Zach isn't coming earlier? He didn't want to have lunch with us?"

Cody is oblivious to my desperation. I need to tell Zach what happened. I don't want to rush it, and Laura is coming over for dinner. Instead, he simultaneously scans the area around my injection site with his X-ray vision. "You're good for a band-aid, the alcohol swab worked."

"He's coming for a swim. I don't think he said he'd come for lunch," Cody mutters absentmindedly.

Putting the alcohol and the swabs into the first-aid kit, I glance at Cody and say, "Yeah, that's weird." I want to tell him it's because she was feeding a dog in the shed last night, but I must cling to my goal of exposing her, and I can't do it yet. I need to have hard evidence. A photograph, a videotape, something.

Upstairs I open my underwear drawer. I see Laura's swimsuit that she left a few weeks ago. She has so many swimsuits. Those are the perks of a government job; you have more disposable income. I wonder whether she's going to join us today. She is obsessed with work, and often stays late. Maybe that's the reason she has so many perks; she works for every scroble of it. I stop rummaging through my drawer as a thought comes to mind: what if she is working for MicroScrep? What if the man on the other end of the line, who she called father, was in some way trying to gain control of Harmony? My heart pounds with fear as I think about this scenario. What if her mission is bigger than just for her and her father's gain?

Finally, I find my swimsuit and step into it. Pulling the straps up over my arms, I stand sideways and glance at my reflection in the mirror. I've gained a bit of weight. I notice my tummy bulging out. It must be the hormones. A sour look on my face reflects in the mirror. I can't tell Cody, and I start to doubt if I should tell Zach. I don't know enough to tell him. I don't have evidence. It's my word against hers.

There is a knock at the door and it creaks open as I swivel around, wrapping a towel around myself. Looking at me with large, foxlike green eyes is Zach.

"Zach! You scared me again!"

Shifting his weight uncomfortably, his eyes turn down, revealing long dark eyelashes against his marble-like complexion.

"I'm sorry, Adriana. I didn't know you were undressing."

"I'm not! I was just putting on my swimsuit. Hey, do you know where Laura is?"

Ever since Laura started working two years ago, she's been strangely absent from her family's life. That's why I believe the person she was speaking to yesterday couldn't have been her father. It must be a code name for someone. "Gosh, half the time I don't know where Laura is, but today she mentioned she'd join us at the pool later today."

I am about to tell Zach about what happened last night, when I hear Cody stomping up the stairs and walking into my room. "What are you two doing up here? The pool is a perfect temperature today!"

⦸

Splashing into the pool, I give a yelp, shocked by the cool water. Cody squirts water at me as I submerge, kicking my feet to make a getaway. Circling around and surfacing behind him, I push him down by the shoulders. We both reemerge laughing. Watching from a distance, Zach smiles broadly, holding on to a floaty and lightly kicking his feet. "Don't get me wet, the water is too cold for me to dunk my head into, I'll get cold-shock-response."

"I have a plan," I whisper into Cody's ear. We both go under and push the floaty out from under him. Seconds later Zach is screaming into the water, and reemerges sputtering.

"You two are evil!" He laughs and spits out water in our direction.

We are startled by a splash. Laura has cannon-balled

into the water, leaving a ripple in her wake. Reemerging, she smiles, squinting her eyes as Cody freestyles towards her.

"Hey, darling, how was work?" he dutifully asks while scanning her for viruses.

"Ah, the same old, same old. Solar panels need to be repositioned and more panels are now needed to generate electricity for the Surrogacy Centers. There seems to be a boom in pregnancies this year."

She wasn't talking about solar panels yesterday on the phone with Daddy. I feel anger towards her lies. She said she wasn't happy being matched with Cody, or at least I assume that's what she meant.

Cody takes her hands and looks softly at her. "Perhaps this year will be the year we'll have our baby."

Swimming up towards his sister, Zach asks, "Have you ever asked to see the Surrogacy Centers?"

Laura is mystified by his question for a moment, but she quickly regains her composure and jokes, "No, silly. That might disturb the Surrogates, to have a bunch of scientists look in on them like lab rats. They need to be in a happy state of relaxation for the good of the babies."

"But I'm still curious to know," he mutters, eyes downcast.

"You're such an odd duckling, Zach. Men aren't usually interested in the whole surrogacy experience." She laughs playfully before mocking, "Hey, you never know. Maybe in the future men can be Surrogates."

She turns around, and says before diving into the water, "Maybe one day you'll know."

Zach changes the conversation to the happenings of the parade. We are all silent, but I intentionally watch

Laura, who stays very quiet except for her comment, "That dog was so incredibly large, I don't think anyone could have prevented it from getting away."

"Yeah, thank goodness that the dog didn't seriously injure that little girl or Kevin. I think MicroScrep should ban animals from the parade. They are so unpredictable!" Cody says.

In the five months it'd been since Cody and Laura's Bonding Ceremony, I learned that Kevin is always wrapped up in an endless stream of work, except for the times he plays soccer with Cody and Zach. I've heard he has quite the reputation for himself as an engineer at MicroScrep Laboratories. His ability to quickly repair glitches in the system is commendable.

"Maybe there's a way for him to formally complain," Zach remarks. "I don't think it's safe to have dogs at the parades anymore, maybe they can be replaced with holograms."

Laura purses her lips. "Aren't we supposed to be having fun?" she says as she flips back into the water.

"But isn't this important?" Zach says as he furrows his brow. I raise my brows suggestively and nod my head. I know he'll believe me; he must sense her absolute disregard for anyone but herself. It also makes me adore him more. He is so ethical, thinking of the little girl and of Kevin.

My thoughts are interrupted by Cody shouting, "Water fight!" Suddenly everyone is laughing, splashing water at each other excitedly.

Losing my balance and slipping into the water, I open my eyes, the chlorine stinging, while air bubbles float up to the surface. I am about to kick and resurface when I see an odd protrusion near Laura's navel. Wondering what it could be, I hold my breath and take one large breaststroke towards it. Something odd is lodged in Laura's belly button and dials outwards. It points its crystal face at me and flashes successively. Reemerging to the surface, I feel slightly lightheaded. I gasp for a breath as Laura laughs and pushes my head down again. Instead of closing my eyes to keep the sting of chlorine out, I keep them open. Again, I see the digital movement of the tiny crystal-face device and a succession of flashes. Pushing off from the pool bottom and forcing myself up, my face is hot, even under the cool water. A sense of threat overtakes me. I feel invaded, like she purposefully went where she shouldn't go. I sputter as I reemerge, gasping for air. My kinky curls bob on top of the water as time stands still. Without giving notice to me, I watch the other three continue to laugh loudly and splash each other.

"Hey, Adriana, don't just stand there!" Cody laughs and splashes a giant wave in my direction. But I don't move, lost for words, and the others look on at me with puzzled faces. Time is motionless, I stare out at them, and they stare back at me. For a moment I have forgotten where I am. I try to remember what happened, and why we are in the water.

Finally, Zach breaks the awkwardness. "What's wrong?"

Peering blankly, I stutter, "It, it, it must be those injections I'm taking. I don't know where I am. For a moment I couldn't seem to recall why I was here."

Furrowing her eyebrows, Laura chimes in, "Oh, come on! I took them too. They aren't that bad!"

My mind flashes back to the chip in Laura's navel, and

I wonder what she just did to me. Did she just take pictures of me, or did I just imagine that? I shake my head. "Um, I need to go. I, I, I'm not feeling great." With that, I swim to the pool's edge and pull myself up.

"Okay," Cody breaks the awkward silence, as I clamber off, "but you're missing out!"

To my relief, they resume splashing and kicking. Entering the house, Mother greets me by scanning me for microbes.

"Adriana, you've got some bacteria under your nails. Let me disinfect it." She follows me into the kitchen and takes her spray and a cotton swab. She cleans under my nails. I am happy she hasn't noticed my anxiousness. Why am I so worried?

Is there a chance Laura took photos of me and is going to share them amongst her friends to taunt me? Laura works for the state as a scientist; what scientific information is she gathering on me? And why would she be gathering information on me, anyway? Is it because I'm an anomaly with my freakishly different colored eyes? Racing thoughts overcome me. I don't remember why I ended up in the pool with them.

Mother covers my hand with disinfectant gel and berates, "I hope you cleaned your fingernails before the parade, absolutely disgraceful for you walking around like that!"

"What parade?" I ask.

Mother looks furious. "Don't be smart with me Adriana! It's enough that you risked your life staying back after that little girl was getting mauled by that terrible beast!"

A memory flashes back into my mind. Kevin holding a

dog's jaw and keeping it open, a little girl's arm is released from the dog's grip. Then another one, but instead of the dog's jaw, it is half a human jaw, lips purple and skin tinged greyish blue.

"Ouch, Mom, you cut me!"

"Oh dear, I'm so sorry, the clippers cut into your nail bed. My eyes are not like they used to be." She slowly fills the cotton swab with antiseptic, and I hold it in place while Mother scurries off to the medicine cabinet.

My mind goes back to the succession of flashes. Perhaps the sunlight was playing a reflective trick? But I saw the gadget dial out and the crystal flashing like a camera.

Mother returns and diligently applies a bandage over my nail. My head is rushing and spinning; I don't know what to make of the images in my mind. I am not even sure what has happened. Should I tell Mother how I'm feeling and what I'm seeing? What good would that do though? I'm so confused. Mother thinks I am tricking her. She'd never believe that Laura just flashed a secret camera at me. Even if she believed me, it would certainly cause friction between her and her daughter-in-law. I remain silent. My suspicion is only just that, a suspicion. I don't even know whether the images that flash in my mind happened. Mother wouldn't know either. She didn't mention a human jawbone, only the dog, Kevin, and the little girl.

I decide I'll ask Dr. Marks about the experience in the pool with the flashing lights when I go in to have my eggs extracted tomorrow. I'd heard from some others that Dr. Marks is a good scientist. He'll know if this is part of some data collection for Harmony.

I've always had a curious mind; it isn't such a good trait to have in MicroScrep. Trusting the process comes with the territory of being a good citizen. So, what does that make me?

Chapter 6:

Extraction

The hospital smells of strong disinfectant covered by the artificial scent of synthetic lavender. It is eerily quiet, like being in a library. It's as if I am on an insulated spacecraft. I scan the doorknob for microbes before knocking politely, but when there's no answer, I help myself in. The secretary doesn't look up from the holographic computer keyboard until I clear my throat loudly. Clicking out of the screen, she looks robotically through me.

"Ms. Adriana, am I right?"

"Yes."

"Here to see Dr. Marks at one p.m.?"

"Yes."

"Please help yourself to some water, in the refrigerator there."

Looking towards the small refrigerator in the seating area, I am overcome with the institutional banality of the clinic.

"No, I'm all right. I'm not thirsty."

Smiling warmly, the secretary motions to the waiting area. “Please have a seat. Dr. Marks will come out to greet you soon.”

The waiting area is quiet. The barrenness of it is made worse by the stifling heat, as if all the dreams of childhood are caught somewhere in a fog over this place. There’s one other girl in the room, sitting across from me on the wooden seats. She looks content, drinking the complimentary water in large, measured gulps.

“Hello,” she cheerfully acknowledges me.

“Hi,” I reply shortly, not in the mood for exchanging pleasantries.

She looks at me curiously, not deterred by my tone. “My name is Louise.”

“I’m Adriana.” I look to the ground, avoiding eye contact. After a few seconds of awkward silence, I ask, “Are you here to see Dr. Marks?”

“No, I’m here to see the psychiatrist, Dr. Beata.”

I tilt my head in confusion. “Oh, they have them here too?” I didn’t know they did more than egg extractions here. A psychiatrist in a fertility clinic? Maybe there is a deep psychic wound opened by the thought of a reproductive cell being stripped of you forever. Children show this fear when they are being potty trained. Some children can’t bear the thought of a part of their body being flushed down the toilet. Perhaps, it is the same sentiment for some women during their egg extraction.

She raises her eyebrows at me, seemingly shocked that I didn’t know this, and just says, “Yes.”

“Oh...I see.”

After a few seconds, Louise says, “The medication is making me anxious; I’m having a hard time sleeping. I feel quite moody. Dr. Marks says that I can't take any sleeping pills until after my eggs are extracted, so I'm working with the psychiatrist on strategies I can use to help me sleep."

A quiet squeak of a voice interrupts Louise from explaining further.

"Ms. Adriana?"

My eyes move towards where the voice is coming from. A frail, mousy-looking man in a white lab coat with poor posture stands in the hallway connecting the seating area with the offices. There's something about the way he holds himself that makes me hesitant to identify myself. But everyone has said that Dr. Marks is the best at his job, and I dismiss the feeling.

"Yes, I'm Adriana," I respond, my voice matching his tone. It is a response to his slight figure, concerned he may startle if I use my normal voice.

"Please follow me," he says.

Walking behind him down the hall, I notice he has a slight shuffle and that he keeps his right hand jangling with something in his pocket, as if he is hiding some terrible secret in his lab coat. We arrive in an office with a full window view of MicroScrep tower. The roundabout of Purity below us is billowing with citizens and honking horns.

Snapping his gloves on, he says, "So, today is egg extraction."

"Yes."

"Did they take a blood sample two days ago?"

"Yes, they have. Was that to take my oxytocin levels?"

"Yes, my dear, soon you'll know your place in society," he whispers almost inaudibly.

"Take off your clothes and put on this gown. He leaves,

returning after a few minutes later, once I've changed into my gown.

Strapping a mask over my face, he says, "Okay, now sit here while I start the calming gas machine."

Feeling my body unwind from Louise's random confession and the general sense of distrust I have for this doctor, I relax into the thought that this will all be over soon enough, then I won't have to be on the medication anymore. The doctor opens my legs and inserts a long narrow tube inside me. A vacuum-like sound starts and I'm in and out of consciousness. All I hear is the doctor counting. "Three, four, five eggs...goodness me...eleven, twelve, thirteen...oh dear...fourteen, fifteen, sixteen...my, my...eighteen, nineteen..."

The next thing I remember is a nurse bringing me a fruit platter. I'm still in my gown.

"Eat up, dear, you'll need to replenish," she says.

The doctor enters abruptly.

"Hello, Adriana, how are you feeling now?" His voice is louder and more assertive than what I remember it to be.

"Good," I manage to slur the word out between a spoonful of watermelon.

"You had many eggs and of such rare quality!" he exclaims. His voice is not only louder, but he's speaking much faster than how he had before.

"I have a question," I say, my voice a low drawl. The room is slightly swimming with the concoction of medicines.

Dr. Marks cocks his ear up in the air. "What's that? You'll have to speak up."

"I have a question," I say slightly louder, but slower

with the heaviness of the sedation.

"Go on."

"Does the state follow all young women of egg extraction age with cameras?"

"What on earth do you mean?" Dr. Marks's face screws up as he questions me.

"A scientist, my sister-in-law, has been snapping photos of me behind my back—secretly." I emphasize the word secretly, despite the exhaustion of speaking.

Concern fills Dr. Marks's eyes. "Adriana, dear—this is very odd of you to ask. Sometimes these sorts of psychotic sensations take hold when you're taking the hormones. Some women hallucinate visually or auditorily. This should have been reported when it happened, not now that I've extracted the eggs from you." He takes a deep sigh in and gathers his thoughts, as if he is going through a protocol. "In this case, I'm not the right person to respond to this. I think I should send you to our psychiatrist, Dr. Beata. She'll help you deal with this." Taking my hand into his, he pats my back. "Don't worry, there's help for this sort of thing. I'm just not the right person to address these matters now."

My mind is a fog, I remember the click and flashes of Laura's camera, but I don't remember the days preceding it. It is almost as if the last thing I remember is weeks ago. Come to think of it, I barely remember the parade. My face flushes, I only remember feeling panic. Then as if a picture emblazons itself in my mind. I am watching through a peep hole in a derelict building. Another flash and a human jawbone. My teeth chatter as I break out into a cold sweat. Maybe I am imagining things. Am I losing my mind?

Taking out his holographic phone, he rings his secretary.

"Please have Ms. Adriana see the psychiatrist today if possible."

A half an hour passes and I'm in Dr. Beata's office. She is a tall, red-haired lady. Her wavy hair is impeccably twisted up around her face with bobby pins and flowers, and she is porcelain white, her mouth upturned in a permanent smile that makes her look somewhat angelic. She looks at me with a blank expression, a poker face against the pale institutional backdrop of the room.

"Hello, Adriana." She speaks my name like pulled taffy, a slight nasal intonation in her voice.

"Hello," I respond, overcome by the beauty of her face, manner, and voice.

"Please seat yourself," she says, again drawing me in with the velvet intonation of her voice.

I pull out my chair and seat myself, somewhat trancelike, the drugs still raging in my veins. My eyes feel spellbound. I am still agitated by the jumbled flashes of memories that I am not sure took place.

"I've read over the notes Dr. Marks made about you." She switches on the holographic keyboard, typing quickly. "Can you explain what you've experienced with your sister-in-law, Laura?"

Her words snap my mind out of its trance. Tingles move up my spine.

My heart races as I ask, "How did you know her name?"

She stops typing and looks at me, her eyes narrowing to a slit. "You must have told the doctor, or I wouldn't..."

I searched my memory, but I don't recall mentioning Laura's name. Could this be some sort of conspiracy? Does Laura wield far more power in MicroScrep than I am aware? I didn't say her name to the Doctor, I am sure of that. How does Dr. Beata know Laura's name? Does she have access to some information on Harmony's database about me and how I am affiliated with her? That's the logical explanation, but why is Dr. Beata denying this?

There are a few moments of quiet, at which she resumes her typing. Breaking the intensity, I say, "Oh, I must have." I want to have as little to do with Dr. Beata and Dr. Marks as possible now. The sinking feeling in my stomach must be my distrust of them.

"Yes, of course you have, or I wouldn't know otherwise." She rolls her eyes and laughs. "I am smart, but unfortunately not a psychic."

Biting my lip nervously, I say, "Laura works for the state as a scientist, and we went swimming together. I noticed in her navel a small camera taking successive pictures of me—not once, but twice." Dr. Beata's typing slows down to a halt.

"Hmm," she says, the angelic smile plastered on her face still.

Sporadically typing, Dr. Beata reads off a list of questions.

"How are you generally eating and sleeping?" she asks, poker-faced.

"I'm fine. I'm eating and sleeping well...apart from that day that Laura took pictures of me secretly...I felt my privacy was invaded, and it just made me feel suspicious, I guess."

"You mean the day you *think* that Laura took pictures. Don't be so sure; self-assurance often brings on delusion." There's a cautionary tone in the doctor's voice. Opening a holographic image, she shows how light can sometimes play tricks on one's mind, especially in water. The holographic clip showed someone swimming, seeing what seemed to be a sharp ray of sunlight, but upon surfacing, the light was all around.

"See, Adriana, this is how water can reflect light off surfaces, making it seem like a flash from a camera." Squinting at me, she continues, "Do you think that this could be a possibility—that the reflection created the illusion of flashing lights from a camera?"

Dr. Beata's question is a rhetorical one. I can tell she's expecting me to agree with her. Inside, though, I feel the same hollowness that I felt when that camera captured me.

Even though I don't agree, something cautions me to lie. "Yes." I nod my head. "It must have been that."

"Good." Dr. Beata's mouth resumes cheerfully, "Let's forget this happened then, or else I'll have to resort to medications, and that's not good for anyone who might become a very important member of society."

Her hand covers mine, and I repress the urge to shudder and pull away. She waits for my response, and I sigh and nod my head. In MicroScrep self-expression is frowned upon.

Dr. Beata spears me with a look. "Let's forget this then, Adriana."

The vacuous feeling in my stomach rises and engulfs my lungs with grim pain. "All right," I whisper almost inaudibly. *Is it that I'm going crazy?* But I am certain that Laura snapped pictures of me. I just can't make out why, unless the flash of images I saw are true, and there is some conspiracy afoot to have me doubt myself.

"Breathe, dear," Dr. Beata senses my uneasiness. "Breathe."

I take a deep breath, and she lets go of my hand after patting it a few times.

"Now be a good girl and don't speak of this to anyone else, yes?"

Feeling like a deflated balloon, I nod my head in agreement. Dr. Beata motions towards the door and excuses me from her office.

Making my way to the elevator, I cannot shake the empty sadness growing in the pit of my stomach. Suspicion grows in my heart. I want to cry out like a crazed woman, but my senses get the better of me. What if the doctor somehow knew Laura and was just covering up for her? But why? What would be her motivation? And that would mean both Dr. Marks and the psychiatrist were covering up for Laura. That was very unlikely. If I had only seen the camera flash once, then I would be able to disregard it as a play of light of illusion, but I saw it twice! I remember it graphically. But why would Laura want pictures of me? Did it have anything to do with the stage of ovulation I was in?

Thinking back to all my interactions with Laura, there was a sense of veiled secrecy about her. She was pleasant enough, but from the first day of her unity with Cody, an air of confidentiality shrouded her. Cody laughed it off as integrity for her work, but for me, there was always a sense of something else brewing in the background. She lived and breathed work and was often late to dinner parties at our home because of it. She was a faithful citizen of MicroScrep, but at the same time, I had the feeling that she knew more and played a more important role in Harmony than she let on.

Am I going mad? The psychiatrist said that if I don't

make peace and reframe the episode as a play of light, then I'd have to take psychotropic medicine. That would be disastrous for my health and my ability to cope well in a Perfect Family Match. It might even lower my chances of Harmony finding a suitable match for me. I think of Zach, and how much I wish that Harmony would pick him for me. I wonder how he'd react if I told him about the camera and the pictures. I'd love to tell him what had just transpired at Dr. Marks's office and the conversation with Dr. Beata. Perhaps he would know better what to do. If he thought it was a figment of my imagination, maybe then I'd forget about this whole experience.

When I return home, Mother is cleaning the windows with the most powerful disinfectant in MicroScrep.

"It's very strange," she says to me. "This window seems to be constantly dusty." She shakes her head in disbelief. "It's almost as if it's been smeared by some prankster pre-teen in the neighborhood."

I'm half listening to Mother, my mind absorbed by the conversation with Dr. Beata, and mumble, "Oh, that's very strange, Mother."

"It could just be a terrible practical joke," she reassures. "The same thing happened to the neighbors two doors down."

My mother must have noticed my pale complexion because she says, "Darling, please don't be so somber. The hormones are awful, I know, but egg extraction only happens once. This whole ordeal will be over in a few days as the hormones leave your body."

"I know. I'm just not feeling well, Mother." My eyes tear up and a lump starts in my throat. Thankfully my mother thinks it's because of the hormones rather than the truth.

She finishes wiping the window, then looks at me with her conciliatory eyes. “Come on, sweetheart, let’s go inside and get you a cup of water, and then you can take a nap; you’ll feel better.”

I do feel slightly better after drinking the water, and I excuse myself to my room. I hear Cody enter the house, laughing as he slams the door behind him. I hope Laura isn’t with them.

I hear three bangs and then Zach’s voice saying, “Hey, let me in!”

Cody giggles. He must be holding the door closed so Zach can’t get in. I listen for Laura’s voice, hoping that she isn’t around.

“Be quiet, you two,” Mother says, whispering to them something I don’t hear.

Placing my head on the pillow, sleep overcomes me, a respite to troubles that ring in my head.

I wake up to the feeling of being watched.

“Laura,” I blurt out as I jump up in bed. My dreams were a jumble. A parade, a little girl, a camera flash, a dog. I am remembering something in my sleep. She doesn’t want me remembering something. My pulse is thumping so hard that I want to cover it with my hands. Panic sets in and a cold sweat washes over me. Jumping out of bed, I go to my ensuite bathroom and splash cold water on my face. Then I hear a knock, two green eyes are the first thing I see, and then his face comes into focus.

“Zach, thank goodness it’s you!” I hold my chest and bend over.

“I’m so sorry, Adriana. I didn’t mean to scare you. I was just leaving a cup of water for you. Your mother told me you were feeling out of sorts.”

He picks up the cup of water on my bedside table and gives it to me. Reluctantly, I take the glass, my eyes welling up with tears. I sip harder, trying to take my mind off the terror still gripping at me.

"Adriana, are you okay?" Zach whispers.

My chest heaves with heaviness. Everything has become too much for me: the doctor, the psychiatrist, the flashes of light, the blanks in my memories, the nightmares. It's no use holding back because the tears are already streaming down my face. I am wracked with grief and pressure. Zach puts a comforting arm around me, but my body is intent on letting the storm of my emotions run through me.

"Adriana, you're all right...Adriana, I'm here. Please, please don't cry." Zach softly strokes my hair and cheeks, wet from my fitful sobbing.

"I'm so sorry, Adriana. Please let me help you; please stop sobbing. I'm beside you now. Everything will be fine." His voice calms me. The heaviness and heaving in my chest slowly ebb, eventually my tears dry up.

My mind is filled with concern over Laura, the camera, and the succession of photos she took of me. I need to know what Laura's motives are and what exactly she's doing to me. Should I tell Zach about it? I search his eyes. I feel deeply about his regard for me. He's my protector, but what if he thinks I'm crazy like the doctor and the psychiatrist did? No, I won't tell him—it's too soon. I'll wait till I find out more about her, to paint a vivid picture of what she is trying to do exactly.

"Sshhhh." He holds me and rocks me. "It's going to be all right; everything will be fine."

Zach has a way of calming me, and his presence has a

grounding quality to it. Minutes later, I stop crying and stare out blankly, my eyes eventually moving to the closed bedroom door. Zach must know the door is closed because he touches my hand even though it's forbidden among non-family. His touch is light on my hand at first, then he holds it, intertwining his fingers with mine. An electric rush travels its way up my spinal column. It's a pleasurable feeling that I haven't felt before. His free hand travels up my arm until he holds me in a tight embrace, stroking my back calmly. He takes a deep breath and exhales.

"Adriana, I know this is strange, being so close to you, embracing you."

Clasping my chin, he tilts my head so I'm looking straight at him. After checking the door behind him, I stare deep into his eyes. Feeling calmed by his eyes, I want to say something but am unable to form words to express my inner world. Zach breaks the silence.

"I don't know what's come over me. I want to take care of you, to make all this uncertainty and upheaval go away. I feel I've known you for a long time, that I understand you, that we are fated for each other."

I scan his facial features, brushing my fingers over his eyebrows, as his eyes search mine. His pupils are large and there is a softness to the edges as they melt with the green of his irises. "I don't know what to call it, and I know this is not normal to say, but I can't bear to be in a Perfect Bonding Pair with anyone but you."

I lightly trace his jaw line, glancing up into his eyes again. I understand what he means because I feel the same way about him. He takes my hand, softly intertwining his fingers with mine again.

"Say something, Adriana."

I look up to the ceiling as if expecting to wake up from a dream. "Zach, I'm afraid," I croak out in a whisper. Before Zach can say anything, I continue, "And I'm afraid because I feel the same way, and I don't know what to do about it." I quickly steal a glance at Zach, whose eyes are round with attention. "I'm so confused," I whisper. "I hate that Harmony has so much control over my fate—our fate. I want to be paired with you too, but now I'm at the mercy of Harmony. What if Harmony's calculations are wrong? In my heart I know we'd be best for each other. I know it." Then I feel the fear grip my gut again, and I breathe deeply. "But we've been told Harmony has never made a mistake. Your sister works for Harmony, and what if I'm going mad?"

Zach's eyes take on a concerned look. I hope he understands my fears. Perhaps he's as worried as I am.

"Adriana, I don't know what to say..." Bowing his head into his hands, he hides his angst.

"But what if we are actually meant to be a Perfect Bonding Pair and just haven't discovered it?" I say, trying to relieve the tension.

His head rises and his large eyes zero in on me intensely. "Perhaps I can persuade Kevin to let me in and see who our Perfect Bonding Pair will be? Working at Harmony, in the Calling department, he must have access to that information."

"Zach, let's keep our desires to be together completely between you and me. Don't mention it to Laura or anyone else you might think is influential."

A look of disappointment crosses his face, and he studies me for a long moment. Finally, he says, "Of course, Adriana. I won't tell anyone about this."

I breathe a sigh of relief. I don't need anyone discovering our transgression from the way things are. Not with Dr. Marks and Dr. Beata already concerned about me.

⃠

It's been thirty-six hours and I haven't seen or heard from Zach. My mind starts flipping through possible reasons for the communication gap. Have his feelings for me changed now that he knows I share them? Does he think I'm mad? Did he tell Laura about this, to help me with finding answers? She has targeted me, why else would she have taken such sneaky pictures of me at the pool? I'd be furious if he did say anything.

I am home the entire day; I don't want to go out. I bake my father's favorite tart, write in my journal, and stare longingly out the window, looking for any sign of Zach. Day turns to evening, and I am exhausted from worrying about what's become of him.

"Adriana, time for supper." My bedroom door creaks open to reveal my mother's plump rosy face. "Come on, being cooped in this room isn't going to improve your mood, sweetie."

Nodding my head, I force a smile. "Is anyone else coming for dinner?" I ask, hoping she mentions Zach's name.

"No, it's just the three of us today. Laura is working tonight, so Cody has a lavish dinner planned for her."

At the mention of Laura, my stomach is again in knots. This feeling lingers on through dinner and through the evening until sleep gives me some relief.

Waking up to the sound of laughing, I stretch my arms out—until I hear Zach's chuckles and leap out of bed to race toward my wardrobe. His laugh is very distinct. He gasps between suppressed chuckles. His laugh is donkey-like, humoring me. Then I hear two sets of feet skipping up the stairs and soon there's knocking at my door.

"Hey, Adriana, let's go for a swim. The pool's just been cleaned." I wrap a robe around me and open the door to Zach and Cody pushing each other out of the way, teasing for a place in front of my bedroom door.

"You two go. I'll be about fifteen minutes." Closing the door, I breathe a deep sigh of relief, still not sure why he hadn't communicated for two days, but at least I know he's all right now. Laura isn't around, so I'll go to the pool. It might jog my memory of the strange flashes.

Thirty minutes later, I yell, "Cannon ball," as I jump into the water, splashing Zach and Cody.

"You surprised us!" Zach mops his hand over his face. "I thought you said you'd be fifteen minutes, not a half-hour!"

Smiling, I quip, "Well, I'm very bad at keeping track of time."

Understanding dawns in his eyes. He knows I'm disappointed I haven't heard from him. He says, "I guess sometimes things are out of our hands."

The way he's looking at me so softly, I realize I can't hold a grudge against him for long. Cody is oblivious to our banter and dives deep into the water, emerging like a humpback whale.

Zach touches my hand as Cody dives down again and

whispers, "I have something to tell you after swimming, so don't storm off."

I press his fingers reassuringly. After a half-hour, Cody proclaims that he's hungry and that we should go back to the house to get some snacks.

Zach says, "That's a great idea. Why don't you go and get some potato snacks while we soak up the sun?"

About to object, Cody looks at me, already reclining on a sunbed, obviously feeling better than I have for two days.

"All right," he mutters, "but save a bed for me." And with that, he plods away towards the house.

Making sure Cody is out of earshot, Zach turns to me. "I've been busy the past two days convincing Kevin to let us into Headquarters. He thinks I'm absolutely crazy."

"What did you tell him?" I ask, thinking that I'll finally get some answers if Kevin lets us in.

"I've told him that I'm desperate to know who my Perfect Bonding Pair is, and that I would pay him well for his help." Zach looks left and then right and then continues, "It took him a bit of convincing, and my mother's sapphire ring, but he finally agreed."

"How the hell am I going to get in? I don't have a darn sapphire!" I whisper through clenched teeth, feeling more hopeless by the moment.

"Relax, I said that I need to bring you along because you want to check Harmony's database to find out why you have one blue eye and one brown. That, and all the scrobles I have saved, was enough to convince him." Zach looked around again before continuing. "Tomorrow evening at 6:30 p.m., just after dinner, meet me at Purity Burger. We'll change into uniforms the scientists use at the main laboratory, then we'll walk to gate nine where he'll drive us to his basement suite, where he works when he needs to get away from the office.

My heart starts beating faster as I think of the ramifications of being caught. For a moment, I doubt we should trust Kevin; he works for Harmony, and he knows Laura. What if he decides to spill the beans to her? Besides, it's against the law to insist on knowing your fate before it's officially conveyed through a government holographic text message. Others have tried, but those who have not been successful have become cautionary tales. On the news, they show it to be selfish and doubtful of Harmony, which has saved mankind from extinction. Those who doubt Harmony are publicly named and shamed. They're taxed twenty percent of their earnings for the rest of their working lives. Sometimes, if repentant enough, the tax is lowered to fifteen percent, but that is for Harmony's algorithm to figure out how repentant a doubter is.

Cody returns with potato skin snacks, and we sit in a circle to eat them.

"These are delicious," Zach comments while he dips one in ketchup.

"Yeah, it's the new recipe that Laura made. It's a special seaweed flavor, full of omega-3s, great for brain health." He glances at me. "You look happier today, Adriana."

"Yes, I think the sun and water really helped my mood." I dunk the potato in enough ketchup to cover the seaweed taste.

We play a bit more in the water, challenging each other to swimming competitions. Of course, Cody wins. After drying off, he pulls on a t-shirt and struts triumphantly to his car, smugly saluting us as he gets in the driver's seat and races off. Zach and I watch him speed away, then he turns to me.

"Look, I've got to go home now, but remember, tomorrow at Purity Burger." He grabs my hand and squeezes, letting go before any prying eyes notice. "And get a hold of your nerves; you'll spoil everything if you let your fear control you."

The next day, Mother wakes me up. "We won't be productive members of society if we are constantly lazing around," she berates.

"Mom, I'm just sore from swimming yesterday."

"Adriana, dear, you know the science of our immune systems. We need balance to fight off any viruses or bacteria that may be overlooked, goodness forbid!"

Antiseptic spray in hand, she sprays the air with disinfectant. I plod along to the kitchen where I make myself an alfalfa and tomato sandwich. Scanning the bread for mold, I eat breakfast quickly and decide to take a walk outside, to breathe in some fresh air. Traipsing through the front lawn and onto the pavement, I notice a little girl, not older than five, playing with a dog. It's uncommon to see dogs in MicroScrep, except in veterinarian households. Perhaps the dog belongs to her parents. As I get closer, I scan the dog and see it has a tick attached to its ear. Ticks harbor terrible diseases—diseases that young children are the most vulnerable to. Striding faster towards the girl, I tell her to stand back as I pinch the tick off the dog's ear.

"What's that!" she cries out.

It is then that I notice she has a patch over her eye. In an instant, a flash of memory returns. We are at the National Day Parade, she is smiling and then skips off to her seat near the last plexiglass divider.

"Oh, kill it," she screams in horror. Her voice snaps me out of my memory flash.

Holding the blood-filled insect, I grab a lighter from my pocket. "It's a tick, and you're lucky it didn't bite you, or else it could have made you sick!"

As I burn the tick with the lighter, I ask her, "Is this your dog?" My eyes fall to the collar around the dog's neck. On it is stitched the initial "M" and then Mills. The only "Mills" I know is Arthur Mills, the founder of MicroScrep. I wonder what the M stands for?

Innocently looking at me, the girl says, "A scientist gave it to me. Please don't tell my mum and dad." Her large eyes rounded, she pleads to me, "It's so fluffy and friendly. Besides, I want to be a vet when I grow up—Mom and Dad say I can't be a musician because Harmony makes all the music."

"A scientist?" I ask, bewildered. Another flash of memory interrupts my train of thought. The little girl is whistling a tune to me at the parade.

"Wait, were you at a parade a while back?" I blurt out.

She looks up, her eye searching her memory, "I...I...don't remember."

"What about the scientist? Do you remember who he or she was?"

"Yeah, she comes to this neighborhood sometimes." Her big blue eye peers at me inquisitively.

I shake my head. "You'll have to tell your parents. You can't keep this a secret, especially now that there were bugs on it. They could have spread anywhere!"

The girl looks up at me with her large blue eye. "No, the scientist said I could keep it near the compound pool. She made a house for it behind there. She took a picture of me with a fancy camera before showing me the dog for the first time. I only take it for walks after everyone has gone to work."

I think about the shed. Nobody ever goes there, but there is a familiar feeling about it, as if I witnessed something significant there. It's derelict, with no tools in it. What a strange request. Why can't I remember what is so important about it? Why would a scientist ask a young child to look after a dog that harbors insects? Unless the girl is lying to me, playing a prank as little kids do, to pass the time. Somehow my gut tells me she's not. Ticks can spread terrible bacteria, and this poor child could have been hurt if I hadn't seen her with it.

"Do you know the name of the scientist who gave you the dog to look after?" I ask.

The girl searches for a name. "She comes here often. I saw her come to your house this week."

Suddenly, my stomach turns. Laura! Why would she do this? She knows the laws around animals. She would know that dogs can only be pets to veterinarians. Unless she's trying to get rid of someone or hide something. My mind flashes and I remember the parade. Laura is there. She is pulling something, but I can't remember what it is. Then the plexiglass. Laura looks coldly at us, me and the girl with the patch over her eye. A cold sweat makes my forehead dewy.

Heart pounding, I say, "I am sorry, I've got to go." I'm running down the street towards my house before the little girl can respond. I've got to tell Zach, he's the only one who'll listen. If Laura does something terrible to me or the little girl before I tell someone, it'll be all my fault. I shut the door behind me, forgetting to scan for bacteria.

Two hours later, I'm at Zach's house. He answers the door.

He's frowning. "I thought I told you to meet me at Purity Burger?"

"Zach, I've got to tell you something," I gasp out.

Zach furrows his brow. "What?"

"A little girl today, she was walking a dog near my house. It wasn't her dog. It had a tick on it. She would have been hurt if it bit her."

"Her parents must be veterinarians, Adriana. They'll know how to deal with animals."

I take Zach's hand and pull him outside with me. "No! NO! She said Laura gave the dog to her!"

Zach's face turns a deep shade of red and he shakes his head. "What? Why would Laura give a random girl in your neighborhood a dog!"

I look at him, realizing I must sound insane. "I, I, don't know, but I keep on having flashes—memory flashes—so is the little girl...I think it has something to do with her eyes. She has a patch over one eye. Like me, she doesn't have normal eyes."

Zach's features bunch up as if he's just tasted something very bitter. "The little girl must have been confused, one of her parents must be a vet or else there's no way that she'd have a dog. It just wouldn't happen, Adriana." Noticing that I'm not convinced, he sighs. "Let's get to the bottom of this." He pulls out his car keys and leads me to his car and we're off towards my home.

After circling the neighborhood for fifteen minutes or so, there is no sign of a dog or a little girl. Zach's face gets more and more stern with disappointment with every round we make. I am equally frustrated. How can he not believe me! I am furious, so indignant, that I feel like bursting.

"Stop at the shed!" I say, remembering the girl saying that they kept the dog at the old shed beside the pool. We walk around to find a dilapidated building. We enter it and there is another door where I hear whimpering. I motion to Zach to follow me, then squat down and open the door. I hear a shrill scream as I'm greeted with the gruesome image of the little girl from earlier, half-eaten by the dog. Everything circles around, the color of blood, the smell of the dog's disgusting saliva, his canine teeth exposed, the blond hair tainted with blood, Zach retching, and still the shrill scream of someone, louder and louder. I look at the images swimming around me, searching for the person screaming. Minutes before everything goes black, I realize the screams are coming from me.

Chapter 7:

Zach and the Database

She looks like an angel; I think to myself as I cover my hand over Adriana's. I think back to the gruesome sight that we'd seen this afternoon. How I'd helped Adriana to the ground after she'd fainted. How I grabbed the dog, leashed it to a tree, and ran off to get help. How terrible it was for the parents of the little girl. The mother's screams of anguish, the father's pain as he doubled over in tears. The sounds of the sirens, the ambulance taking Adriana on a stretcher. The child's body covered in a body bag. How the doctor said it was best for Adriana if she remained asleep for a few hours longer. Considering her recent mental health, they had administered selective amnesia. I think of her theory, of how she thinks the girl was targeted because of her eye. How could that be? She has a totally different problem with her eyes than Adriana does. The little girl had a lazy eye, and Adriana has two different eye colors.

"She won't remember this, so don't reference it ever again." The doctor's stern warning is directed to everyone in the room—Adriana's mom, dad, Cody, and me. "It may cost her sanity if you do," he says rebukingly.

We all sit in silence as the doctor injects the selective amnesia into her side. He's placing a band-aid on Adriana when I feel the vibration of my holographic phone and with one touch have answered Kevin. I'd forgotten we were supposed to meet him today.

"Where the hell are you? It's seven p.m." He doesn't even bother with pleasantries.

"I'm in the hospital; something awful has happened," I say with a tinge of frustration in my voice. "Can we postpone it to tomorrow?"

"Well, you should have told me," Kevin barks.

"Sorry, it was out of my hands." I get up and walk into the hallway, fearing that Adriana's parents may overhear the conversation.

"Then it'll cost you another of those gold coins."

Kevin doesn't even wait for my reply before he hangs up. This behavior isn't normal for Kevin. We've always been pleasant towards each other. He's the one who befriended me through Laura, when she mentioned that Cody and I played soccer. He's the one who asked to join us during the weekend matches. There has always been something comforting and calm about Kevin, he feels familiar, but this telephone call is very unlike him. He must be on edge, worried about the ramifications of being caught. People here don't go against the rules, even Kevin. In fact, Adriana is the only one who I know who speaks her mind, at least in private. It might get her in a lot of trouble one day.

I shrug to myself and go back into Adriana's room just as her parents and Cody decide to get something to eat. I tell them I'm not hungry, but really, I want to be here to protect Adriana. Every ounce of my being wants me to be the one on the bed and not her.

On his way out of the room, the doctor notices me staring and frowns. "Go ask for repentance for Harmony's sake!" As if he knows I'm too attached to her. "Go wash your face and take some millidot," he orders, telling the nurse to see to it that I'll be given the sedative to numb my attachments.

Even though I tell her I don't want it, the nurse administers the millidot. In a few moments, a sense of flattening, of conformity rushes through me temporarily. There's a sense of detachment. I look at Adriana on her hospital bed, and I'm filled with a sense that she is just like any other MicroScrepian, flesh and duty.

Adriana's eyelashes flutter before she slowly opens her eyes. She takes one or two blinks before she sees me clearly.

"Hey, Zach, what happened?" she says groggily.

"Not much, you just fainted, no big deal."

"Why am I in a hospital?" Adriana attempts to get up but closes her eyes and sinks back against the pillow. Her brown, curly hair is like a large crown around her face.

"You fainted because you haven't been eating properly. The doctor said you'll be okay to be discharged soon."

Adriana sighs before closing her eyes. Her freckled petite nose shiny from the humid hospital room.

"I have a feeling that we were supposed to do

something today, but I don't remember..." Her eyes are still closed.

"Oh, don't bother yourself. We'll go see my friend tomorrow."

"Oh, yes, now I remember. I'm going to find out some information before it becomes official." Adriana looks around the room. "They don't have a camera here, do they?"

"No, we're fine. Just don't go around talking about our appointment tomorrow." My voice is tinged with sarcasm. Adriana nods and closes her eyes softly, coughing a laugh at herself. There is a knock at the door. "Yes," I call out. I hear Cody and Adriana's mother's muffled voices outside the door.

Adriana's mother, wringing her hands nervously, enters the room, Adriana's father and Cody following closely behind her.

"Hey, Mom and Dad," Adriana greets them with tired cheer.

"Honey, I am so happy you got some rest," her mother gushes.

"Adriana, you'll be out of here in no time, and then we can swim again," Cody says cheerfully.

Adriana's eyebrows weave together as if she's remembering something bothersome.

Cody continues, "Well, maybe not then. Just would be nice to have you out of here."

The doctor knocks on the door and enters. "All right, which one of you wants to stay the night?" His joke goes unappreciated by the dead silence in the room. "I didn't mean in the morgue, I meant in the hospital room."

Adriana's father politely chuckles to cover everyone

else's awkward silence.

"Okay then, you must be Adriana." He lifts her hand and looks at her wristband label. "That's how you pronounce it, correct?"

"Yes." She nods.

"You're fine to be discharged. Just remember to see reception and they'll untag your label."

On the drive home, the millidot they gave me is starting to wear off. The feelings I have for Adriana return, and I prefer it this way. I don't want to be the flat robot that the millidot makes me into. Adriana is still very groggy. Her eyes drift in and out of sleep. Cody and I help her out of the car and to her room, where she slinks down on the bed and falls asleep. On the drive back to my house, I leave a voice memo on her holographic phone, reminding her to meet me at Purity Burger at 6:30 p.m. tomorrow.

The day goes by very slowly. Jittery and unsettled, I think of all the things that can go wrong. What if security finds us catching a ride with Kevin, won't that be enough to provoke questioning? What are we going to say if that happens? Apparently, Kevin has a few faithful security guards, so he's confident from that angle. The worst worry of all is the probability of Adriana being put in a Perfect Bonding Pair with someone other than me. How am I going to go through life without her near me? Our connection will slowly be lost if she's given to someone else and starts her own family nucleus.

Worrying does terrible things to my appetite. I can barely eat, and I am forcing down food as my blood sugar plummets. The thought of finding out who I am going to live my blissful, harmonious life with is intimidating as well. I find myself again questioning whether I am abnormal for desiring so desperately to know what my fate holds. Most people my age just trust Harmony's choice. Questioning like this is abnormal. Or is it? Adriana questions too; this might not be a coincidence. Citizens in MicroScrep believe that the system works. We have no economic or social distress in our society. There is no crime, no terrible suffering. Then why am I doubting it? Could it be that the oxytocin that I'm taking isn't working? If it did, I wouldn't be doing these silly, reckless actions—bribing an acquaintance to let me see private information not meant for me yet. Then I think about Adriana. Sweet, beautiful, unique Adriana. Her curly hair, her angelic face, her eyes, so starkly uncommon, so rare. I dream of her face. I long for her smell. Touching her hand is the pinnacle of my day. Her soft hand, so warm, resting on her beautiful chest.

It is 6:35 p.m. and I am getting nervous. Adriana hasn't arrived yet. The sound of chatter envelops me. The Purity Burger is bustling, and I sit near the kitchen on a barstool. The sound of the barbecue is sizzling and the chefs clanking and cutting are barely audible.

6:38 p.m. I'll have to leave if she didn't make it by 6:45. The door suddenly opens, and I see Adriana enter while folding her umbrella. It must have started raining in the last ten minutes. I motion her towards me. I had ordered her an iced tea, not realizing that it might be the last thing she'd want in damp and cloudy weather.

"Hey, sorry I'm late. The taxi driver was acting strange, as if he didn't know the location of Mills Boulevard or Purity Burger." She shakes her head in disappointment. I smile at her, lost for words, my heart still pumping quickly.

"What time should we go?" She breaks the awkward silence.

"In about five minutes." My voice cracks. She can tell I am nervous.

Politely sipping on the iced tea, she thanks me and pushes it to the side. "I guess we should get going."

After a few minutes of walking underneath Adriana's umbrella, we hear Kevin's car beep behind us.

"Okay, phew—thank goodness it is raining. The cameras won't be able to see your faces up close if they suspect."

We arrive at Kevin's house, but take a stony path that leads us to the small, detached office that he has made behind his home. When inside the building, our rubber boots make an awful squeaky noise against the laminate floors. We find Kevin's computer tucked away behind a large generator. Adriana asks whether this is connected to the Harmony database. Sitting down, Kevin's fingers shake. I am not sure if it is his fear or the coldness of the weather.

"For goodness sake, yes, it is." His voice is harsh and low-toned. Kevin already has two seats set up in front of the holographic screen.

"Give me your citizen number," he barks without a word of explanation.

"Well, good day to you too," Adriana sarcastically

mumbles to Kevin as I choke back a smile.

He looks up from his screen, his face stern and overbearing. “It’s against the law for any of us to be doing this, so I can’t waste time with cordialities.”

With a few clicks on the holographic screen, he has Adriana’s personal information and a long list of numbers, forming a family tree. No pictures, no visuals, only numbers. The next tab is algorithms for various subheadings: personality traits, body language, voice recognition, retinal scans, and Perfect Bonding Pair, and before I can read the rest, he clicks on a tab that says psychometrics, which again displays dates and series of numbers. Some are color-coded.

“Yes, I can see you’re a bit of a rogue, a bit of a rebel,” he says with an edge of nerviness in his voice. “You weren’t always this bad either, something has changed recently,” he says under his voice. My stomach twists, does he know Adriana’s feelings towards me? Or worse yet, does he know that Adriana is suspicious of MicroScrep and Harmony? Sweat gathers at my brows, and I suddenly feel hot.

He starts typing hysterically on a black side-by-side screen. “Okay, now for the imminent future.” He takes a deep breath and types in a code on the black screen.

A projection pops up, words capitalized overtop of a moving holographic 3D image of Adriana. “SURROGACY CENTER (dangerous oxytocin levels unfit for a Perfect Bonding Pair).”

“Congratulations, Adriana, you are honored with the fate of becoming a Surrogate!” Kevin says loudly, but in his eyes, there is a lost sense of sadness.

Adriana looks neutral, her eyes moving back and forth

as if she's trying to make sense of this new revelation. Staring at the screen, a calmness takes over her features, but the more she relaxes, the tenser I get. My heart feels as if it has been broken, my mind races as my stomach does twists. Surrogacy for Adriana means I won't see her ever again after she leaves for the off-grid center. It means we cannot be a family; we cannot live out our lives together.

"What?! There must be something wrong." My voice trembles.

Kevin gives me a flippant glance. "You should be happy for her. She'll become a heroine, immortalized forever in MicroScrep. Don't tell me you want her to live out the rest of her life in domestic service." Kevin glares at me, his face red, expressionless, and deciphering. "Were you two looking for something else?"

Adriana quickly straightens up and puts on a victorious smile. "Don't be so jealous, Zach, let's see what your fate is."

I'm not sure what Adriana is thinking deep inside. Perhaps she is as heartbroken as I am, but she encourages me with a smile and a brief knowing glance.

Kevin huffs incredulously and starts furiously typing. He inputs my number, and, in a few clicks, my holographic image rotates in 3D. The label on top of it reads "EUNUCH." My heart starts beating faster and faster, I'm spinning just as my 3D image does in front of me. My breathing becomes shallow. Kevin looks concerned as my head gets very faint, and he moves to hold me up, but I'm already on the ground hyperventilating.

Kevin paces back and forth, freaking out, cursing everything in sight. This gives me a slightly out-of-body experience, seeing a calm Harmony engineer be so foul-mouthed and anxious. I regulate my breathing as I watch Kevin explode into frenzy, probably because it takes my mind off myself for a few moments. Adriana reacts quickly, going through the drawers searching, and finally producing a paper bag, which she holds over my mouth to regulate my breathing. When I am finally breathing regularly, Kevin still pacing around the room, she brings me a cool drink of water.

"Leave immediately," Kevin says after I drink the water. Then he sighs, running his hand through his hair until it's sticking up crazily. "Darn it, wait," he moans.

Something, perhaps pity, has changed his mind. "I'll give you guys a lift home," he says, his eyes wild and distraught.

I try to imagine what could make him change his mind so quickly. Maybe it isn't pity; maybe it's fear that we'll be spotted and linked back to his office.

He insists on leaving his office before we do. He explains that he doesn't want anyone to see all three of us together.

"Don't do anything stupid, just wait five minutes and meet me outside and down the road. Don't say anything, don't do anything on your way out. I'll make sure we won't be flagged if we aren't walking to my car together." He then slinks out of the room. I immediately grab Adriana's hand and pull her close to me.

"Adriana, what are we going to do?" I whisper, choking back tears. Adriana's face is flushed and her eyes dart back and forth as if trying to make sense of our assignments. She squeezes my hand.

"We'll be okay. We're going to sort this out." She's

breathing faster, and I see a faint sweat gather at her brow.

"Surrogates only live to birth a child; you'll be dead by the time you're twenty." My voice cracks on the word "dead." I can't imagine a world without Adriana. I don't want to. Shaking my head, I say, "And I'm going to have to live my life as goodness knows what! I won't even have a family to soothe me when my work is done."

Adriana is quiet for a few moments and then whispers, "We still have a few days; we'll figure something out."

"Figure what out? In two days, they're going to send a holographic message to our parents, and our names will be published in the newspaper, and they'll come and collect us amongst fanfare and fake joy. We'll have to put on an act, as if we don't know that this is coming, and to make things worse, we'll have to act like this is a great honor! Adriana, all I've ever wanted in life is to be with you." I step back and gaze deep into Adriana's different colored eyes. I see little parts of blue against the cosmetic contact lens. It's like she has the strength and life of two people. Tears are slowly rolling down her face and plunking off her chin.

"And all I've wanted is to be with you."

I feel a magnetic pull, and all of sudden, a loud beeping startles both of us. We hold onto each other and duck instinctively.

BEEP, BEEP, BEEP.

Then there is the sound of deafening sirens.

Opening the door, we see the lights are turned off, except for the red emergency lights that flicker in the hallway towards the exit.

"Get back in, Kevin told us to wait five minutes, it's only been two."

Closing the door, we huddle under Kevin's desk. We hear the sound of several feet trotting loudly into the office. I look at Adriana who has her hand over her mouth, afraid to breath.

"Hmm, Kevin's little hideaway." A deep voice bellows.

"Ha—he's taking working from home to another level," the other snickers.

A bead of sweat rolls down my brow and cheek. I wipe it off.

One rummages around his books, the other clicks on the keyboard of his computer.

"Locked." The deep voice murmurs, teeth gritted together.

"The little weasel," the other jeers before they look around and leave.

The door clicks closed. Adriana's fret.

"That was close" I whisper, my heart pounding in my ears.

Adriana's jaw is tense. She nods her head. She opens her mouth to speak, but closes it. "We have five minutes," her voice trembles as she speaks.

At exactly five minutes, I help Adriana to her feet, and we steal out of the office and out onto the street. Kevin is waiting for us in his car and as soon as we get in, he speeds off. When we can finally see his house in the rearview mirror, Kevin looks at our faces. "What's the matter with you two?"

My voice trembles with emotion. "I want Adriana to have a good long life. Surrogates only live to birth a child."

Adriana is deep in thought, but squeaks out a moan.

Kevin hits the brakes and turns to look at me. "Do you think living in a Perfect Bonding Pair and Family Match for forty years has any added glory? It's what the common people do. At least Adriana will be immortalized, someone like me is just another cog in the wheel."

There is a heaviness and tension in the air as Kevin starts to accelerate, and I lean my head back, my thoughts bouncing wildly around my head. Outside it's raining, and the window wipers slosh the rain back and forth. The quiet is interrupted by Kevin choking back tears. His eyes meet mine in the mirror. "I'm sadder for you. You'll live your life in the Eunuch barracks, alone for many years. Eunuchs are known to live longer than the average male, but they don't have a family system to shelter them. You'll have a limited future. It's not what I wanted for my biological son."

Adriana and I shoot straight up and look at each other, completely flabbergasted. I can see the thoughts buzzing in her mind, but before she can say anything, I ask, "What, you're my real father?"

Understanding dawns in Adriana's eyes and she says, "He works as a Harmony engineer, so he must know where his sperm ended up."

Kevin looks in his rearview mirror at me. "Yes, that was supposed to be confidential information, but I have access to it. That's why I befriended you, and why I helped you. I couldn't say no to my own flesh and blood."

Thousands of thoughts are swirling in my mind, all that Kevin is saying is totally against MicroScrep culture. It's illegal to know who your biological child is for a regular citizen, to even ask to know is a treasonous sin. Everybody belongs to everyone else. Blood does not matter. Love—pure, clean love—for all of society is idealized.

Adriana suddenly breaks the silence. "Kevin, can you

overwrite the algorithm in Harmony?" I open my eyes wide at the thought. Kevin stares hard at the front windshield, a tear trickles down his face. He nods. After a few moments, he says, "If I'm going to do that, I need one thing." He looked at me again in the mirror. "I need you to steal your sister's amulet."

Chapter 8:

The Amulet

During the ride home, Kevin agreed to help us rewrite our fate. "Adriana, fate has dealt you a rainbow. I knew there was a reason for all this," he said looking over his shoulder as he changed lanes. He'd have to hack into our files, but to do this he'd need us to find our way into his office the following day so that he could access our files through our retinal scans. Kevin told us that we did not have much time, the official memo of our citizenship assignments was going to be sent in the next two days.

"It was originally Arthur Mills's amulet," Kevin said as he wove manically through the traffic.

"How would Laura have Arthur Mills's amulet?" Zach had asked.

"She's the only surviving genetic link to Arthur Mills, and because of that, Arthur Mills's amulet was passed down to her. It's the only thing that can override Harmony's database without tracking and linking the change. If I have that amulet, I can change your fate without anyone being the wiser."

"What if I can't get it?" Zach's face looks sick from the uncomfortable heat in the car and the sloshing of the windshield wipers.

"Then I won't change anything in the database." Kevin's eyebrows weave together and he continues, "It isn't just my life on the line here; you both would be killed if found tampering with the system."

We all fall silent for a few kilometers, listening to the continued downpour of the rain on the car. It's calming amidst all the worry and hazard that surrounds us.

Once we change our fate in the Harmony database, the amulet will be returned safely and no one will talk of this ever again. Kevin makes us promise this.

In the history of MicroScrep, there'd never been an attempt to tamper with Harmony, but the consequence is public death by stoning. The thought of being pummeled by stones is more nerve wracking than dying in a hospital bed off grid.

It's the thought of us getting caught that causes me to have yet another panic attack early the next morning. Zach isn't around to console me, and I'm alone in my room, wondering how Zach is going to manage to get the amulet before nightfall.

I feel dizzy, as if a great wind has blown into my room and turned my belongings into a funnel of shapes and colors. My breath becomes shallow as I claw my way to the bed. I fall on my back, hold my sides like a wounded soldier. Panic takes over and I call out to Cody.

"Hey, what's going on in there?" he shouts as he bounds up the stairs.

When I don't respond, he bursts into my room, his face contorted with surprise. He helps me to a sitting position which makes me dizzy again. My eyes scour the room, I point to the paper bag in the corner of the room. Cody gets up and brings it to me. After a few minutes of breathing into the bag, my normal breath returns.

"Okay, Adriana, seriously, you need to see a doctor." He slides his back down the wall and sits on his bottom, overcome with confusion. My forehead has a slight dew on it, and I swipe the sweat away with my forearm.

"Cody, I've been having panic attacks lately," I mutter miserably.

His face turns from alarm to worry, "Why, what's going on? You can tell me, Adriana."

The awkwardness in the room is palpable and I look towards Cody. "I guess I am anxious about the naming ceremony."

Cody opens his mouth to protest, but just then his holographic phone lights up and rings. He taps on it to see who the caller is. "Darn it, it's Laura. Sorry I've got to take this." From the progressive reddening of Cody's face, I can tell something is deeply wrong. After a few moments, Cody says, "Who could have broken into your safe? And why would they steal nothing but your amulet?"

I can hear Laura's voice shouting on the other end of the phone. Cody stays silent until she finishes her torrent of anger. "Okay, well at least they didn't take our wedding gems and all the gold we store in there." Her voice becomes irate and Cody distances his ear from the phone. "I'll be there in ten minutes, don't call the MicroScrep hotline over such a petty theft. They have bigger fish to fry." He hangs up and looks at me. "I really think you should see a doctor soon." He turns to leave, but hesitates a moment at the door, torn between staying with me and assisting Laura. Being the dutiful husband, he excuses himself and leaves.

My fingers jitter as I call Zach immediately, "Where are you?"

"I'm coming to pick you up. We've got to get to Kevin as soon as possible, Laura knows the amulet is missing."

"How did that happen?"

"I thought she was at work. She was supposed to be there, anyways."

"How did you know the code?" I ask bewildered.

"That's the freaky part, I didn't. When I went upstairs to where the safe was, it was already open. Either somebody was there before I was, or Laura forgot to lock it."

I gasp. "Okay, I'll call Kevin."

Hanging up, I dial Kevin's number, and when he answers, I say, "We have the amulet. Laura knows it's missing. What should we do?"

Kevin curses. "You'd better get yourself and Zach to my office as soon as you can, I'm leaving now."

I hang up and instinctively grab my backpack. Running down the stairs, I decide to steal out the back door and walk to the front gates of the compound where Zach pulls up and flings his car door open for me.

"Why the hell did you bring a backpack?" Zach says annoyedly.

"I don't know, I just did," I say. "We might have to camp out at Kevin's office for a while."

"Don't be stupid. We're going to hack into Harmony, change our fates, go back home, and I'll return the amulet back to the safe tonight."

Zach parks his car down the road to where Kevin's car is parked, and we get out and move quickly. As we pass a cafe, a tinge of sadness overcomes me. I can't pinpoint what it is, but I think it has to do with all the young people our age sitting inside, chatting and laughing with no care in the world.

For a moment I worry whether Zach and I are safe to do this. What if Kevin can't get in? *I am not going back home*, I think to myself. Something about Laura having the key to do as she pleases in Harmony bothers me to my core. So, how does being a genetic offspring of Arthur Mills gives you such rights? Aren't we all supposed to belong to each other? Aren't genetics irrelevant in the whole sham of a society we live in? These questions furiously arise as I walk towards Kevin's home office. I guess we'll find out what it can do when we meet Kevin in his office in a few moments. One thing is certain though, I have no faith in the system anymore, and I certainly am not going to let Laura and MicroScrep win.

Stopping before the stony path that leads to Kevin's office, a dizzying sense of anticipation hits me.

"Adriana, what's with you?" Zach says. Noticing my jaw clenched, he says, "Adriana, snap out of it!"

Shaking my head, my eyes tear up and I'm filled with anger. Anger at their lies, anger that I let them silence my questions in childhood.

Zach tuts and takes my hand. "Take courage, Adriana." Every step becomes increasingly more certain. I am sure Zach senses my indignance as he laces his fingers with mine.

Standing in front of his office, Zach presses the doorbell. When there is no response, he unlatches the door and we walk in.

Kevin has his back towards us sat facing the computer. As Kevin swivels around, we are petrified by his expression. His eyes are bloodshot. He's been working on hacking the system for a while now. His hair is greasy and harried. Zach runs up to Kevin. "What's wrong?"

Kevin's eyes tear up and he doesn't speak, instead he brings his hands to Zach's pocket and pulls out the amulet. He is already at the screen that requires it. He scans it, his mouth twisting into a smile. His eyes wide and awestruck.

"I've been trying to change things for a while now," is all he mutters.

Suddenly, everything goes black, and the sirens start blaring. There is a sound like a hollow clap. Kevin's wide eyes look from my face to Zach's. He's scared. He falls to the ground, dropping the amulet.

Kevin crawls to a trap door and motions me towards it. He picks up the amulet and gives it to Zach, staring into his eyes for a moment.

"It's fake," he sputters, blood seeping between his teeth. "Harmony knows I was not faithful to the system, and it fired a bullet at me."

His eyes suddenly change as if he's realized something more ominous that his impending death, "Shit, Cody's in deep shit...the note I gave him at our last meeting—it's—" his voice breaks off as we hear the thump of boots, progressively getting louder."

"Go!" He points to the trap door and the bunker where he wants us to shelter. He closes the trap door behind me and Zach. Seconds later, we hear security enter the office, followed by the sounds of a struggle. I hear a thump and a moan. I imagine security has Kevin on the ground. Then I hear the terrible sound of Kevin choking and sputtering. I shut my eyelids tight and plug my ears. I do not want to listen to his last stifled breaths. Silently weeping, Zach rubs the amulet for false comfort.

For the next few hours, we hear the horrific sound of security trying to find any other accomplices to Kevin's crime. They turn everything over, even dismantling parts of Kevin's computer in frustration.

Zach and I look at each other. Nothing had changed, and by tomorrow both of us would be carted off: I to the Surrogacy Center, and Zach to the hospital to be castrated.

After what seems to be a few hours, we hear someone say, "He must have been stupid enough to think he could change the database. Don't let the media know he's dead. We'll be in charge of the rest."

My anger comes in ebbs and flows. MicroScrep hurled these abuses on us for years. They cheated me of my childhood. How many lies have we been fed about this subjective database when Laura can simply change what doesn't suit her? Everything here is fake.

Zach and I didn't dare to speak for an hour after security had left. We only whisper when the silence of nighttime takes over. I rummage through my backpack and find a Swiss army knife, some bottled water, and a flashlight. I turn the flashlight on and look around the bunker. There's a cardboard box about a meter away. I motion towards it and Zach crawls with me to it. I cut through the tape with my knife and find what looks like an album. The pictures in it are of Kevin when he was younger. The first picture is of him being born, the date and time of birth labelled under the picture. The next pages show him as a schoolboy. The next pages are of family portraits with his Perfect Family Match. His younger pictures are carefree, a wide smile or laugh, a sparkle in his precocious eyes. But I notice his expression becomes more and more serious as he develops into a young man. In some of the family photos, his eyes are chillingly vacant. The last picture before a stapled envelope and letter, shows Kevin with dark circles under his eyes and undeniable terror present in them. I look at Zach, who rips the envelope out of the album and opens it up. Shining my flashlight on the unfurled letter, we read:

Dear Zachary,

If you are reading this, you've found me, or I've found you. My greatest wish in life was to know you, my own flesh and blood. I am sure you understand this somehow—either epigenetically or subconsciously—you must know that I fought to keep you safe. I had my eye on you, making sure what happened to me didn't happen to you, but your Perfect Family Match are just regular people, detached and gullible about all the evil that is inherent in the lies the State feeds us.

I am writing this to tell you of the horrors that I've had to endure and to make you aware of the struggle in MicroScrep between the forces of good and the forces of evil. I also want you to know about how depraved humans can be, even when controlled by a database. I am now a grown man; I have my own Perfect Family Match. I have a wife and children who have been given to me and who I've raised with all the love that was denied to me as a child.

I cannot help but think how different my life would have been if I were able to marry and have children with someone I truly loved. How different my life would be if I hadn't been educated as a Harmony engineer in MicroScrep. You see, even though MicroScrep has done away with romantic love and sexual desire, there are still people who search for love, and there are still men who are perverse. As a child, I grew up under a man who was the second biological link to our founder, Arthur Mills. This man, Milton Mills, was my chosen father in my Perfect Family Match. A chill runs down my spine when I think of him even now, years after his disappearance. He was a terrible, perverse man. He raped me daily from the time I was ten years of age. He used to tell me that if I told anyone about his transgressions, he would be able to change my fate in Harmony and have me stoned to death. You see, he had the amulet that could allow for the algorithms in Harmony to be tampered with. I suffered through life with Milton Mills. Acting as if I was blessed to be a citizen of MicroScrep, blessed to be given a Perfect Family Match that supported me and loved me unselfishly. As a child, I'd read history books about life before the pandemic and wondered if degenerate humans, who had genetically common children, were really all that depraved? I remember fantasizing about my real genetic parents, and I doubt they would have treated me as terribly as Milton Mills had. My goal in life was to get that amulet and change his fate to make him suffer. I could not; he disappeared before my twentieth birthday, and his amulet was taken by MicroScrep Security Forces.

After some research with my loyal friends, those that are working to overthrow MicroScrep, I've been able to find that the amulet was given to Laura, your Perfect Family Match sister. How strange that MicroScrep is built on the idea that biological relations are not important, however those who have power are somehow related to Arthur Mills.

The day I graduated as a Harmony database engineer was the day I traced myself to you. My sperm and Perfect Genetic Pair's egg was used to create an embryo and transferred to Surrogate who gave birth to you in a Surrogacy Center where she died quickly after. You were given to a Perfect Family Match, and I was adamant about following you, making sure you were not mistreated as I was. In an interesting twist of fate, Laura, your matched sister, was the second survivor of Arthur Mills's bloodline and was given the amulet. Whoever has the amulet can make changes in Harmony. Right now, a consortium of engineers think they have power, but Laura is the one who can change anything she wants because she has the amulet.

I am happy to see you did not have to endure what I did. Then, a few years ago, we befriended each other. Those were the happiest moments of my life. Watching you, a part of me, thrive in the world. I know we are taught to love all unconditionally, and I do want the best for all citizens of MicroScrep, but I see this as a duty. The love I have for you is different, it is mingled in my heart and favors you over my own matched children.

I want you to be happy, so please pursue what you desire, and know that I want you to be happy, that might mean that you have to go after MicroScrep, or Laura. Remember, with great knowledge comes great responsibility.

With Love,
Your Father,
Kevin

Stunned by the rawness of the letter, Zach quietly weeps.

"What are we going to do now?" I ask. My fingers jittery as I bring them to Zach's shoulder.

Looking at me, Zach takes my hand. "We have two choices. Nobody knows we're here. It's past midnight. We can go home and wait until tomorrow when we'll be carted to our fate. The second option is to run away together off-grid and find our way. We have enough water; it will last us a few days."

My face reddens. I want to do what Zach suggests, but we are only two people. I need to know more about what Kevin means by the forces of good and the forces of evil. I need to know what I am up against.

"What do you think, Adriana?"

"We won't know how to survive off-grid, and if we manage to stay together, it won't be long until they find us. Then we'll definitely be stoned to death."

Starting to object, Zach pleads, "But we'll be together."

"I know that," I counter, "but even if we were to be off-grid, we don't know how to survive. How would we find food or shelter?"

Zach's green eyes glow with sadness. "I'm worried I'll never see you again."

I take his hand in both of mine and interlace my fingers

with his. "Let's promise to find each other." I raise our hands up towards the trap door for no reason other than to solidify the moment, ingrain it in my mind.

"How?" His voice cracks. "With me in the Eunuch Center and you in the Surrogacy Center..."

"I'll either find out where you are, or you'll find out where I am. We'll escape to find each other."

Zach moans. "You'll be pregnant and then dead after giving birth."

I embrace him and whisper, "You have such little faith in me. I am strong; I'll stay alive."

My mouth muffles against his shoulder, hot tears stream down my cheeks.

"We'd better get going and get back to our homes. Tomorrow is the big day." I glance down at my watch, 12:25 a.m. We open the trap door to pitch darkness.

Closing the trap door, I turn to Zach, who whispers, "I'll go first." He climbs out of the trap door, pulling himself up and lying down on his stomach until I'm beside him. We sneak towards the door. Zach points to the exit, and we walk outside and tiptoe on the stony path and then run towards Zach's car.

I pause for a minute taking in what will probably be our last moments together. "Get in, Adriana, I don't want to be spotted now."

Zach reverses quickly before we are flying down the empty roads.

When I arrive home, I steal in through the back door and quietly creep up the stairs into my room. I get my holographic phone out and message Zach, "Did you make it?" I can't sleep until I see his response, it comes quicker than I expect.

"Yes, go to sleep now." I close my eyes and drift off.

I wake up to someone knocking at the door. I open it to my mother, Cody, and Father holding a gigantic chocolate cake. "Happy Calling Ceremony Day!" they whoop in unison. Their faces are wreathed with smiles, while my insides twist and toil. My thoughts automatically turn to Zach. Is he experiencing a similar wrenching pain?

Mother picks up on my mood. "Darling, we're so happy that you'll finally learn your fate and calling today. I know you'll be marvelous at whatever is chosen for you."

Swallowing the lump in my throat, I croak, "Oh, thank you, the cake looks delicious. Too bad I'm not that hungry."

"Well go get changed and come downstairs. You can't be in pajamas on your Calling Ceremony Day," Father chimes in.

"Of course, Father."

He looks quizzically at Cody and Mother. "Gosh, if it wasn't for this cake, I'd feel like we were going to a funeral, what with Adriana's glumness." He laughs.

They turn to leave, and I close the door. Being a Surrogate will buy me time. It will also show me what exactly goes on off-grid. I take a deep breath, battling with myself. It isn't that bad, I say to myself, being a Surrogate. I won't have any duties other than taking care of myself and the baby. That will give me free time to think and logically figure out how to struggle against the injustices in MicroScrep. I hear the Surrogates are treated lavishly. I'll gain strength there. They do have short lives, but they are decorated and commemorated. Their pictures line the walls of the Surrogacy Centers. Every year, on Arthur Mills Day, their names and pictures are projected and honored in the sky like constellations. I take off my pajamas and get into a jean dress. Besides, my parents will receive special privileges on World Cleanliness Day. They'll receive a specialized humidifier that consistently detoxifies the air from microbes and bacteria. They will always have valet parking for free wherever they go. At the grocery store they are given special queues and always have first pick of the vegetables and fruit. Even during tax season, an extra sum of money is paid to them. Having a daughter become a Surrogate is a great honor in MicroScrep. It will work well. I just need to be smart about what the next right move is.

I splash cold water on my face, looking at myself in the mirror. My eyes are bloodshot. I take out my contact lens. The blue and brown are as distinct and divided as my heart and mind are. My mind flashes back to a memory of a little girl with a bandage over her eye. *They were trying to destroy her*. But I don't remember if they did or not. I apply lotion on my face, rubbing upwards on my cheeks. *What's Zach doing?* I can't bear to think we might never see each other again. Walking mechanically down the stairs, knees and body tired and restless, I reach the last step, compose myself, straighten up, and put on a smile.

"Surprise!" yell twenty people who greet me as I walk into the dining room. My eyes zero in on Zach and his family, then Cody and Laura, and then my family and a few of my school friends.

"We wanted to all be here to share in your joy, so we decided that since Zach, Tara, Aimee, and Steve are all the same age, we'd have a bigger celebration," my mother says, her cheeks rosy with joy. "I'm so happy security let us have such a large gathering, considering the public health concerns around large groups."

"Oh, this is lovely." I smile. Zach's eyes look down, and I must consciously look at others to distract myself. Mother hobbles off to the kitchen and returns with a cake. Cody and Laura help her portion it to everyone. I help with the tea, but Mother shoos me away. "It's your day, my sweet, you can scan for microbes if you want to help, and please remind everyone about social distancing."

My father clinks on his teacup to draw everyone's attention. "It is almost ten a.m., but before we receive our text messages, I would like to make a speech." He clears his throat and takes my mother's hand. "Twenty-five years ago, I was given this woman as my Perfect Bonding Pair. Harmony has never failed me. To this day I'm grateful because the algorithm can never be wrong, my life is a testament to that." Mother's eyes beam with happiness and her rosy cheeks glisten with pride. My face reddens. Yes, Mother and Father seem to have a happy life together, but it is such a surface happiness they have. They don't share any similarities or interests, other than their patriotism. "I dedicate this Calling Ceremony to loyalty. Without loyalty we will never survive as a race. Long live Harmony, long live MicroScrep." A sense of guilt strikes me, but soon after follows rage. I wonder if Father would say these things if he knew the evil that MicroScrep has stood for. What would he feel about it if he knew they ruthlessly killed Kevin, who was terribly abused in childhood from Arthur Mills's descendant? What would Mother say if she knew Laura had the amulet that could change her life in a flash, if she felt so inclined to?

Cody and Laura are the first to peel out with cheers, and everyone joins in clapping loudly. My father clinks on his teacup again. "It is ten seconds to ten a.m. Ten...nine... eight...seven..."

Everyone joins in. "Six, five, four, three, two, one." The dread in the pit of my stomach weighs heavier with every passing moment.

A chiming sound is heard, and Father flips his finger up. The holographic message verifies his retinas and projects the message.

Dear MicroScrep Citizens, it has been determined that five young MicroScrepians are in attendance at your Calling Ceremony. Their callings are as follows:

#7770655 Tara Adison - Perfect Bonding Pair to Jason Sonoma #4765555

#6432410 Aimee Shylo - Perfect Bonding pair to Tommy Grator #3145641

#4612341 Steve Woo - Perfect Bonding Pair to Kaylee Mari #6411461

#6666777 Zachary Molten - Eunuch

#7777661 Adriana Buckowski - Surrogate

Father's eyes fill with tears, and Mother wraps her arms around me. "Adriana, what an honor," she whispers in my hair.

Cheers, hollers, and claps surround the table. Zachary is smiling mechanically, while his mother and father hold his hands. But I can tell he's not okay. He's looking down and his knees are shaking. My father walks over to his father, scans and shakes his hand. Out of the corner of my eye, I see Laura's eyes fixed on Zachary and then on me, a wry smile on her lips. Why would she go after Zachary?

It's me she wants. I am the freak with the funny eyes! Could Harmony have flagged our love for each other? The others all help themselves to more tea and sandwiches, unaware of mine and Zach's turmoil. I hold my breath out of fear that I'll scream.

Today is the last day I'll see him.

Chapter 9:

Zach's Questions

The hardest part of sitting through the Calling Ceremony was watching my fate slip out of my hands like water through the bedrock of a stream. Adriana mostly avoided my eyes; the one time I did catch it, they shimmered before she diverted her glance and blinked furiously to dry up her tears.

The second hardest thing was to witness Laura's smug self-assurance. She's so sneaky. It was hard realizing that for most of my life, I didn't know the real person behind the false exterior. She had no sense of right or wrong. She was a terrible, ruthless, person who was drunk on getting and keeping power. If it weren't for Kevin's letter, I would have never believed it.

The party lingered on with fake fanfare. Everyone scanned for microbes, terrified that a group of twenty might be too large and some virus or bacteria could be ingested unknowingly. Adriana entered the dining room with a toothy grin on her face, all the while her body language stiff and uncomfortable. Her father's speech made me jealous of the life he'd lived. The life that was being stripped from me and her. It wasn't the fact that I'd have to become a Eunuch that bothered me. What was the use of vestigial organs like testicles anyway? The perverse dance of intercourse was just a forgotten primitive necessity before in-vitro fertilization, and I had no interest in that type of barbarity.

Then what was the mysterious pull that had me wanting to be with Adriana? Perhaps it was compatibility, the shared interests, the allure of her smile. Maybe it was her walk, her words, that stoked the fires in my heart. Then why wasn't I chosen for her as a Perfect Bonding Pair? There must be a reason, something I don't know, something only Harmony does, or did Laura change that around? The fake amulet. Why was the door to the safe left open? Was this her plan all along? My face burns with anger. I want to scream out, but I can't. My hands are tied. She's won.

"Meet me in the garden," Adriana whispers as she nears the sandwich tray and grabs a cucumber sandwich. She floats away before I can respond. Walking over to the punch bowl, I pour myself some punch and scope out the room. Everyone is busy chatting. Adriana's mother is scanning for microbes, a disinfection spray bottle held in her hand. Slipping out through the screen door towards the garden, I see Adriana is already inside the gazebo. She smiles sadly at me.

"So, this is it," she says. I take a few steps towards her, hold her hand, and we both sit down in the chairs.

"This isn't it yet, Adriana."

She looks at me curiously. "What do you mean?"

"We can still resist."

"Don't be silly, how can we resist? Our names and holograms are being projected on the screens at the roundabout of Purity, near Harmony headquarters. Everyone in MicroScrep will know our fates." Tears well in her eyes, but she blinks them away. Now the only thing I see in her is defeat. "The ambassadors of Eunuchs and Surrogates are coming to pick us up tonight." Adriana places her hand on mine. "This is it, Zach, accept it."

My voice breaks as I say, "I can't, I won't...Run away with me tonight before they come for us. I have enough water and bread for us to survive on for a few weeks."

Adriana looks intently into my eyes. "And then what? We'll be hunted down, brought back to MicroScrep, publicly shamed, and stoned. My family will be dishonored. They'd never live down my disloyalty. We need to be smart about this, Zach."

Hands shaking, face as hot as a flame, I refuse to give up. "What if they don't find us? You could live longer than one year, Adriana. Right now, your life expectancy is dead in ten to twelve months."

Adriana turns her gaze from me and shakes her head. "I won't do it, Zach. I won't run away now. I'm in for the long haul; I won't give up until we can be reunited, and we can fight against the injustices here."

Looking left and right, I take her hands in mine. I need to convince her, but what can I say to do that? "Then this is the last day we'll see each other."

Looking towards the house, she holds my hands more firmly. Nobody has yet noticed our absence. "No, we'll see each other again. I'm going to escape the Surrogacy Center within six months of being there. If you don't see me in seven months, then you come looking for me. Deal?" She turns back to me and stares into my eyes. I would rather we leave now, together, but I don't want to argue with her anymore. She won't back down, she's a fighter.

"Deal," I say as I squeeze her hands with both of mine.

Hearing the screen door open, we whisper our goodbyes, promising to hold fast to the timeline she laid out. The best thing I can do now is to solely accept my fate and learn as much as I can about the off-grid Eunuch world. The more I know about my new world, the easier it will be to get to her. Knowledge is power and the only option for survival now.

The ride home with my parents is silent except for my mother's periodic sobs and the sound of yet another tissue being plucked out of the tissue box.

We arrive home at 9:30 p.m. I can take one possession with me, everything else I need will be provided for at the Eunuch Center. Looking around my room, my eyes settle on a wallet Kevin gave to me a few months ago. It is made from peacock leather and feathers, one of the most prized animals in MicroScrep. Opening the wallet, I notice a picture folded neatly into one of the pockets. Taking it out and unfolding it, I notice it's a picture of a young boy with dark, sad eyes. Turning the picture over, it says, "Kevin, age: 12." Under that is a terrible scrawling penmanship that reads, "Please God. Help me." The word God is foreign to me. It takes me a moment to remember what we learned in history class; that primitive man believed in God because they lacked the technology of a perfect, unbiased, mostly autonomous system like Harmony. Harmony provides what primitive man hoped for in a god: a system where everyone has a place, a duty, and a legacy.

People believed in a set of morals that if followed would allow them to have a good afterlife in "heaven," a place where all that was desired would be granted by God. Those who went against the rules would end up in "hell," a place of perpetual suffering. God was a ruler, a judge, that watched and decided on the fate of humans. Harmony is like a god, but far more impartial.

Putting the picture back into the pocket, I realize that the concept of God is very much like the concept of Harmony. Why would Kevin appeal to God when he knew that God was an unproven fairytale? Perhaps with no faith left in Harmony, he turned to God, but that would make Kevin a rebel from his teenage years... A honking horn interrupts my musing.

"They're here, Zachary. Hurry, we want to properly bid you farewell." Hearing the urgency in Father's voice, I place the wallet and picture in my bedroom drawer, I can't take this with me, it belongs here in MicroScrep. If anyone finds it, they will be curious as to Kevin and what really happened to him; perhaps it may aid someone else in their search for what's really happening in MicroScrep. I run downstairs to where father and Laura are standing.

"Where's Mother?"

Father pats my back as a tear slips down his chin. "She's unable to say goodbye, Zachary. She is quite shaken." Laura stands with an ice-cold, distant look in her eyes. She hugs me stiffly. Sniffing his tears away, he continues, "Quite unnatural by MicroScrep standards. I'll see to it she cuts some of her oxytocin tablets."

I look out at the large tank-like vehicle waiting outside for me.

"Okay, so this is it. Thank you, Father." I look at Laura,

and steady my voice, “Farewell, Laura. I will do MicroScrep proud.”

“You’ll always be my Perfect Family matched boy.” Waving me off, his shoulders bend forward, eyes staring out into the night.

Looking back at him, I holler, “Give my love to Mother.”

I am welcomed into the tank by a tall middle-aged man named Toru Torishi. The tank can be used mid-air like vehicles in MicroScrep, or it has wheels that can cover harsh and wild terrain. He has model-like Asiatic features: a square jawline, eyes that burn like coals, large lips, and a strong broad nose. I slip into the passenger seat just as Toru gets into the driver seat. Before I can fasten my seatbelt, he scans me for microbes.

“I’m Toru, the ambassador for this year’s Eunuchs.” I look behind him; there are three other boys my age huddled together.

“Introduce yourself,” Toru says.

“Hello, I’m Zachary.”

“I’m Ben,” a boy with blond hair, blue eyes, and a ghost-white complexion says.

“I’m Alistair,” a chubby boy with reddish hair and freckles says.

“I’m Daniel,” a black boy with large eyes and curly eyelashes says timidly.

Toru stares out, concentrating on the road ahead. “It’ll be about four hours until the off-grid hospital used for castration. I recommend getting some sleep.”

“Do you mind if you answer a few questions?” I ask Toru.

Toru frowns, his face becoming severe. Settling back

in my seat, I realize I've spoken too soon. Apart from the occasional cough, the boys behind me are silent. Taking my cue from the quiet atmosphere, I focus on the sound of the wind's humming sound that churns on for what seems like hours.

I awake to Alistair snoring and the other boys squished together in sleep. Toru gives me a passing glance. His profile is strong, despite his long-limbed, bony arms.

"You had a question?" he says.

I clear my throat. "Yes, I did."

"Continue," he grunts.

"We never learned much about Eunuchs in school, MicroScrepians seem to ignore that Eunuchs even exist until the Calling Ceremony. All I know is that they live off-grid; are we off-grid now?" I ask, not wanting to seem overly zealous.

"Not yet, a few more kilometers. You'll see the barbed-wire fences," Toru replies.

"Why do Eunuchs live off-grid?"

"Because they don't have families."

"Yes, I know, but why can't they have families?"

"Listen, boy, not everyone can be everything to everyone. We are specialized for service."

"But service to who?" I ask.

"Don't be so impatient, you'll see soon enough."

Disappointed with Toru's response, I am about to object, but realize that I may need an ally soon.

"Does castration hurt?" I ask quietly.

Toru looks at me for a few moments and then back at the road ahead. We are in front of the gigantic barbed-wire fences that separate MicroScrep from the off-grid world. We've moved from being suspended in air, to having our wheels on the ground. Off-grid doesn't have the electromagnetic power that helps on-grid cars fly. I also realize that my X-ray vision is glitchy the closer we get to the off-grid world. A security guard marches out of his shelter and flashes a light at us. Toru's eyes are dark as ever as he squints them. The guard raps on the window and Toru lets it down.

"Papers," the security guard shouts.

Toru pulls up his sleeve to unveil a glow-in-the-dark tattoo imprint on his arm.

"The others?" the guard says.

Toru produces what looks like a crumpled paper where our names and faces are shown under the heading of Eunuch.

The guard takes one brief look, then says, "All right, off you go."

There is silence for a few moments and then Toru says, "Pain is temporary. Honor is lifelong."

I remember reading in school about Eunuch culture being quiet, meditative, and secretive. That's why perhaps Toru doesn't mince words. The road is not paved, and the tank gets noisier on the dirt and stone roads, dodging tall timber trees and scraping past bushes. I once see the flash of doe eyes before it dashes off into a clearing. The road is also bumpy. The three boys in the back wake up, wide-eyed. They, like I, have never seen the forest, or have been off-grid. Then in the distance, I see a large watchtower with lights around its fortified walls. A large cement block of a building in the center.

"This is the hospital," Toru says.

He parks his car in the dirt patch in front of the hospital, and we all get out. On entering, we are misted with an antiseptic solution. We are directed towards a machine that looks like an old lamp post. Toru tells us to roll our sleeves all the way up, past our shoulders, and stand skin flush against the post. Alistair is first and he howls in pain as a bundle of needles puncture his deltoid muscle with a tattoo. It takes only a few seconds and then he looks down on his reddened muscle. It glows a serial number.

"That is your Eunuch number," Toru says. "Next."

I'm next, the searing pain only a flash as I bite my lip so as not to call out in pain. At least I am prepared, unlike poor Alistair.

"Good bravery," Toru says. "Eunuchs must be brave."

Everyone else finishes with not a word of complaint. We enter the waiting room that is sparkling clean and minimalistic. There are not even chairs to sit on. Toru stands against a wall and motions to us to do the same.

There is a greyness to the room, as if sadness was embedded into the lackluster walls. Toru walks up to the grey door and knocks. A team of four men in lab coats stand in the background. A young servant boy opens the door.

"Are they finished with their tattoos?"

Toru nods.

"We will take the four of them all at once."

We enter the room as Toru waits outside. The door closes, and we are directed to pick one hospital bed to lay face-up on. The ceiling is grey with splatters of black. It looks like the inverse of the cosmos, as if in a silvery grey blanket there are splatterings of darkness. Is this the metaphor for life as a Eunuch? Dreary and dull with terrifying moments of darkness? Who would design a ceiling like this? Each doctor stands beside a bed. A keypad appears and they input numbers. Metal cuffs hold our wrists and ankles to the bed. Alistair gasps. My heart is beating fast. The doctors take scissors out and cut our clothes off our bodies. I hear Alistair squirming in the bed beside me.

"Don't resist," instructs the man in a lab coat. "It is worse when you do."

The other boys seem to know this because they make no noise. The doctor produces a sickle-like knife and with a swift blow, cuts away our manhood. A needle is stuck in our urethral tube, and we are bandaged up. The screams are loud and deafening. Alistair is hyperventilating, the others groaning in pain. I have bit down on my lip so hard that blood seeps into my mouth through my teeth. The doctors work quickly, mopping us clean and smoothing a calming gel over our severed parts. The pain is no longer lacerating, but a deep ache that makes one weak everywhere. It's like a wound to the soul, one that focuses all one's concentration and energy on it.

The doctors dispose of their gloves. One of them stands before our beds, saying that we will have three days of recovery. During the first two, we are not allowed to drink or eat. After the second day, the needle will be removed and we'll be able to urinate, or not. If we are unable to urinate, we will have to die a solitary, painful death. Nothing can be done to help. Alistair is weeping out of fear. I hear him whimper in pain for hours until I fall asleep from sheer physical and emotional exhaustion.

When I awake, I hear Alistair speaking with the others. "They say that Eunuchs live a long life, why then did the doctor say we could die?"

Ben's voice cracks as he responds, "That's if you make it to the Eunuch Center I suppose."

Daniel's voice is deeper than the others. "Alistair, if I were you, I wouldn't show my weakness to anyone. I've heard that the Eunuchs have a hierarchy and that the more trustworthy and brave you are, the better your chances of being given easier tasks. It isn't like MicroScrep, where everyone is equal."

Ben objects, "If Alistair cries or not shouldn't be your concern, Daniel!"

Alistair disregards what Ben says. "Ah, he's only trying to help, Ben. Isn't it weird that nobody knows anything about Eunuchs other than the fact that they exist?"

Ben turns his head slowly to look at Alistair whose bandages are soaked with blood. "Yeah, it's strange. And have you all noticed how weird Toru is?"

Daniel shushes everyone. "They could be listening in on us. You wouldn't want to be punished here; just look at how close to death we've gotten with this 'surgery.'"

Closing my eyes, Daniel's voice breaks the silence. "Zach, what do you think?"

Taking a few minutes to formulate my response, I mutter, "I think the fact that we've had this surgery means something. We're being initiated into a new world. I think you're right, there is a hierarchy. Judging from Toru's speech and actions, I would say the best way to survive would be to follow rules."

As the boys chime in with their thoughts, my mind slips to a few days ago. I was going against the rules in MicroScrep in order to have a life with Adriana. Tears sting my eyes. Where is she now? What is she enduring? Following the rules now is meaningless unless I can be reunited with her. She is my reason and goal in life. This gives me hope and the will to carry on. She is going to find me within six months, and if she doesn't or can't, I will go after her, whatever rules I need to break. Suddenly, I realize the only way to survive and find her is to be quiet like Toru, brave like he encouraged.

Chapter 10:

The Surrogacy Center

Zach's words echo in my mind: "We can still run away before the evening when they come for us." Looking at the clock, it is ten p.m. now and they'll be here any moment to collect me. Mother can't contain her pride; she bounces her hands with joy as I descend the stairs. Father, Mother, and Cody are standing beside me, dressed in their best clothes, faces wreathed with smile. There is a loud beep outside.

"All right dear, we love you." Both my parents shelter me in their arms. Cody embraces me, holding my shoulders. "I know you'll survive your first pregnancy and make us proud." Trying to form words, I cannot speak. My mind is abuzz with the events of the last few days. Casting my head down, I sling my backpack across my shoulder and run out to meet the long-limbed chauffeur holding the door to the limousine open. He greets me with a tilt of his head, a row of yellow stained teeth set into a warm smile. As I sit on the plush faux-leather seat, I notice across from me are two heavy-set girls munching on crackers and cheese. In their hands is a long-stemmed wine glass filled with bubbly. One of them is oddly familiar. As if I've seen her before, somewhere in the recent past, but I can't seem to put my finger on when.

"Hello," the girls say in unison, making eye contact and then breaking out into laughter.

"Hi, I'm Adriana," I say as the chauffeur closes the door.

"Hi, I'm Sheryl," the slightly chubbier one with red hair says, smiling broadly.

"I'm Tanya," the other girl says, her white hair pulled up into a high ponytail.

"You can help yourself to a drink of champagne," Sheryl says.

"No, no, I've just brushed my teeth," I say, slightly astonished that they can drink alcohol. Alcohol is outlawed for anyone other than scientists, or so I thought.

"Brushed your teeth? Oh dear, the fun is just starting," Tanya says.

"What do you mean?"

"There's a special sendoff ceremony in our honor tonight in Mills Park. You didn't know?"

"No, what are they doing that for?"

"It's just another way to thank us. Apparently, this is the first time they're holding a ceremony for Surrogates." The girls clink their glasses together and smile.

The limousine stops, and the chauffeur opens the door. Before us, the park is filled with dozens of people holding candles, all of them sitting in front of a great stage with red curtains. Speakers blare that terrible electronic music that Harmony has composed for the festivities. As we walk quietly on the red carpet that cuts through the part in the crowd, everyone stands at attention with their lighted candles. The experience is out-of-body, the way everyone is revering us as if we are prophets. We finally come to sit on the three reserved seats at the front of the crowd. Looking through the crowd, I see my parents, their eyes glistening with pride. A sense of loss fills me. This is the last time I'll probably see them.

When the music lowers, Stevie, our chauffeur, makes his way to the stage. He taps on the microphone and clears his throat.

"Ladies and gentlemen, thank you for attending our send-off ceremony. This year's ceremony is in honor of the three ladies here who have been chosen by Harmony's perfect algorithm to be Surrogates. This is a new way that MicroScrep will celebrate each neighborhood cluster's Surrogates. Tonight, we would like to celebrate their valiant selflessness for the good of MicroScrep. The first to pay their homage to them is a newly matched Bonding Pair, Cody and Laura, who we anticipate will receive a child for their Perfect Family Match from one of these Surrogates seated here."

Swallowing a gasp to mask my surprise of Laura and Cody presenting, I bite my lower lip as Laura takes the stage with Cody trailing slightly behind her.

"We've written a poem to honor the Surrogates, one of whom is Cody's sister." Laura looks at me and smiles, but her eyes are a blank stone, cold grey. All of a sudden, a flashback of Laura pushing me under in the pool as the micro camera she has snaps pictures of me. Her voice breaks the flashback, "The title of this poem is 'The Valiant Heart.'

To open your heart to other's fortunes,
To cultivate the womb for growth,
I heard the name, 'Mother of Orphans'
Is what it is to take a Surrogates oath

Your sacrifice is worthy
Of honor, light, and love
All of life's a Journey
But without you, we cannot evolve.

So, thank you for your grace,
And thank you as we displace—I mean, praise.'"

I am shocked by Laura's fumble with the rhyme. Displacement is obviously playing on her mind to cause such a slip of tongue. Laura chuckles at her mistake and curtsies at us.

"I did mean praise," she says as she moves her hand up to the amulet that is strung around her neck. She looks at me out of the corner of her eye, a sly smile moves across her lips. I am awestruck, she has the amulet! She knew that the one she had in the safe was fake. She planted it there. She's responsible for Kevin's death! She may even be responsible for Zach and me being sent off-grid. A sense of doom overcomes me. My mind races; what if the Surrogacy Center is a control mechanism of the state? To get rid of us, to eliminate the doubters, but Sheryl and Tanya don't seem to be particularly rebellious. Then it dawns on me, maybe Laura changed my position in Harmony to get rid of me. I close my eyes and see a dog in the shed, Laura feeding it half a human jaw. Is she in charge of getting rid of people who are a threat to MicroScrep? Another memory flashes; a girl with an eye patch, the dog behind the plexiglass, struggling against Laura to attack her and me. It is all becoming clear now. Is there something about my eyes that makes her want me to suffer and die?

As Laura and Cody step off the stage, large, red fireworks burst behind the stage. The gunpowder looks like blood dripping down the sky. The crowd peals into oohs and aahs and loud clapping. Sheryl and Tanya's eyes fill with happiness, while my heart feels like it has been pierced. My mind is still confused by the events of the past weeks. The speakers play a song of blessing as Laura and Cody descend the stage back to their seats. Sheryl and Tanya's parents deliver speeches, both holding their candles reverently towards us with outstretched hands. Father repeats his speech from the Calling Ceremony while Mother stands beside him, both as joyous as ever. When it is time to leave, we are waved off by the crowd who hold their candles at us, the children throw flowers at us, thanking us for perpetuating the cycle of life in MicroScrep.

Stevie opens the door to the limousine to let us in.

"Wasn't that such a great experience?" Sheryl gushes. Tanya nods her head, smiling from ear to ear. Leaning back in my seat, I stay silent, watching the lighted streets outside.

I keep my mouth firmly shut because I feel that I'll lose control and scream. The lies I've been fed; I am angry that Kevin was killed by Laura. I am furious that they've separated Zach and me. I want to scream out the window to the audience to not be fooled. That there is a terrible corruption of power, and that Harmony is used to control the masses. I can't though. I must wait and find a way to fight back. To scream out now would be self-defeating, and I've promised Zach I'll find him. Two heads are better than one. We'll find allies, and then we'll go after Laura and whoever else might be working with her.

Something flashes in my mind, but it's gone before I can focus on it. I stare out of my window, trying to call it back. Half a memory flashes before my eyes again, but this time I can see it. A little girl, a dog salivating blood.

My pulse is racing. Is this something I've repressed? Is this part of a timeline that I don't remember? Or is it a nightmare I've had in my childhood coming back to haunt me? My gut tells me these images are something more than just pictures, they're something hideous.

I try to grab on to them, but the harder I try, the more they seem to slip away.

"So, are you just going to sit there looking out the window?" Tanya says, her white ponytail bobbing as she speaks. She's slightly drunk, I can tell by her slurred speech.

"I like looking out as we drive past. Besides, it's probably the last time I'm going to see MicroScrep, seeing as we'll probably be dead in less than a year."

Tanya's eyes widen and she frowns. "You don't have to be such a downer about it, everyone's going to die sooner or later. We can enjoy the party as long as it lasts."

Sheryl nods her head. "Yeah, you don't have to be such a kill-joy!" She looks at me through narrow eyes. "And honestly, I'd rather die and make history than die without a legacy."

Ignoring them, I let silence be my response, but drunkenness doesn't allow for such peace. A few moments later Tanya says, "More champagne and cheese?" as they both peal into laughter, clinking their glasses together.

An hour or so later, we arrive at a barbed-wire fence. We're about to leave MicroScrep for good.

The guard holds a scanner up, and Stevie pulls his sleeve up to his shoulders. A glowing tattoo with a serial number on his deltoid shines under the guard's flashlight as he scans it and motions our car to move on. The girls are too busy drinking and eating to notice anything but themselves, but I'm perplexed. A tattoo serial number? I've never heard of anyone having a tattoo. I thought they were obsolete now. In primary school, our teachers told us about prisoners getting tattoos so they could be identified, back when humans were still degenerates. I wonder if I should ask Stevie about it, or would he be offended? I decide not to ask.

Large forest trees stand stoic and silent around us as we continue off-road. The headlights illuminate the old branches and brush that swish and scrape the vehicle's exterior. In the distance is a grey clearing with a square container-like building in the middle of it. Stevie parks in the dirt plot in front of the metal entrance door.

"Okay, first stop here."

Sheryl and Tanya wake up, disorientated.

"Are we there yet?" Sheryl rubs her eyes.

"No, this is just a stop on our way to the Surrogacy Center." Stevie looks at us from the rearview mirror. "Get out."

Tanya looks from me to Sheryl, confused. We were expecting Stevie, our chauffeur, to rush out and open our door, as is his habit, but he sits and looks through the mirror at us with contempt. The awkward silence is broken when he gets out of the limousine and makes his way slowly to the metal door of the building.

Tanya looks at Sheryl in horror. "Where are we? This place looks hideous."

Deciding to leave the two girls with their indignation, I open the limousine door and walk towards the building. The smell of the evergreens fills my lungs as I inhale deeply. The air is light and crisp, and as I exhale, I see the condensation of my breath make its way to the metal door where Stevie waits. When I reach him, he is whistling carelessly, as if he's been met with this type of bewilderment thousands of times. It comforts me in a bizarre way, his whistling against the backdrop of the grey skies and bleak surroundings. The two girls shuffle up to the metal door, arms wrapped around each other's shoulders.

Stevie's whistling is interrupted by Sheryl's voice. "Where on earth have you taken us?"

"You'll see soon enough," Stevie says as he pushes on the metal door that scrapes, booms, and echoes a metallic opening. Four feet ahead of us are two metal posts with an imprinted foot molded in the cement floor. Apart from this, the building is empty, its greyness envelops us.

"Adriana, you go first. Take your shoes and socks off and walk to the posts. When you get there, place your right foot into the imprinted one in the cement." I nod my head at Stevie's instructions. Hearing the thumping of my heart in my ears, I bite down on my lip to squelch my fear. Placing my foot in the embossment, a hundred needles bob back and forth, puncturing my ankle. Gasping in pain, the needles stop, and it is over, except for the pain that lingers on. Gingerly taking my ankle out of the mold,

I retreat to where Stevie and the girls are waiting. I look down at my ankle, four drops of blood make their way down towards my foot arch. A set of numbers are scribbled with blood and grey ink.

"I'm not doing that!" Sheryl screams.

Stevie doesn't say a word. He instead nonchalantly pulls out his handcuffs and shackles Sheryl. Screaming and digging her heels into the cement ground, Stevie pulls her forward, placing her between the posts and coercing her feet into the imprint. She screams and howls for a few moments as the needles puncture her ankle. Tanya all the while runs towards the metal door, thumping on it.

"I want to get out here," she cries. "Someone help me!" She slides down the metal door onto the ground in a heap of emotion.

Stevie unshackles Sheryl and then goes for Tanya. Flailing her arms and legs, Tanya kicks Stevie, scratching at his face. They jostle like this for a few minutes, until Stevie is on top of her, reaching into his pocket. He takes out a taser and shoots it at her. Her body jerks with the current, lifting her a few inches off the ground. When the surge ends, she falls to the ground unconscious and a trail of blood seeps out of the side of her mouth.

Shrieking loudly, Sheryl crawls towards Tanya. "How could you?" She cries as she curls up beside Tanya. "You animal, you terrible man!"

She turns Tanya's lifeless head towards her. Sheryl's mouth gapes open like a dead fish.

"You killed her...you killed her...you killed her," Sheryl chants, as if calming herself with this mantra.

Heart racing, my eyes switch back and forth from

Tanya to Sheryl and then to Stevie. Stevie's eyes stare blankly at the spectacle before him. He walks to the limousine, hands flinging up to the sky. He's talking to himself angrily, but I can't make out what he is saying. Sheryl is weeping beside Tanya's motionless body. I stagger towards the limousine.

Stevie's voice becomes more and more clear, "But, your Excellence, it was a mistake. I used my taser to get her to the tattoo machine since she was resisting. I didn't know she was going to die!"

An indecipherable voice responds, but I can't hear it. Eventually, Stevie says, "Yes, I'll bring a vial and the syringe back to the Center, I'll get to it immediately."

The other person speaks as Stevie paces to the trunk of the limousine and opens it. "Yes, your Excellency. I'll bury her afterwards, we won't mention it to any of the Eunuchs, they don't need to know the real story. For all they know, she committed suicide, so we'll have two Surrogates and not three coming." Stevie sees me from the corner of his eyes and waves me over, his face looking as grey as the sky.

He clicks off his holographic phone. "Take these." He shoves two syringes into my hands. Grabbing a shovel from the trunk, he scurries ahead of me to the building. Sheryl is still sobbing over Tanya's body, smoothing strands of Tanya's white hair that have escaped her ponytail from her face. Kneeling beside Sheryl, I put a hand on her shoulder. She shakes me off, looking confoundedly at the two syringes I have in my hand. Stevie lays the shovels on the ground, and Sheryl jumps at the sound.

"You terrible man," she says with a whisper of disgust.

"You killed Tanya."

Disregarding her curses with a curled lip of contempt, his shoulders tighten as he crouches down beside me, taking the syringe and sticking it into Tanya's abdomen. Blood and fluid fill the syringe.

"What are you doing now you...you...terrible murderer!?" Sheryl screams like a raving lunatic.

Clenching his teeth, anger filling his features, Stevie shouts, "Shut up, or I'll kill you too!" He takes the other syringe and sticks it deep into Tanya's leg, all the while looking at Sheryl with stone-cold eyes. Sheryl's eyes go wide and she quiets herself, except for her stifled sobs. Silence is everywhere as thunder strikes outside and the pitter-patter of the rain starts falling on the metal roof of the building. Stevie instructs Sheryl and me to take Tanya's arms and legs and drag her out to the first patch where the limousine is parked as he shovels the dirt, which is quickly turning to mud. His brown hair wet and matted to his face, he looks like a sinister murderer, not a peaceful agent of MicroScrep. When the grave is long enough for Tanya's body, we drag her into it. Stevie smooths dirt over the body. The rain washes some of the mud away, revealing a finger and a toe.

"Get back into the limousine," a soaking wet Stevie says, droplets of rain streaming off his drenched hair.

The mood in the limousine is somber, made worse by the torrential rain that falls ceaselessly on the roof. The bumpy dirt path that we follow becomes wet with puddles that splatter against tires. Squinting at the window shield, Stevie's jaw clenches like a fist. Aside from Sheryl's periodic gasps and sobs, the sound of the limousine lurching and splashing through the potholes, there is only silence.

In MicroScrep we had learned from a young age that rain brought in its wake an increase in bacteria. So, out of compulsion, I scan for bacteria, except that my X-ray vision doesn't work for more than a few seconds at a time. Everything goes black and white, magnified as I scan, but then it flickers and fails, my eyes resuming their normal ability to see color. I do this a half dozen times, like a baby trying to stand up and having her knees give away, but to no use. Stevie observes me momentarily, my eyes switching from the blank state of X-ray back to a more human expression.

"It won't work anymore after a few miles," he says, detached, as if he was reading the morning news to me.

I sigh. There's no point in protesting; it wouldn't solve the issue, and it would make the drive that much more unbearable. Besides, I'm too exhausted to form words. Thinking back on the past few weeks, it seems so surreal, as if I'm in a dream. Am I in a dream? Pinching my thigh, I feel the sharp pain of my nails on skin. I notice Sheryl looking at me inquisitively, then switching quickly from X-ray vision to normal vision over and over again, as if she is trying to prove to herself that it's still working. Sheryl's mouth is contorted into a hollow O, petrified and amazed at the same time. Stevie glances at her and shakes his head. He must be thinking of how stupid she looks, not believing her own eyes as the saying goes.

Through the thick of the trees and the pelting rain, I see in the distance what looks like a large black box, a wall scaling around it, barbed wire adding to its terrific presence. As we follow the path, the building goes in and out of view. It seems as if we are following a road elsewhere, but then the road bends, and we arrive at the wall.

Stevie parks and we all sit quietly. At least we aren't in the awful rain and are sheltered by the limousine. Stevie gets out something as large as a deck of cards, with a long antenna that he pulls up. On its surface is a touchpad with numbers. It reminds me of a device I had read about in the school library, a walkie talkie. Soldiers had used them to communicate during some war a hundred years ago. I still remember the name because I had been amused by it. Walkie talkie sounded like a type of pigeon English that only brutes would invent or use.

There is a static sound from the walkie talkie, and then a voice says, "Stevie, roll them in." *We don't need to be rolled, we can walk perfectly fine,* I think to myself. Then I see two orange cloaked men with pointy hoods roll out two wheelchairs to our limousine. Opening the door, they ask Sheryl and me to take a seat on the wheelchairs. Too tired to object, we do as we are told.

"Keep your feet off the ground, or else you'll be blown to smithereens," one of the cloaked men says. I don't understand what smithereens means, but I reckoned it would be an equally worse place to go to.

"Then how can you walk?" I say, the low nag of my voice surprising me.

"We are Eunuchs. The ground out here doesn't blow us up, but it will do for you, Surrogate."

I look at the ground in shock, wondering how that could be possible. Perhaps the explosives recognize our ankle tattoos. That's the only explanation I can think of since the Wardens can walk freely on the grounds.

We enter through a large arching metal door. It looks

like an antiquated medieval Arab entrance to a fort, the rusty paisley etched into the cold metal. We enter the black box of a building and immediately are confronted with a large wall stretching up towards the roof, like a shrine. To our left and right is a hallway.

"I will go right with you," one of the Eunuchs says to me. "And the other Surrogate," he points to Sheryl, "will go left with him." He points to the Eunuch holding onto Sheryl's wheelchair. The smell of burnt sage fills our nostrils. It is burning behind the wall, smoke curling up to the roof.

I watch Sheryl being rolled away down the hall. The Eunuch responsible for me turns me around and pushes me down the other end of the corridor. The smell of burning sage becomes more accentuated, clarifying my nasal passages. I pass a door to my left and can see a statue with sage offerings around it. Women with humongous bellies stretch like Yogis, their bodies emaciated. Some in different prayer positions, breathing in and out to a timed ringing of bells. I pass by many rooms on my left and right, each door closed, a number plaque the only distinguishing feature. There are trays left outside some of the doors, all of them with such meagre portions. As I pass, a putrefying smell gathers in the hall, and I gasp as I see a cockroach scurrying over a half-eaten sandwich. Scanning with my eyes, I realize too late the futility of my endeavor and the hopelessness of my situation. Stripped of my X-ray vision, I have no power to protect myself anymore. As we proceed down the hall, the smell of sage changes to the smell of mildew and something that I can only describe as off. The Eunuch lifts his cloak over his nose. Finally, we arrive at a door plaque, the number 127 etched sloppily on it.

"Here, now this is your home for the next nine months or so." He pulls his cloak down and produces an old key chain, which he opens the door with.

I'm sure my eyes are wide with horror. Noticing my demeanor, he says, "Don't be saddened," and he gives me a kind look before casting his eyes down with embarrassment. I flick the light on. It takes a second before the flickering becomes a steady stream of light.

"I'll be back with dinner, and then my shift will be over. Do sleep. I'm sure it's been a difficult day for you," he says as he turns to leave.

Despite my utter shock, his kindness gives me some comfort and a spark of hope. He doesn't seem as jaded as Stevie is. I watch him close the door, then turn to the room. With a sigh, I note that it closely resembles a cell, but without bars. A broken mirror stands in the corner beside a plain single bed, with a simple red sheet on it that smells of urine. Above me is a light bulb hanging on the end of an electrical wire. The walls are greyish cement slabs. The door is made of plywood and there are no windows. A mostly empty wardrobe sits beside the plywood entry door. The door of the wardrobe hangs at an angle and at any moment the hinge could give way. The room is cold.

It is nothing like we are taught to believe.

A few seconds later, there is a knock at the door. I turn, hoping they've come to tell me there's been a mistake. That a Surrogate should not be in these dingy quarters. The Eunuch opens the door and slips my backpack on the ground first without saying anything and then puts down a tray of bread. He avoids my eyes as he leaves.

There is no mistake. This is the life chosen for me. I stagger towards the bed and cry myself to sleep.

Chapter 11:

Zach and Shamok

A week after castration, I still lay in bed. The medicine that they have given me makes my eyes grow heavy, even though judging by the position of the sun it's midday. Daylight, minutes, hours blur together into a lazy blackhole; I move only to the pulse of my blood and breath.

Alistair has died, that I know for sure. I witnessed his fevered face, sweat dripping. Then the flames, the funeral pyre, the melting of his skin, the liturgy of orange cloaked and hooded Eunuchs chanting, sending him to Shamok.

"He will reside with the leaders and heroes of MicroScrep," Toru says to me afterwards. That is where good Eunuchs go after their life of service. "Alistair is no different," Toru confirms, glaring at me. "He served by offering up his body." This is a bedtime story that he repeats time and time again, but I don't believe it. Their medicines can't change my mind about that, not after what I know about MicroScrep through Kevin's letter. The smell of sage burning is often brought into the room. Ben says it wards off infection. Then why didn't it work for Alistair?

When I asked Ben this the other day, Toru was listening from behind a cherry blossom room divider, and he startled me with his answer.

"He was fated to be with our leaders in Shamok." Toru's eyes squint as if to decipher my reason for asking.

His voice booms in the small room. My legs buckle underneath me with fear, I promised myself never to ask such questions again, especially if I wanted to find a way out of here and find Adriana.

I am given tea, spiked with something that makes me terribly tired. The smell of it is slightly musty and metallic, but I drink it because it takes away the weight of the pain—I don't dwell on my questions. I can merge with the lights and sounds around me, wavering in between sleep and the constant groan of the orange cloaked and hooded Eunuchs. Toru called the orange cloaked Eunuchs Wardens. They are one stage above Toru, who is an Ambassador.

My thoughts are chaotic: sage, blood, sickle, orange, flames, Adriana's eyes, her tears, Alistair's bones.

"Get up now," Toru beckons, splashing cold water at my face. "You must walk."

Taking my hand, he gently helps me stand. In the light of day, his face is more feminine than I had realized the first night we met. Perhaps it was the darkness that gave him a more masculine look. He did not have any facial hair and his fingers were long and narrow, like that of a teenager. His limbs were long, noticeably so, as if he should be able to swing from branch to branch, instead of walking his gingerly amble.

Toru encourages me when he sees that walking is

difficult. The pain in my lower abdomen is making me bend over protectively. "Brave, yes brave, and special. You'll one day become a Commander."

"What is a Commander?" I ask.

Toru laughs his sardonic chortle. "The highest class that a Eunuch can be, except for Numen Eunuch, and don't think of becoming a Numen," Toru tittered. "There is only one Numen, and he's healthy and strong, thanks be to Shamok."

The pain in my abdomen shoots down my legs, and I'm annoyed by Toru's teasing. I'm not in the mood to know about all these classes of Eunuchs, although it might be useful if I need to find Adriana in the end. My heart warms with the thought of her. It seems ages ago. I look down at my wasted body. I have lost at least two kilograms since the castration. What will she think of me now, a useless, scared shadow of a person?

Toru sits down on a cushion and motions for me to take a rest on one beside him. He offers me metallic tea that soothes the pain.

Besides the castration, I have not suffered greatly. My X-ray vision is gone; it doesn't work off-grid. It was a slight adjustment, habitually wanting to switch to it, but the fear of contamination didn't overcome me. Maybe it has to do with the teas, making me careless and lethargic. Besides, the only goal left for me was to live long enough to be reunited with Adriana. Toru says that a mark of a great Eunuch is courage. Living without X-ray vision is a testament to that and a signal of faithfulness to the idea of Shamok. My courage only comes from the need to be reunited with Adriana; I don't need a heaven besides that. The idea of Shamok is so new to me. In MicroScrep there was no concept of an afterlife. No mention of divinity, except for that strange instance when I flipped over Kevin's picture to see his invocation to God. Perhaps he needed to believe in some mystical force of good to carry him through the disillusionment he felt in MicroScrep. I think of Kevin. Poor man, so far ahead of his time and so abused by his father, Milton. I wonder what he would have thought about Eunuchs? This is an area that MicroScrepians don't know anything about. They are held in high regard, but their function in the sustenance of MicroScrep is veiled in secrecy.

When I ask Toru about what exactly Eunuchs do, he quiets me with a frown. "Impatience is no good; you'll see in time."

After some moments of silence, Toru continues by saying that we are on a different level off-grid; we are detached and serving MicroScrep's peace, just by existing.

"This will become more apparent as time goes on, and you're given your position. In the meantime, you must prove yourself."

Toru takes my hands into his palms. "MicroScrepians do not know about the afterlife because they live in perfect harmony already. Those that live in harmony stay in that state of peace even after death."

As we sit in this quiet contemplation, Kevin's sufferings come to mind. How could MicroScrepians live in perfect peace, as Toru says, when I know what terrible injustices took place during Kevin's childhood? And what about myself? I certainly didn't live peacefully after knowing I'd be separated from Adriana and finding out about Laura's tyranny. I'm about to object but realize that Toru won't accept my arguments. Confiding in Toru would be silly. My goal is to get to Adriana, and I can't trust that he'll believe what I want to tell him about MicroScrep.

Toru sighs and presses my fingers as if realizing my hesitation. "We are given a greater free will off-grid, Zach. We need to make sure our service and intentions are in harmony with MicroScrep...it will give us freedom. It must be tempered with pure intention and servitude."

He looks at me; his cheeks blush. "Drink. Stop thinking; too much thinking is against nature."

His voice is so calming, and when taken with tea, it becomes an earworm, penetrating my subconscious. Drinking the tea makes me sleepy, so Toru pulls out another cushion and helps me lay my head down.

"You are brave. You will be a Commander if you are loyal to your true fate," he whispers and then kisses my ear as I drift off into deep sleep.

Waking up, I hear the sound of deep moaning reverberating around me, as if a group of humpback whales are being tortured underwater. A chill runs through me from head to toe. Looking around, Toru is curled up beside me, his eyes closed, in deep sleep. How can he sleep through this? Crawling to the partially open door, I prod it open with my elbow.

Standing up is still too difficult for me, especially without the aid of Toru. Crawling down the smoky hall, the smell of burning sage is overbearing. Not knowing what time it is increases my anxiety, and as I advance down the hall, the terrible smoke gets stronger and stronger, while the guttural moaning gets louder and louder. Turning a corner, I peer into an orange room and see a hundred orange-cloaked Wardens sitting trancelike and cross-legged. Their upper bodies move in a circular motion, counterclockwise. A turban-clad Warden sits at the head of the room. The smell is acrid, bushels of sage in gold vases let off smoke from the four corners of the room. The Warden at the front also sits cross-legged, his arms outstretched and resting and on his knees, his upper body circling like a wild animal caught in an outer space vortex. I gasp as he takes a syringe from behind his back and injects himself with it. Suddenly his movements are faster, his muscles bulging. His chanting becomes louder and louder, his circling faster and faster, until he opens one eye and sees me. Bringing his hand up, he points to the exit, willing me away. Crawling backwards, I retreat halfway down the hall until I find a nook where I can regroup and hide.

A clear and distinct voice booms in my ears, "Till death we are chosen, after death to Shamok."

Instinctively I know it's the turban-clad Warden. These words cue a prolonged moan from the crowd seated in the room.

"Tah mord parasta akhar mord tah Shamok." The leader says it three times and the others join in, chanting it together. The voices sing this incantation in a low growl, and I wonder if it's a special language that only Wardens speak. The sounds make me very sleepy, even though I had just woken up. My head throbs with the mantra. All of a sudden, I am so focused on the sound that I'm completely empty, as if someone has cut the top off my head off and has poured the contents of my brain out, replacing it with the sound of the Wardens singing their invocation. I am not present in my body, no mouth or neck or hips. The singing abruptly stops and slowly my mind returns to my body. The smell of sage has lessened, or maybe I've grown

accustomed to it.

Crawling back to my room, I pray Toru is still sleeping. I'll ask him when he wakes up about the ceremony because now a deep curiosity to know what the syringe was filled with develops in my mind.

Toru wakes up, startled, because I'm watching over him. He rubs his eyes and yawns, playing his exhaustion down.

"Why are you awake before me, you surely need more sleep than I do." I don't say anything, and Toru continues, "Let's go to Ben. Today I will show you the routine and your Eunuch's education classes."

My mind is racing with dozens of questions: the use of the sage, the chanting, the strange language, the syringe. Perhaps the classes will teach us what had just happened. And hopefully, I'll also learn more about the Surrogates, and clues on how to find Adriana.

We arrive in Ben's room. His eyes light up when he sees us. "I couldn't sleep with that strange groaning choir last night."

Toru's eyes look disappointed. "It's our ceremony. This is part of an initiation to become a Warden."

Ben shuffles uncomfortably. "I just meant that it was hard to sleep—no ill will towards the Eunuchs."

Toru ignores Ben and helps him up from bed. Ben and I stand slightly hunched over; the pain of standing straight is still too difficult. "To become a Eunuch is not just a bodily castration," he says earnestly. "To become a Eunuch, you must unlearn your previous life in MicroScrep. You must be brave enough and smart enough to relearn and become wise. You were chosen by Harmony because you have this ability, but you must apply new knowledge if you want to succeed."

Toru takes a wooden staff and hits our bottoms. We straighten in pain, both of us howling in unison at the shock and agony.

"See, just as it is natural to have pain, it is natural to adapt once conditions are different. We are the engine that keeps MicroScrep going. We are the body of MicroScrep. If one part of the body is ill or weak, all other parts suffer, and the body as a whole is weakened."

Both of us speechless, Toru makes his way in between us, holding our hands and helping us to the cafeteria.

The cafeteria smells like curry. Inside the hall, there are round tables set up with wooden chairs. Apart from the clinking of utensils on plates, there is no sound. Ben looks around with a blank expression. The buffet is very simple, toast and warm lentil broth. A sign is posted: *Take only what you can eat—wastage is unvirtuous.* I scoop one ladle of soup into a simple red clay bowl and a piece of toast. Trotting slowly to the utensil tray, I take a spoon and decide to sit at an empty table. Every face is strange, and I feel the absence of Adriana deep in my gut. I am certain she is eating and sleeping better than I am. Taking a spoonful of lentil soup into my mouth, I let the warm broth comfort me. My body is depleted, and this simple dish fills me with gratitude. I wonder what Adriana is eating, how she is getting on, whether she has been given an embryo. I can see in my mind her beautiful face smiling and her body growing rounder and plumper.

"Can I sit here?" Ben asks while I take a large bite out of my toast. The aroma of the bread is yeasty, fresh, and fluffy. *Nothing is better than fresh bread,* I think to myself. Nodding my head in response to Ben, we both eat silently until Toru appears.

After a few seconds, I break the silence. "Yesterday, I woke up in the night to chanting. I saw a turban-clad Warden inject himself with a syringe. Is this part of the initiation?"

Toru swallows and looks into the distance. "It must have been the blood of a Surrogate. She might have committed the worst sin."

Ben's eyes widen. "What's the worst sin?"

"Suicide."

I swallow hard. "Why would she have killed herself?"

Toru's eyes look into mine. "Ungratefulness."

It almost feels as though Toru knows the struggle inside me. But I know that isn't possible. Still, guilt rears its head inside me, and I tap it down. Hoping my features don't give me away, I say, "Then why would he have injected her blood into himself?"

"To make sure she is forgiven and that she goes to Shamok. See, even those who are ungrateful, we make sure through our services they continue on."

Eating the rest of our meals in silence, I hope Toru doesn't notice my hands shaking.

We follow the smell of the sage to our first class. My mind feels clear and my tummy satisfied from the filling breakfast of lentil soup and toast. We arrive in a rather large rectangular room. Vases are set in the four corners of the room, a constant trail of smoke curling up and disappearing in the air. Low red divans surround the perimeter, and Toru walks to the one furthest from the door and shows us how to lay down on them, splaying our legs out lazily, rather than folding them uncomfortably to the side. Getting increasingly more comfortable and accustomed to our sitting arrangements, we observe a few newly-bandaged Eunuchs filter in.

Somberly, three Wardens march in, their heads bowed low and their steps minuscule. The eldest one holds a porcelain jar. Copying Toru, we sit up in respect. The Wardens sit directly in front of us, choosing to kneel on a rug instead of sitting next to us on the divan.

"This is a small group, but as you will soon discover, small groups are what keep great systems like MicroScrep alive," the oldest, greyest Eunuch says. "Lesson one is a history lesson as well as a premonition about your first initiation into the order of Eunuchs. When Arthur Mills's tower fell, thirty scientists were never found. It was later discovered that they, the scientists, established a vigilante society off-grid with the aim of bringing down MicroScrep. They procreated using savage means. They are filled with diseases, and their bodily fluids, saliva, blood, urine—everything about them is a pathogen. To rid the world of their vileness is what one of our goals as Eunuchs is, nobody in MicroScrep will touch them, only the brave. They taught their offspring that one day, when strong and large enough, they'd raid MicroScrep. Do not be fooled, although acting like barbarians, they have advanced technologies. They burn with hatred for Surrogates and Eunuch and all MicroScrepians. Tomorrow's lesson will be about the failed raids."

So that was what had become of the mysterious thirty scientists not recovered in the tower collapse. That is why only seventy graves still commemorate the ill-fated scientists in Mills Cemetery in MicroScrep. Every year at the National Day parade, they are barely mentioned. A mystery made more elusive with time, but now I understand, and fear runs through me cold and unstoppable.

"Now let's pray these lessons will help us become strong," the old Warden says.

"Shamok soooollll, Shamok hummmmmm, Shamok sooollll, Shamok hummmmm." We all begin chanting deeply, and my mind starts to feel incredibly focused. The sound reverberates in my ears, and I am lost in between time.

A porcelain jar is passed, and the old Warden takes the lid off and retrieves an orangey-pink pill with the letters MM stamped on it. One by one, the Wardens take a pill and swallow while chanting. Hesitating for a moment, the old Warden takes my hand and guides the pill to my lips, encouraging me to take it and swallow, just as they have.

Several moments later, the colors in the room become vivid, circling around and shifting. The now multi-colored divans levitate between ceiling and floor. Children are playing in a MicroScrepian compound; I see them through the colored haze. Smiling lovingly at them, their Perfect Family Match parents clap their hands to a tuneless chanting. Then, a Bonding Ceremony appears in the corner; two partners who look incredibly alike, almost to the point of being fraternal twins, get married. Their eyes have the same twinkle and color, their smiles and builds almost identical, were it not for their gender differences.

"MicroScrep needs us to be their heroes."

"We are the brave knights that support society."

"Our enemies are ever-present, always cunning and

tireless, always ready to infect us."

"The off-grid scientists are destroyers of peace and Harmony."

Toru and the Wardens repeat their sentences amidst the colors, shapes, and figures that dance around in the room before my eyes. At one point, I start chanting with them. My mind is focused on bravery, on honor, on the sweet calmness that is present in the room, along with the shapes and colors circling me.

Then it stops. Darkness engulfs me, and I am hit with terror. A scientist in a lab coat is mixing vials of blood. In a petri dish, a dead embryo is floating. My hands are shackled. Adriana is crying. The scientist is torturing her.

"All MicroScrepians must die," he shouts as he brands her stomach with a burning coal.

"All babies must die, MicroScrep will have no more Surrogates, they will be punished when we rebel and take back what is ours," the scientist says.

I struggle against the chains that hold me down, coughing, screaming, sputtering, foaming at the mouth.

"I'll kill you, you twisted scientist," I shout. My mouth forms the words, but no sound comes out. I feel as if I'm shouting underwater. The more I try to scream, the less anyone can hear me and the more petrified I become.

Shaking and fevered when I wake up on the divan, the comforting smell of sage surrounds me. My breathing is labored, and Toru is looking at me, concerned. Turning my head to the right and to the left, I see that each Warden is watching over a Eunuch. Wetting a sponge, Toru presses it over my forehead. Not a word is spoken as the cool sponge soothes my burning temperature and my shocked nerves. The water trickles as he wets the sponge again and hums what we were chanting before we took the pills. The water and humming are comforting.

"What you saw in your vision is true," Toru says, as if blessing me with the nightmare I just dreamt. The shock I experienced with the vision is agitating, but I have a hard time believing it is true. It is more likely that the off-grid scientists are struggling against MicroScrep's tyranny than trying to torture Surrogates. But maybe they see Surrogates as a part of the MicroScrepian system, and this makes them want to eradicate the Surrogates? My head hurts. I can't bear to take any more of their medicines, or Toru's suggestions, let alone my own harried thoughts.

That night while brushing my teeth, I peer at my own image in the mirror. I look foreign. My eyes are aged, dark circles underneath them. My facial features a hollow similarity to what I looked like in MicroScrep. A yellow hue sickens my color. My youthful past seems ages away. I glance at the jar with the remains of my manhood preserved, and a ripple of defeat runs through me. There is so much more to MicroScrep and its history than I had known or been taught. Maybe there is a way to make me whole again, if I prove myself, if I am able to move up the ranks. The sound of the scraping bristles against my teeth brings me back to the present. I place the toothbrush back in its container, realizing that I've lost the impulse to scan objects and the sickening thought that comes with it, that the off-grid scientists are full of disease and that we can't protect ourselves.

There is much more life off-grid than I had been aware

of. Off-grid vigilante scientists, Eunuchs of all shapes and sizes. Perhaps Adriana is being harassed, like what I saw in the vision. I hope nothing terrible is happening to her, not by the scientists or by MicroScrep. Looking into the mirror, I frown, we should have run away when we had the chance. I am angry at myself for listening to Adriana; she is brave, but she is also foolhardy. Were we being too naïve to trust that we could even run away from these terrible people, these terrible circumstances? I need to find her, or at least find information about her. My only hope is to stay calm and keep my eyes and ears open to news about the Surrogacy centers.

Adriana's face comes into my mind. Sweet Adriana, her image still makes me feel like mush inside. She inhabits a sacred spot in my core. The nightmare vision I had was more terrible, not because of the chains I was in, but because of the pain I had to witness her go through. I can't trust the system, and I don't even know who to trust—which might be worse? I splash my face with water, exhaustion takes hold.

As if in a trance, I walk to my bed. Kevin comes to mind. Now that I know he was my biological father, a sense of sadness fills me knowing that he was so tortured in life by his Perfect Family Match father. Milton Mills, the name makes me recoil with hatred. I wonder how Harmony could not have known the avarice in the man. I think back to what my mother would say sometimes, "Trust the process." Leaning back into bed and covering myself with my blanket, I soothe myself with her words. Smelling sage and exhausted from contradictions in my mind, I fall fast asleep.

Chapter 12:

Stevie and Isidro

During the night, I wake up several times. The sound of lashing followed by screams and howls makes my heart palpitate. It sounds as if a wild dog is being zapped with an electric cable. Past the point of exhaustion and the hope for sleep, I rub my eyes and decide to take an evening walk through the halls of the Surrogacy Center to search after the noise. Hitting my toe against the food tray, I double over and grab my foot, cursing the orange-cloaked Eunuch who had left it there for me. As I flick on the switch, I feel guilty for cursing him. He had gentle eyes, slightly downturned and droopy, and I didn't get the menacing sense of evil that I do when Stevie is around.

Immediately after turning the light on, I feel something hard and oily sit on my hand. I hold my breath as a winged cockroach flies toward the bare bulb light hanging over my bed. I look down at the tray. Blackened toast and no more than a spoonful of baked beans. The sauce, like thinned blood, oozes over the side of the plate.

My hungry stomach growls, but I cannot bring myself to eat the food on the tray. I turn the knob on my door. The light from the room shines into a dark corridor.

A particularly sharp scream resonates down the hallway. Then there's a mechanical clap-like sound and again the muffled howl, most certainly coming from the stairwell at the end of the hall. My heart races as I argue with myself: go downstairs, or stay inside the room? The thought of the oily cockroach somewhere on my bed persuades me to explore where the sound is coming from. I open my tiny wardrobe and find a thin black veil hanging from a coat hanger. It smells like mothballs. Draping it over my head to conceal my identity, I tip-toe to the end of the corridor. The sound of a whip cracking, hitting flesh, makes a shock run through my nerves, and my head fills with blood. Pacing quietly down the steps, my hand skims the rounded wall as I spiral down the stairwell. I stop just before where the sounds are coming from. Heavily breathing, I bring my shirt over my mouth to conceal it. There is a dripping sound and soft measured sobs. No words are exchanged, only heavy breathing, dripping, and repressed moans. Then, there is a sound of heavy boots turning and traipsing off in the other direction and eventually disappearing.

Sitting down on the cold cement step, I place my head in my hands. I'm so confused. Weren't Surrogates meant to be the most revered and beloved of MicroScrep? The treatment that I've witnessed has gone from poor to worse in less than two days. What would Zach think of this? He probably believes I'm in a resort, lazing by a pool, being served caviar and cheese. *What is he enduring? If this is how Surrogates are treated, how must he be doing?* Stevie and the orange-cloaked man are Eunuchs; they don't seem starved.

A cooing sound reverberates near me, then quiet weeping, and the sound of suckling. Getting up carefully, I take a few steps forward until the floor gives way under me and I'm slipping and skidding into a dimly lit room. On all fours, I look up and see a black and blue face staring at me from behind steel bars. Her red hair falls over her exposed bosom. Tears slowly trickle down her face. In one arm she cradles a deformed cooing baby, and with the other carved and cut-up arm, she defensively shelters him from me. She breathes heavily, holding her defensive pose, her eyes as large as a ghost's. The baby pushes its smashed and crooked face up to her breast and suckles in between whines.

"Who are you?" she whispers.

"I'm a new Surrogate," I say hesitantly. "What's happened to you?" Unveiling myself and searching into her eyes, I notice the black of one pupil is larger in one eye than the other.

"Poor creature." She shakes her head. "You will suffer here. This child has been born of me, but he's not fit for MicroScrep, so I will die with him."

"Why? Why would they do that? Who would do that?" My voice grows emboldened.

"Ssshhh. You'd better leave soon. He'll be back."

"Who'll be back?" I ask.

"The Eunuch, Stevie, he'll do away with me tonight." She turns herself around in her cell. Deep gashes ooze blood and drip down onto the cement below. My face heats in rage. As she moves the baby to her other breast, she notices.

Her eyes dart behind me, wild like a caged animal. "He takes orders from Numen Eunuch. Go! I fear he'll be back soon."

"What can I do to survive?" Pressing myself up against the bars, I'm choking with pain.

"Escape as soon as possible, make your way out of here, off-grid, they'll just kill you eventually if you don't. They hate us, even more than the other Surrogates. We have differences, we have different eyes, we cannot be influenced as easily. Find your way off-grid, go into hiding, I suspect there are others. Hide!" I hear boots in the distance, along with a jangling of keys. Without another word, I fly towards the stairs and hide in the darkness.

"Now you sorry excuse for a Surrogate." Stevie cracks his whip and the Surrogate groans. The baby cries.

"This child is a product of your system, not of mine!" she screams. "I am sure of my knowledge." The crack of the whip comes down hard. Blocking my ears, anxiety fills me. She's going to be tortured to death, I know it. How long would that take? I can't find out. Instead, I quietly move up the stairs and down the hall. The cockroach in my bed is the least of my worries.

When I wake up, I notice that the tray is gone. It's dark in the room, but this doesn't mean it's night. Who has taken my food? Stomach gurgling uncontrollably, my head feels like a cement block.

Last night's occurrence weighs heavily on my heart. A chilling sense of doom surrounds me. There is nothing I can do but wait and plan my escape back without Zach.

But we had a promise made. I can't go back on my word. I'll have to find him. We can face the future or consequences together; perhaps this way it will be more bearable. The door creaks and the orange-cloaked Eunuch comes in, face downcast, shy, and unassuming.

"Did you eat your food last night?" His voice is so quiet, I must strain to hear him.

"No," I mutter.

"You must eat to keep your strength, Adriana." He says my name gently.

"Someone took the tray before I could."

"Oh, I apologize, some new Eunuchs are on night shift."

He looks at me, his eyes are not only droopy, but a warm hazel, like my mother's. He turns to leave.

"Excuse me, what's your name?" I ask.

"Isidro," he says softly. "Don't go anywhere, or else you won't get anything until lunchtime." He closes the door behind him before I can respond. I stand up and look around, trying to make sense of Isidro's gentleness.

A few minutes later, he enters with a pouch and a warm flask. The pouch is full of dates. The flesh is meaty and satisfying. The flask is filled with warm cinnamon milk.

"This will give you energy, but please don't mention it to anyone." He looks intently at me. "I will get in trouble if you do."

Something about his mannerisms reminds me of a story I wrote in primary school about a friendly troll who decided to befriend a little girl who was lost in a maze and needed to find a way out to get to her family. A kind spin on the ancient Greek Minotaur myth.

"Today you will be impregnated with an embryo," he says. "Do not ask the doctor any questions; they do not speak the truth." My mind flashes back to Dr. Marks in MicroScrep, referring me to Dr. Beata. Now I see it was all a cover. They were cogs in a wheel, trying to get rid of me as a Surrogate before I could expose anyone. I wonder if that strange girl, Louise, who was in the waiting room at the doctor's office for Dr. Beata, is a Surrogate too.

Isidro takes my flask and the empty pouch, puts it in a large mesh bag.

"Will the doctor come for me?" I ask.

"No, I must take you to get cleansed, and he'll come there to collect you."

He looks at me and I nod.

"I'll be back as soon as I can," he says and exits the door so gently that I check to make sure the door is completely closed.

I look in the wardrobe and find a tattered towel. I'm not sure if it's grey from filth or by design. Bringing my nose to it, it smells musty. Moments like these make me mourn the loss of my X-ray vision.

Isidro is back. And he has a better towel, bleach white and warm to the touch.

"Hide this in your backpack, and roll the tattered one under your arm," he instructs. "Follow me."

My instinct tells me to trust him. His gentleness has already surprised me, but I still leave a little room for suspicion, especially after all I've been told about the off-grid world has been a lie. We steal down the opposite end of the hallway to a bamboo door. He opens it and clinks it closed, pulling a latch down to secure it. I turn and notice wooden partitions dividing the room into four parts. In each section is a bar of soap, a large porous sponge, and a porcelain tub. I undress myself as Isidro casts his eyes down and walks over to the tub. Filling it with water, he instructs me to get in and proceeds to sponge me from neck to toe. Every so often he stops to rub the bar of soap onto the sponge, or to submerge the sponge into the tub of water, squeezing the sponge on my head.

"I can do this," I say.

"No, this is my duty." Placing the tattered towel on the ground, he takes out the clean white towel from my backpack.

"Stand up," he instructs, holding the white towel outstretched. I wrap myself in its warmth.

"The doctor will be here soon," he says, and I hear an edge of anxiety in his voice. "So please dry off quickly so that I can take the towel back to my room, wash it, and hang it to dry before anyone discovers what I've done."

"I thought the towel was meant for me," I say.

"No, this is my towel, the grey one would have given you an infection."

"What?" My face screws up in indignation. Why would they give me a towel that could infect me?

"Yes, this is how Surrogates are weakened. They don't want you to survive for more than ten months." His eyes take on the look of a lost child. "They derive enjoyment from putting you through as much pain as they can before you finally give birth and most probably die." Isidro looks down to the ground, his voice wavering as he mutters, "I am tired of seeing suffering."

My throat constricts, and all of a sudden, my mouth feels dry. I don't stand a chance against the system. They're trying to kill me here, my worries should be on survival here-and-now, and if that's what I'm up against, how will I ever find Zach? Isidro senses my shock and places a hand on my shoulder in comfort.

We hear the sound of footsteps outside the door, and I quickly gather the towel and crunch it into a ball, stuffing it into my backpack. Isidro picks up the towel on the ground and hangs it over his forearm as I throw on my shirt. There is a knock on the door. Isidro zips up the backpack and proceeds to unlatch the door as I pull my skirt down.

"Adriana," the doctor says, inspecting me from head to toe.

"Yes, that's me," I say, pushing a lock of soaking wet hair off my shoulder.

"You've done a terrible job of cleaning up," the doctor says, his large nostrils flaring. "I hope that isn't how you'd take care while pregnant with a future citizen of MicroScrep."

"Sorry," I say, looking at Isidro, who is staring straight ahead into the distance, like a demoralized soldier would after a great battle is lost.

"Come along then, we have to work on you," the doctor says. I'm not sure if he's referring to Isidro or me.

We walk down the corridor, up the spiraling stairs that I descended last night. We arrive in an office that has an old leather table with two stirrups at the end. There's a screen connected to various wires, a row of test tubes on a table near the stirrups, and a long cannula attached to a wire that runs to the screen.

"Eunuch, you can go now," the doctor says, motioning me to sit on the table. Isidro leaves without a word.

"Now you must take off your skirt and lay down, so I

can scan your tattoo with this." He holds up a device that makes a weird static noise and emits a green light. I lay down and he guides my legs into the stirrups. An electronic sound comes from the scanner as it's pressed against my tattoo. A serial number and a litany of letters and numbers show up below my name on the screen. The doctor inspects the test tube labels and finds one. "Aha, all right, this will work," he says to himself. He places the cannula into the test tube and the liquid is sucked upwards into it. He works fast, inserting the cannula into my cervix.

"This will only take a minute, breathe and relax."

Almost immediately, the screen flashes various other numbers and letters and then abruptly stops.

"There. All done!" He says this triumphantly, as if he is the creator of the embryo that's been now deposited into my uterus. He pulls out the cannula, and I am left trembling.

"That's just the hormones at work," he says as I look, teeth clenched, at my shaking knees. "Lay here for a half-hour. I'll put the timer on and be back with a Eunuch to help you to your room." He sets the timer on the screen for thirty minutes and leaves.

The door clicks, and I slump back. A sense of relief overtakes me. I realize that they can't kill me while I'm pregnant. They may weaken me, but I have valuc as a receptacle for a MicroScrepian. My body is a hollow tube that has been temporarily filled with what they need to perpetuate their power, therefore, by default I hold value for nine months. The best thing I can do is to stay calm and work towards escape and finding Zach. I am not completely as vulnerable as I think, I have my body and this embryo as ransom. Now, all I need is an ally and some knowledge. The doctor returns after thirty minutes, and this time I am oddly calm.

"The Eunuchs are all engaged now," the doctor says. "You look strong enough to make your way back to your room." Extending a gloved hand, he helps me off the table.

"There you go," he says as he ushers me out of the room. I stop to let a group of Eunuchs roll a gurney down the corridor. Someone is covered in a blue blanket, and as it gets closer, I see a hand fall to the side of the gurney. It is a very delicate female hand, blue and bruised. Immediately, I notice a small motionless lump on top of what must be the lifeless body. Suddenly, I gasp, realizing that this must be the Surrogate I spoke to last night.

"What a shame, the baby is dead," the doctor says, completely disregarding the large body underneath, cradling her baby even in death. He looks at me. "Oh, I mean they are both dead, what a shame." In all my life, I haven't heard a more insincere sentence uttered.

Shuffling down the hallway, I open the door to my room and flick on the switch. The light bulb flickers and shines. This might be a grand metaphor for my life: a flicker, a flash, and then it ends. I touch my torso, wondering who this child will grow up to be. A mindless MicroScrepian, going about life on-grid, not knowing anything about the suffering of Surrogates? Or could this child end up with Laura and Cody? I shiver at the thought of the child that I carry only considering me as a vessel—something that delivers and flashes out like a mechanical light bulb.

Crawling under the covers, I now don't care if there are a thousand creepy crawlies under me. My indifference is interrupted by a polite knock at the door. Isidro, with downcast eyes, enters with a tray. He doesn't leave it on the ground like he did yesterday. He brings it to the bed.

"Don't eat this, I'll bring you something else later on tonight, when the other Eunuchs are getting ready to sleep after their meditation."

I look at him blankly. "And why shouldn't I eat this? I'm starving; it doesn't matter if it's burnt."

"It's not burnt," he says. "It's moldy. Someone high up, maybe even Numen Eunuch himself, has ordered that your food be the worst. They are trying to get rid of you before nine months, or at least deliver the baby from your weakened body prematurely. I've seen it done before."

A hard lump forms in my throat. I thought I was immune to their treatment for nine months; that if I was a vessel for their sick system, I could find a way to get out of here. Now, I feel like I'll never win against these terrible people, this tyrannical system! I close my heavy eyes, hunger groaning in my core. Tears that I've suppressed flow down my face and my chest heaves with sobs.

"Don't cry, Adriana, please." His comforting words remind me of Zach's gentleness.

"Why am I being treated so terribly? Don't they value human life? I'm carrying one of their own. Why...why... why?" My voice rings out like a siren. I am shaking now, and my tears are making my hair and pillow wet.

"Shhhh." Isidro dries my face with the tissue he has in his cloak pocket. "I don't know why, Adriana. They are terrible to Surrogates, but they are particularly cruel to you. Do you...do you have any enemies in MicroScrep?"

I think back to Laura, a memory of her flashing incognito camera under the pool, and the wry smile she had when I was named Surrogate and Zach was named

Eunuch. The slip of tongue when she gave a speech at Surrogate send off. It is Laura, my sister-in-law, who is my enemy, but I decide not to tell Isidro; what use would it have to tell him? He won't have any power to change what's happened.

"No, I don't think so," I say before a lingering sob escapes my throat.

"I don't know how long I can continue to help you before I get caught," Isidro says all the while avoiding my eyes, "but I will help as best I can." I catch his glance as he looks intently at me.

He leaves with the tray and later brings back a paper bag and a flask. The paper bag is filled with baked treats and a croissant. The flask is filled with warm ginger milk. I devour the croissant and greedily eat the treats with the milk. The heat of the ginger warms and soothes me. My crushing tension headache subsides slightly.

"Isidro, I have a secret to tell you." I take his hand and hold it. "Promise me you won't tell anyone about this."

Isidro glances sideways. His shoulders hunch up defensively. He's reluctant. "Please, you're all I have."

His shoulders lower and he sighs. "All right, I promise."

"In MicroScrep, I had a very dear friend, Zachary. We wanted to be a Perfect Bonding Pair. We wanted to be given children, according to what Harmony deemed a good fit, to complete us in a Perfect Family Match. But I was chosen as a Surrogate, and he as a Eunuch."

I pause and assess Isidro's eyes, trying to find empathy, or resonance. "You know as well as I do that I'll probably be dead in ten months or less. I want you to help me find Zachary and escape this place. I want my last months to be with him."

Isidro's eyes search the walls behind me, unable to look at me even for a second. The knot in my stomach tightens.

"Adriana, I...I can't. This would be considered treason... and besides you wouldn't be able to survive off-grid. The forest is too deep and thick. The animals are too dangerous. You'd be dead before you find him."

My mouth is open, as if in a perpetual, muted scream. A tear streams down my face. I let go of Isidro's hand. I am trying to form words. They race through me, buzzing in my ears, but no sound is produced.

Isidro shakes his head, the warm weight of his hand resting briefly on my shoulder. "Adriana, your secret is safe with me, and I'll do everything I can to make these months easier for you here."

Chapter 13:

Zach's Initiation

"During the siege of a Surrogate Center in 2150, several off-grid scientists killed and maimed dozens of Surrogates, Eunuchs, and doctors. With their germ warfare, they infiltrated our ranks, spreading a new variant of a disease unknown to Harmony. The reason that you can't scan for viruses off-grid is because they have the technology to hack our system. Blame the off-grid scientists for any premature death here. They determined to destabilize MicroScrep and will stop at nothing to do away with any Surrogate, Eunuch or doctor here.

Toru grows silent, letting the gravity of the lesson sink into those around. A few other Wardens listen intently, nodding their heads and tutting the injustices of the terrorist scientists. My mind is hyper-focused; the pills today are strong.

"The Eunuchs banded together and fought back. They were able to kill only a few, and the rest retreated into the forest. These cowards realized that the only way to continue their indignations towards MicroScrep was to procreate like savages, without regard for cleanliness or chastity. They performed their perversions with each other, the women scientists falling pregnant and delivering like bitches, every year with a different man."

One of the Wardens scoffs with disgust. I look at Ben, whose eyes take on a fanatical fervor that eats away at his facial muscles. Along with the focus is a sense of restlessness deep in my core. The stories we're told weave in and out of me like possessed demons.

"The scientists are wayward. They are dirty. Even the air they breathe can infect you. Their saliva, or blood, can bring back pandemics that Arthur Mills and MicroScrep worked so hard to extinguish. They have procreated and multiplied exponentially since the time of the siege, intent on wiping out MicroScrep, by any means possible. Our duty is to resist them. Our job as Eunuchs is to protect MicroScrep by facilitating the arrival of babies from the Surrogacy Centers to MicroScrep. To fulfill our fate, we must prove ourselves first, and then we must work in unity to ensure healthy babies are delivered to MicroScrep's Perfect Family Matches."

Ben looks towards me. His eyes are open and animated. He is a good disciple for Toru, even though I feel Toru favors me. How can I exploit this favoritism to learn more about what the plan is, and how I can get closer to Adriana?

"I would like to volunteer to serve in the Surrogacy Centers," Ben says while raising his hand, his eyes still wild with zeal.

"Not so quickly," Toru says, "patience and valor are needed to be a Warden, but first you must prove yourself."

"How?" I ask. My voice cracks, foreign, even to my own ears. A dozen eyes stare at me, surprised I've spoken.

"Ah! See, Zach's patience allowed him to ask the right question at the right time." Toru smiles. "It may be difficult for you to hear, Zach. Are you sure you want to know?"

Curious about this invitation, I nod my head.

"First you must spend two days in meditation, giving your body and mind up to the greater good."

"No food or drink?" Ben whines.

Toru chortles. "No, you've already done this step."

Mockingly wiping his forehead, we laugh heartily, knowing that Ben loves his food and beverage.

"Indeed, a few days ago you completed this portion of the initiation, during our retreat." Toru laughs, his mouth curling into a smile.

"So, then what?" Ben replies.

"You must go through the second initiation. Penetrate the fortress wall that surrounds the scientists' city. Find a scientist and bring its head back to us. That is the only way. It must be done with a knife; they have ways to heal from any other mode of killing."

I swallow hard. Ben's eyes light up. Uneasiness settles in me. I can't harm someone, let alone kill them. How am I ever going to be initiated and find Adriana if I am expected to kill? My mind races, and I feel my throat constrict.

"When will we be doing this?" Ben wets his lips as if ready to feast on flesh.

"Tomorrow evening at dusk you will be taken by tank to the wall surrounding the rebel scientist territory. Once you've penetrated the walled city, you will see primitive gravel paths and huts. They live as savages do. Decapitate someone in the city and bring their heads back with you here. When you've completed this task, you will be fully initiated as a Warden Eunuch, be given the orange cloak and habit, and will be sourced to a Surrogate Center where you can fulfill your lifelong duty of making sure MicroScrepian babies are delivered and sent to a Perfect Family Match."

Ben is drunk with excitement, bouncing up and down on a cushion. Toru rests his hand on Ben's back to calm him.

"But you must do this initiation completely voluntarily. There is no stigma attached to those who do not want this honor. I, myself, didn't become a Warden because I did not complete my mission."

Toru's eyes fall to the ground. My heart skips a beat. I immediately think of Adriana. If I follow through with the initiation, I will be able to find her. I can't believe my luck and can barely conceal my enthusiasm. Ben is smiling broadly and raising his hand to give me a high five.

"Yeah, tomorrow we fight for MicroScrep!" he bellows as his hand meets mine in a loud clap. My face is red, and Ben's is jubilant. I look around to see Toru and the other Eunuchs clapping their hands for us.

Dusk falls and we are ushered into a tank. Toru accompanies us, insisting that if we do not wish to complete this mission, we could still opt out.

"I'm in a hundred percent," Ben exclaims as he jumps into the tank.

"Thank you, Toru, but I would like to complete this last step to become a Warden and keep our Surrogates safe from the enemy." It only took mention of the Surrogate Center for me accept this challenge. I need to find Adriana; I can't delay this any longer.

Burning sage at the door of the tank, Toru touches his hand to the smoke and places it on my head, as if blessing me, "May you be free from their diseases" he hums in a deep guttural cadence. The other Wardens chant as they circle the tank. Sage wafts up and out into the crisp evening sky, the vermillion sunset a bright backdrop to the grey smoke climbing high. As the driver embarks on our journey through the forest, I rest my head back, thinking of the abhorrent deed I must commit to find Adriana. I am sick at heart and conflicted like the path that we follow that zig zags into the woods. We avoid clearings, instead choosing overgrown paths that scrape against the vehicle's body. Ben is sitting up astutely, his eyes follow the green brush that surrounds our now slow-moving vehicle as his hand absently caresses one of the knives we were given to do our duty.

"Be quick," the driver says. "Don't stall in the city, the successful Eunuchs are in and out within fifteen to twenty minutes. My suggestion is to find a house, open the door, and be done with the first person you see."

Ben's eyes turn to the driver. "Should we work as a team, or go about it separately?"

"As you wish, but the most success I've seen comes from those who separate. It's easier that way, doesn't leave room for as much error."

Ben looks at me. "What do you reckon, Zach?"

"I think we should do it together." Somehow, the idea

of killing someone before or after Ben lessens the uneasiness that I feel. That, and if we do kill as a team, I would feel only half-responsible for the death.

"All right, then, we'll go in together," Ben says as he swallows another pill.

We stop at the edge of a clearing. I look through the front window and see a massive wall surrounding the parameter. The wall looks diseased, with weathered and discolored stone. I try to scan the wall and a faint flicker of my x-ray vision confirms my feelings. Then it flickers off again, before I can memorize where not to touch.

"If you aren't back within thirty minutes, I will leave, and you'll have to find your way back to the Eunuch Center. That's if the scientists don't find, torture, and kill you first."

The driver says "scientist" with a considerable amount of disgust, spitting the word out as if it is filth in his mouth. He unlocks the doors, and we steal out into the cool night.

We run fast towards the wall. I can hear Ben sucking in air as we advance. He isn't a runner; each stride is heavy. His heels strike and his shoes flick back clay and grass. The wall is uneven, cracks are easily found, where we can lodge our fingers, or grip, or place a foot against the wall. I find myself at the top and look over. An electric current strikes blue, veiny lines overtop the city. We must find a way around the electrical currents first. There are lights in the distance, near the center of the city. Huts are speckled throughout the tiny gravel roads. Everything is quiet and peaceful, the only lights are from the stars and moon, and a few torches that shine at random points. In MicroScrep, one cannot see the stars, and there is never this quiet.

Ben is so mesmerized and hyped up from the drugs he's taken that he dangles a foot over the wall. There is a light buzzing sound, and before the flicker reaches Ben, I push him back and we both tumble to the ground. I fall and roll onto the short bushes and shrubs underneath me. I hear the staticky sound of Ben falling down on tall grass and his torrent of curses. The leaves are dry and crunch under me as I move to him. I've saved his life. If we had fallen into the village, we would have been fried by the currents. His leg looks like it's been tarred, and it smells copper and metallic.

"Can you get up?" I croak.

Ben winces against the pain.

"Should I take you back to the tank?" I am desperate now. If Ben doesn't come I can't complete the mission. I couldn't live with myself if I had to kill alone.

"No—just give me a hand." He groans.

I lift him up, and he hobbles on his leg. "I think the mud will soothe it, just see if you can scan it."

I turn my x-ray vision on, and it moves in and out of focus, wavering and stopping.

"Damn it, it won't work!"

"Try it again," Ben says through clenched teeth.

I flicker it on again, and to my astonishment it works. I scan along the wall and see a tunnel covered in soft mud. There are no viruses there.

Ben hobbles alongside me until we get to the mud; we both start digging frantically until we find the opening of the tunnel. Ben grabs handfuls of the mud and slathers it on his leg. The tunnel is insulated and cleaner than I expect. I am the first to emerge from it and extend my hand out for Ben, who groans against the pain he's feeling.

We start to crawl towards a house that is not too far away. The lights are completely off, and the cabin looks derelict. Perhaps no one lives there. What if this is a trap?

"Ben," I whisper, "I don't know if we should target this house. It looks abandoned."

"Well, it doesn't hurt to try. Remember we have a time limit, and I'm injured, you genius!" His sarcasm bites me, and then he follows up with, "Come on, let's try the back door." Motioning to the back door with his chin, we stand up and make our way towards it. The door is ajar, and Ben slides in sideways, careful not to make any sounds, but I can tell from the sweat on his forehead that he's in pain. I follow his arrhythmic hobble.

We're in the basement of the house. I can hear a voice humming melodically and the sound of water running. Side-stepping with our backs against the wall, we reach the stairs. Ben touches the knife in his baldric. His eyes are wild with excitement, a wry smile frames his face, despite the sweat dripping down it. We hear footsteps and the clanking of dishes. Motioning with the tip of his nose and a nod of his head, Ben hunches down and climbs up the stairs, one leg trailing behind as I follow along. In front of us is a wall with a small entrance to a kitchen. To the left is a hallway. Ben crawls past the kitchen entrance. The woman has her back towards us, washing dishes while humming peacefully. Ben is in the hallway, and I scurry past the kitchen entrance as she begins to hum another tune. Her feet move to the beat of the music.

Ben motions us into another room and enters it. Touching my knife, my fingers shake on its cold handle as I enter the room. In a crib a baby is standing, holding onto the panels. Its back is towards us, bouncing to the sound of imaginary music, his silky blond hair swaying. The baby is wearing a blue onesie, and a sentiment deep inside makes me want to cry. A loud crowing sound snaps Ben into attention. A parrot sits perched in an open cage.

Ben swiftly grabs the bird and twists the parrot's head off. There is a loud crack and blood trickles on the crib mattress. Feeling weightless, I see pinpricks of light and can taste acrid bile in my mouth. Moments later, I hear a blood-curdling scream come from behind me. Somebody tackles me from behind, legs encircling my hips as I fall over. Her fists are flying everywhere, she is pulling my hair, punching my face. I don't fight back. Then there is the relief of her weight. Ben has her pinned against the ground. She head-butts him. Blood spews from his brow. She spits at him. Saliva mixes with the blood and sweat on his brow. Ben curses, "She's diseased; she's given me a disease! Kill that bitch!" I push her off him and take the knife out of my baldric while she wriggles underneath me.

"Kill her," Ben screams, wiping away the spit and blood on his brow.

My knife is against her neck, but my arms have lost their strength. I look into her eyes and see Adriana's image flash before me. My knife is shaking. Looking up and ahead, I see the parrot curled up into a pool of blood. My knife falls. The lady grabs at the knife fallen beside us. Just then, Ben plunges a knife deep into her rib cage. He stabs her several times, while all I see are pinpricks of light and feel an indescribable heaviness that envelops me and fills my bones. She curses at me as blood pours out from her mouth and nose. My head is weightless, somewhere in deep space, with the lights twinkling like stars, but my body is heavy as lead, my heart a dense magnet that attracts everything dark in the universe and pulls it close. I wish I could decapitate my head from my body and float away into the stars.

Chapter 14:

The Birth

The terror surrounding me the first few days at the Surrogacy Center has been reduced now, but only through adaptation, time, and dissociation.

Isidro steadfastly saw to it that I was comfortable, washing my towel, exchanging it with his. He rubbed my growing belly with oils that smelled like various flowers: one day it was rose, the next lavender, or a mix of gardenia and jasmine. Even though others were suspicious of him, he would steal into my room to bring me bits of food he'd salvage from his portion. His sense of detachment seemed to eat away at him, his weight plunging to an alarming low. He tells the other Eunuchs that he's fasting to allay their suspicions. That he wants to become as attached as he can to his duty and not waste time eating. The days where he does eat in front of the other Eunuchs, he puts some aside in tinfoil and says to the others that he will be feeding the stray cats outside. There is a stairway that connects the outside area where he leaves some food for the cats, and then brings me a small portion.

Isidro does not see me every day, but he always has a way of stealing food into my room. Under my pillow he plants his dates, or raisins, or fresh bread.

Other orange-cloaked Eunuchs also enter my room, but they walk in and out, performing their duties, rarely speaking, ignoring my existence with a lost, far-off look in their eyes. I'm doing the same; the lack of trust and pockets of sheer denial are what keep me from experiencing a nervous breakdown. It's interesting how one can emotionally shut off when it's necessary for survival, finding friendship in an ant, a rock, a swollen belly. I have already named the baby, which squirms and kicks at night. Ophelia. Loved dearly by me, bound to be separated at birth.

I do not venture out of my room, except to see the doctor or to take a solemn walk through the corridors, making sure to avoid contact with other Surrogates. I can't see their suffering, although I know that I am treated worse. I know they are given meagre portions, but I at least have companionship in Isidro. There is an unbearable heaviness that fills me every day. The awe and power of a growing being within my womb brings with it deep aspirations and an unbearable helplessness. I am determined to carry her to term, to allow my body to be her shield, to allow her blood to pump and mingle with mine. I regret not knowing this feeling sooner, not comprehending the power in the carrying of this priceless pearl. My resolve to find a way out of here is also heightened. To find Zach, to be a free human being, even if it is only a matter of time before they find us.

I speak of this only to Isidro when he is bathing me,

the tap water muddling my words so that only Isidro can hear me.

"Last night Ophelia kicked me for the first time. Oh, here it is now!" I take my shriveled fingers and grasp his hand, submerging it into the bath water and onto my rounded belly. He smiles proudly, eyes softening.

I plead with Isidro to help me escape, to find a way out of this prison, but despite his goodness and loyalty to me, he steadfastly resists, fearing I'll die sooner out there, off-grid, than in here.

"I can't let her go, Isidro. I think I'd die if they take her from me. You must do something. Let me leave here. Set me and my baby free."

"If it were only that simple, dear, I'd have done it long ago. Not only will I die a humiliating death, but you and the baby will suffer greatly before I do."

Isidro has also become attached to the infant in my belly. A psychological overcompensation for what his biggest regret in life has been. He tells me he would have loved to be a father in a Perfect Family chosen by Harmony. He wants to care for something: a cat, a baby, a woman. He regrets not being able to see someone through infancy to adulthood. Cherishing their firsts, building memories from their smiles and triumphs, steadfastly holding to them in moments of doubt, or fear.

"I will make sure Ophelia goes to a truly Perfect Family. Forgive my blasphemy. Of course, all families chosen by Harmony are perfect, but what I mean is the most perfect of the perfect," he says skittishly.

"You don't need to apologize to me, Isidro," I whisper.

"What do you think it was in me that made me be chosen as Eunuch?"

"Perhaps you are too perfect, too loving. No one could match or equal you in the mundane and mindless goings-ons of MicroScrep."

His eyes shine and then fall dark.

"What's the sadness then?" I touch his chin. He looks away. I gently push his chin up so he's looking at me again.

"I hate seeing Surrogates die; it's the most painful part of my job." He says "job" and not duty. These little snubs in our vocabulary show that our true loyalties are to each other, rather than to MicroScrep.

"Then help me survive this birth," I say.

"What's the use? You don't understand, Adriana." He shakes his head; his face contorts sourly. "If you survive Ophelia's death, you will be transferred to another Surrogacy Center, worse than this one, ten times as unsanitary and foul. There will be no Isidro there to aid you, to keep you alive. There you will suffer greatly before you die."

"Will you come with me?" I ask.

"No, only Eunuchs who have been valiant throughout their initiation go there to prove to themselves further to Numen Eunuch."

I stand up in the tub. Water drips down my round belly. It shines in the dim light. Isidro stands up to wrap his towel around me. His eyes are deep in thought. As I step out of the tub and slowly pull on my clothes, Isidro's voice is a whisper.

"I might not be able come with you," he says, "but I will find a way to keep you safe."

We walk out and down the hall. I can feel that the weight Isidro is carrying lightens; his arms move gracefully in time with his strides. He has a plan for my deliverance.

I touch my bulging belly. Ophelia hasn't dropped yet. She rides high and wide, what the doctor says is a tell-tale sign that it's a girl.

"The Surrogate in room 111 is hallucinating," Isidro tells me one morning. "I don't know how to help her. I'm already under suspicion for eating so much yet losing weight."

I look at him; he has the stalwart qualities of a quiet hero. I can see sincerity in his statement. He continues to pace the room, sanitizing the handles, spraying for cockroaches. He stops and looks at me.

"If she weren't nine months pregnant, and due any moment, I wouldn't be so concerned. I can't tell anyone else for fear of denouncement by the other Eunuchs." He sheepishly turns and starts to pace again.

"Isidro, I'm happy to give half of my food to her."

He looks at me, eyes downcast. "But then you must deliver it to her in the evenings, when we Eunuchs are in meditation."

He slips me what looks like a watch. Its face is scratched and shattered at one edge. There is a peculiar white background with a ring of numbers from twelve to eleven encircling the outer edge. Two arrows, one larger than the other, are at a right angle.

"This is an old battery-powered watch. It's what people used before electronic ones." He points to the short arrow. "When this is pointing exactly at eight, and it's after your dinner, you can deliver whatever you haven't eaten to the Surrogate in room 111. I will speak to her about this so that she knows to keep her door unlocked."

Isidro's eyes are pleading. If he can risk himself like this, so can I. He's risking a longer life expectancy than I am in the end anyways. On the bright side, I wonder if she will become a good companion. I am hungry for a female friend anyways. Someone who, like me, has known what it's like to be snatched from MicroScrep and brought to this horrid and dark place, to be met with savagery and ruthlessness instead of honor and appreciation. Someone who realizes the crushing reality of being lied to their entire life, finding themselves in a pestilent hellhole.

Isidro walks over to me, his demeanor lighter now, and embraces me. It's an odd feeling, being touched by a man, even one as sweet and gentle as Isidro. It is oddly calming and soothing, something I've never experienced before.

"Tonight, during our meditation, a new Warden will arrive. I've been asked to be his mentor," Isidro says.

My mind buzzes with excitement. "What if the new Warden is Zach," I blurt out.

Isidro's eyes darken. His chest sinks in with heaviness.

"What did I say that was wrong?" I ask as Isidro looks at me.

He clears his throat. "Do you know what Eunuchs must do to become Wardens?"

"No." I cut my explanation short and shake my head in response.

"To become a Warden, you must prove your loyalty to Numen by murdering an off-grid scientist."

I frown in confusion. "Who are they?" I ask.

"Remember the MicroScrep Tower explosion tragedy, where one hundred scientists were killed, yet thirty were never found during Arthur Mills's time?"

I nod my head, eyes wide open with anticipation.

"Those thirty scientists fled the tower before the explosion. There was something that they knew about Arthur Mills's Cleanliness Campaign, something terrible that he had hatched and planned in order to have complete control. They escaped MicroScrep and set up a society off-grid. Their descendants still live in the forests. They've created their own society, have fortified it with a wall. The only way to move up in the Eunuch hierarchy is to prove your loyalty through committing acts of violence against these people, the successors of those thirty scientists."

My eyes move left and right, trying to make sense of this new information.

"Then you've killed someone." My voice quivers. "That's how you've become a Warden."

Isidro looks into my eyes and takes my hand. It takes all my effort not to pull away in disgust.

"No." He shakes his head. "My partner did. We were always sent in twos, but he didn't survive. He was stabbed numerous times but had dealt the two scientists we'd found fatal blows. One of the scientists had a letter in his back pocket, saying what Arthur Mills had done and the real history. It was meant for his killer, a Eunuch, if he ever was killed in a raid. I found it, read it, and placed it back in his pocket before leaving the village. I was named the hero and promoted, when actually all I wanted was to be saved and to endure."

His eyes close as if he's trying to forget the images and memories enshrined in his mind.

"I had my reasons for wanting to be a Warden, as you have your reasons for wanting to escape, but believe me, my Adriana, fate is best untampered with."

I press his hand in mine. A sense of both pain and empathy take over as I look at his soft features worn down by time. I want to ask him more, but I can see he's bent over with the pain of remembering.

"I should go now; I don't want to be late for meditation." He squeezes my hand affectionately and whispers before he leaves, "Don't forget, when the little arrow is on the eight."

I compulsively check my watch, waiting for eight. The shorthand is at the four. Isidro delivered my lunch tray at two, an extra ball of tin foil under one of the overturned cups. He's put it there for me to portion some of my food in it for the Surrogate in room 111.

I lie flat on my back, looking at the bulb slowly swaying back and forth in the circulating heat of the room. The fan hums with a lazy drone. It was put there when I reached the seven-month pregnancy milestone. So much for the luxurious living people in MicroScrep believe the Surrogates to have. Double the blood is coursing through my veins, double the heat. I used to feel like a lobster in a steaming pot, being steamed alive, until that fan arrived. Now, I can wet my disinfected towel and place it against the fan, giving me cool air—a makeshift air conditioner. Desperation breeds innovation.

I know that Isidro must be meeting the new Warden anytime now. I fantasize it might be Zach. I imagine my surprise, my tears. It would be a bittersweet moment. Embarrassed that I didn't fulfill my promise to find him first, I'd shyly look down to the ground and then run towards him with outstretched arms, overjoyed that fate brought us together again. I shake my head. "The chances of this are slim," I whisper out loud, disappointing the hope of my wandering mind.

A curious impulse arises as I watch the sway of the light bulb. What if I made my way down the hall and ran into Isidro and the new Warden? Certainly, I would be chastised by Isidro, but he wouldn't be cruel or punish me. If I came across another Warden, I'd say that I'm visiting the doctor to take my temperature because I feel fevered.

Turning off the fan, I jog around the room until my forehead drips with perspiration and my temperature is high enough to fool a Warden. I open my door to an empty corridor and walk up the stairs at the end of the hall. Where should I go? The freedom and impulse of the moment emboldens me. Isidro's room would be my safest bet. I turn right after a flight of stairs. His room is beside the Bathing Room, close enough for him to steal clean towels from after he bathes me. I turn the latch, expecting it to be locked, but it opens. Hearing footsteps from afar, I quickly enter and close the door quietly, turning the latch discreetly so that it makes no more than a gentle clink. My mind is buzzing. The footsteps are making their way towards me, and then pass. I exhale and turn to look around.

The room is minimalistic. A tidy white bed in the corner, a shelf with a picture of a younger Isidro with his Perfect Family Match parents. He must be no more than ten in the picture. His eyes are bright. His mother has her hand around his shoulder; she is holding him close. His father is looking down at Isidro, a smile of adoration enveloping his face. There is a drawer near his bed. I look through it. A bundle of sage, a matchbox, a journal. I flip through the contents of the notebook, but it's blank. I feel the rush of apprehension hit me. On the one hand, I am so curious to learn more about Isidro, on the other, I am trespassing in his space. I let my curiosity win this time. The second drawer has a jar filled with solution and the pickled remains of his castration. I place it back quickly, feeling the guilt of interfering with his forbidden organ, a sacred relic. I turn around and squat down, putting my ear to the ground, listening to hear whether anyone is coming up the stairs. I then see it. Under his bed is a red box, faded in places. Sliding my arm under the bed, I retrieve it. Taking the lid off the box, I notice that there are papers folded up, and underneath are old pictures. The first picture is of a tall broad-shouldered lady, slender but strong, with dark shocks of dreadlocks and a stunningly beautiful aubergine black face. Her nose is small and precocious. Her eyes are golden brown. She is the most beautiful woman I've ever seen. I turn the photo over. *Ester - age sixteen*, it reads. I recognize Isidro's writing. The next picture is one of her in this very Surrogacy Center, the plaque on the door reads room 111. Ester is pregnant in the photo, though not heavily so. I turn it over. *Ester - a week before escaping the Surrogacy Center*. I open up the folded paper. At the top again is Isidro's back slanted handwriting, it says *The Last Letter*. I read voraciously, gulping the words down as if they were a sweet nectar and a soothing tonic.

My Isidro,

I'm writing with the hope that you'll see me or at least this letter one day—I've made provisions for the latter. Writing to you, I've felt the most alive I've ever been in this makeshift treehouse off-grid. Since escaping MicroScrep and now the internment camp so deceitfully called the Surrogacy Center, I've redoubled my commitment to finding you. I will, if not in this life, then on one of the myriad other planes of existence, as yet invisible to our eyes.

I love you. I am not ashamed to admit it. Before my Calling Ceremony, when we consummated our love, I knew you'd become a Eunuch. Isn't it surprising who Harmony chooses to be a Surrogate, and who it chooses to be a Eunuch? They want us separated, but I will find you, just as I promised. I came pregnant to the Surrogacy Center. The doctor said there was already a beating heart in my uterus when he was about to impregnate me artificially. Yes, I say artificially—I am not taking these words back. What we felt for one another, and all our doings, are natural. Their ways are unnatural! Arthur Mills himself wanted it this way. Control and power in the wrong hands are as dangerous as the most pestilent disease that can be created.

Thank God for enlightenment. The doctor said he'd keep silent but would not be able to enter our child into the Harmony database, it would instantly be flagged and all four of us would end up dead. The doctor instead helped me escape. If you receive these letters, it means that that doctor was good to his words, that he'd find and deliver them to you.

I love you, Isidro. I will say it a hundred times in a hundred tongues. Your baby is growing. I'm finding food, meagre though it may be. I will find you. We will be united—have faith.

Yours,
Ester

I am completely dumbfounded. Isidro's story so closely resembles mine and Zach's that I feel a deeper affinity for them. The horror and indignation I usually experience when sexuality is referenced is totally numb as I read Ester's letter. Their love seems so pure and harmless, their act of consummation is a symbol of their trust and love for one another, rather than a vile expression of animal instinct.

I turn the letter over, and grab the envelope, no notes that might hint at what happened to her, none of Isidro's distinct handwriting. I feel cheated. But where is the next letter? There has to be one, right? What happened to her next? Does Isidro know where she is? My imagination takes a turn; does he live a double life, one as a Eunuch and the other as a family man, stealing out of the center to travel to her at night? He'd surely be saving my food for her though. My mind wanders further. One of the pictures shows Ester beside the room plaque 111. Is Isidro using me to bring food to her? Is this part of an elaborate plot to sustain her, while simultaneously depriving me of finding my Zachary? It can't be, if she ran away, surely the other Eunuchs would know that she's back, and why would Isidro title it the last letter if she was here? What if his hesitation to help me escape is founded in past trauma with Ester? There are too many questions floating around my head, some more plausible than others, but I feel an urgency to find my way back to my room before I'm discovered. Breathlessly, I place all objects back, scramble out of his room, down the stairs, and back to my room. I glance at my watch. The arrow is past five, but not at six yet. My stomach rumbles and I take a piece of the stale bread that Isidro left me a few days ago. I want to keep as much as I can for the Surrogate in room 111, especially after what I've just learned. I wonder if I should confess that I've been to his room. I'm not sure if he'd be angry with me. I've only been here for seven months; it's hard to trust after all I've seen. I'll decide later, I tell myself, turning on the fan to dry my sweat.

There is a polite tap at the door. I glance at my watch; the short arrow is at the seven. I quickly look around the room, the tray is underneath my bed with the tinfoil neatly wrapped around a dinner bun with some peanut butter and jam slathered between two halves. Everything looks as it should, except the wet towel on the fan. I roll it into a ball and place it in the wardrobe. Another tap, slightly more forceful this time. I open it to a shockingly fair man. He is almost translucent, and I stop myself from reaching out to see if he's real or a figment of my imagination. He has a scab on his forehead that looks new, as if someone has seared him with a spit.

"Hello."

He doesn't respond. I wonder if he's lost or disillusioned. His eyes are icy, almost devoid of blue. I can see the blue veins that run below his eye as he stares blankly at me.

"Can I help you?" I touch my belly, my face flushed despite all of a sudden feeling a chill rush through me. Isidro appears in the door frame to my relief.

"This is Benjamin, a new Eunuch. He's under a vow of silence for twenty-four hours. It's a way of showing his loyalty to Numen Eunuch. He can't walk comfortably unfortunately; his leg was injured during his recent initiation."

Isidro looks drained. There are dark circles under his eyes, as if silently showing his displeasure at being tasked with a new Eunuch.

"Are there any others?" I ask, stepping aside so both Benjamin and Isidro can come in. My heart starts beating quicker, hoping that Isidro might say that Zach is here as well.

"No, unfortunately not. We only have nine pregnant Surrogates in this Center that are due to deliver in the next month, so they've dispatched only one Eunuch here."

Benjamin walks oddly, as if he's in a stupor, he favors one leg. He rubs a finger along my wardrobe, then lifts his finger to his eyes and squints, a layer of dust sullying it. I don't think I've ever seen a stranger person. He looks ghostly but walks as if a large weight is holding him down. Robotic, his rigid features and blank expression make me wonder if he is indeed human.

"Would you like some water?" I ask, but Isidro widens his eyes, perhaps warning me against easy familiarity. Ben turns to look at me, his icy cold eyes squinting again as if he's zeroing in on me. He shakes his head slowly, as if his body and mind are at war and can't agree on what gesture he should use to refuse me. He touches his brow, where the fresh scab sits. It reminds me of a chemical wound.

"Benjamin will be in charge of you and the Surrogate in room 111. I will, of course, help him with his duties." Isidro breaks the awkward silence with his voice and continues, "Poor Benjamin, he must be shocked to see a Surrogacy Center. He might have envisioned a more luxurious place than this, but Numen Eunuch has informed us that the off-grid scientists have hacked and stolen a lot of money and resources from MicroScrep, thus there are limited funds available for the upkeep of the Surrogacy Centers." Isidro widens his eyes again, motioning that I am not to respond to what he's just said.

"All right then, Benjamin, let's take you to room 111 before our meditation session at eight." Isidro taps on his wrist, where a watch used to be.

I watch the long arrow move from eleven to twelve, and suddenly the short arrow moves to the eight. I crouch down, bundling the ball of food-filled tinfoil under my shirt. It bulges out under my clothes like a distended umbilical hernia. I move to the wardrobe and drape the black veil over my head loosely so that it falls over my midriff. Slowly opening the door, it gives a creaky, high-pitched yawn. Looking left and right, I shuffle down the hallway, hands over my belly, tinfoil jiggling under my shirt. The door to room 111 is open. Her room is similar to mine. She's sleeping on her bed, all lights off, except for a night light in the corner power outlet. Unmoving, she coughs, a deep bronchial one, as I tiptoe towards her, wondering if peanut butter and jam was the wisest choice. She's sleeping on her side, a blanket pulled up to her chin.

"Hello," I whisper. "I'm Adriana. I believe Isidro told you I'd bring some safe food for you."

She blinks a thank you before falling into another coughing fit and pointing to the door. I go and close it. She's already opened the tin foil and has taken a large bite out of the bun by the time I'm back. She chews noisily before swallowing.

Her frizzy hair puffs up like a crown around her head. She has African features, except for two hazel-colored eyes and a set of long curly eyelashes. Had we not been here, I would have thought they were artificial, but clearly, they're not. Her eyes look as innocent as a doe's. I open a flask of warm water near her bed, pouring it into the cup-shaped lid. She is slow to sit up. Her arms and legs are bony and long. Her stomach is swollen far past her large breasts. She takes the lid with her two hands and drinks.

"I'm Rowani," she says, handing the lid back to me. She touches her belly. "He is due any day now." A faint smile is swiftly overtaken by a fit of coughing. "Excuse me," she mutters in pain. "My chest hurts terribly."

"I'm sorry, I wish I could help." I fill the lid again, giving her time to eat the rest of the sandwich before washing it down with the warm water.

"You are helping by just visiting me here." She smiles, her compassion showing in her eyes between sips of water. There's a moment of silence as her gaze lingers on me, then she says, "I'm certain that you'll survive. You're eight months pregnant and in such good health, I've been on the decline since arriving here."

I take the opportunity to ask her if Isidro is a recent friend, or has she known him before in MicroScrep. She shakes her head no.

I learned that she recently has been relocated to room 111 after a Surrogate died in childbirth.

Before this, other Eunuchs were looking after her. She's sure she got the cough from one of them. Of course, they're fed better, so they recover easier.

"I don't know if this is what was intended by the founders of MicroScrep, but the Eunuchs have sure killed us off effectively," she chuckles and coughs before continuing. "If I'd known in MicroScrep how terrible they are to Surrogates, I'd have hung myself the night of my Calling Ceremony."

As Rowani starts shaking with fever, I pull the blanket over top her shoulders.

"Am I going to die?" she asks, and at the same time, I feel she's asking something bigger than me, something she has hope in, and which is there with us in the solemn room. Perhaps because we've been lied to all our lives, a deep, philosophical belief in a greater power blossoms as we inch closer to death. Her eyes grow large as she lays down on her back shivering. She reminds me of a child, reluctant to sleep for fear of a never-ending nightmare that visits every night. Not knowing what to say, I hold her in an embrace.

"I must go now; I'll bring you food again tomorrow."

The next day, my morning tray is left outside the door. No special tinfoil-wrapped goodies, no nuts or dates or flasks of milk. Ravenous, I pick the mold off the bread, plug my nose, chew, and swallow. This gives me some relief from the hunger pangs. Rowani's face flashes before me, such a strong woman, convinced she'd die. I hope I'm able to take food for her in the evening again.

The door creaks.

"Isidro, it's you! Where's Ben?"

Isidro shuts the door before responding. "He's in medical training."

"Medical training?"

"We are short on doctors; the Eunuchs will have to learn quickly how to deliver the babies expected in the next month." Isidro sighs.

So, there are a group of doctors, perhaps the doctor who helped Ester is still here. Hope bubbles up in me.

"Where did the doctors go?"

Isidro's gaze drops. "They shuffle them around from one Surrogacy Center to the other. They don't want any of them developing any empathy for the Surrogates, and some of the other doctors...well...they don't make it."

Don't make it. The words sound hollow and unpresumptuous. The doctor who examined me didn't strike me as someone who'd have an ounce of empathy. In fact, the comment he made when the dead baby and Surrogate was gurneyed past us was still emblazoned in my mind. His dismissal of her, the comment about the baby being unfit for MicroScrep, absolutely no regard for her cold blue hand and the dead baby lying so tragically on her chest.

"What do you mean—don't make it?"

Isidro's forehead creases, his eyes dart upward. He places a ball of tinfoil filled with something warm on my bed and stands a moment in silence.

"What do you think happens, Adriana?" he snaps. He shuts his mouth and takes a deep breath. "They kill them. They get rid of them if a Surrogate goes missing or if false information is inputted in Harmony. God! Don't you know already these people are ruthless!"

He runs a hand over his head, his shoulders slightly slumping. "I think they're after me," he whispers, his back still to me.

The realization that I am putting Isidro's life at risk hits me; my hands start to shake. I walk toward the bed and pick up the tinfoil ball which drops to the ground, I squat down and pick it up, feeling lightheaded. I hold the ball of tinfoil as his words wash over me. He stands with half an arm crossed and stroking the other arm for relief. His mind lost in anxiety. My longevity is on the line in this prison, but so is his.

"How do you know?"

"Last night after the meditation, I found that they'd been through my personal letters and pictures. I thought I had locked the door. Oh God! They'll see that I'm a traitor; they're just waiting for the right time to kill me."

I feel my face growing hot; it would be terribly unjust of me not to tell him. "Isidro, I have a confession to make. I was the one who went through your box of pictures and the letter. I'm so sorry about Ester." Isidro recoils as I say her name. My head turns down, avoiding his look. "It must be terrible to feel all you have for someone and to not know where they are. I've also felt this way too."

Isidro sighs as if he's a pressure cooker releasing his pent-up steam, and then he laughs, a nervous laugh. It unnerves me.

"So now you understand what I mean when I say they get rid of the doctors. The poor doctor who helped Ester, cut into a million pieces. It was a crude and grim sight I will never forget. Adriana, your revelation gives me hope that they aren't after me yet, but I know that they're after you and the Surrogate in room 111 and all the Surrogates in all the centers off-grid. You're only meaningless cattle for them, once they get what they want from you, you're discarded."

I feel a great relief that Isidro is not angry at my trespassing. I can feel it deep inside my bones. I can feel the pestering jitteriness of anxiety release its claws. I have a true friend now, one who I can confide in completely.

"What happened to Ester?"

Isidro startles when I say her name again, and the expression on his face goes from an air of righteousness to a deep melancholy.

He shrugs helplessly. "That's the question I'd give my life to answer, Adriana. But I don't think she made it. She probably died a horrible death off-grid, alone."

The way he looks at me, the utter devastation in his eyes, unnerves me. He might not help me because he's worried that I'll die off-grid and that he might be held accountable for my disappearance.

"I don't want this to happen to you, Adriana. I don't want you to leave for the unknown."

Suddenly Isidro is weeping, suppressing his sobs into hiccups and then torrents of tears. My hands pat his, and my lap becomes wet with his tears. I feel I am the only one who has allowed him to cry since Ester's death. It must have been awful to wait for her letters month after month, year after year, and receive nothing. What torture he must have gone through to not be able to mourn her openly, or to have no closure. I am struck by his emotion, and a tear trickles down my face. I'm cold suddenly.

There is a howling animal on the loose. It's a trumpet-like sound. A large female elephant with thick skin and wizened eyelids. Her lashes are long. She is older than I am; her eyes show it. Her skin is thicker than mine, a dusty, tired grey. She trumpets. Her legs are in shackles, but she kicks anyways, breaking the shackles. She's coming for me. I'm going to be trampled. No more MicroScrep. No more Surrogacy Center. No more Isidro. No more Zachary.

Waking up, I'm panicked, fevered, and cold. I blink my eyes a few times to make sure I'm here, not there with the elephant. A terrible howl fills the hallways, it echoes. The sound dissipates. Is the elephant here? The sense of pain still lingers. There it is again, a trumpet-like holler. No words, just echoing madness. Have I lost my sense? I am so tired: am I awake or asleep, or in the murky territory between?

Isidro barges into my room. His hands are bloody, they drip.

"I need a towel," he says breathlessly, looking left and right, like a lost animal.

"They're going to kill her." He doubles over, hands on knees. "There's nothing I can do to save her. The baby is stuck. I need the blasted towel! Where did I put it!"

I scurry out of my bed to the wardrobe where I've kept his towel since the last time he couldn't pick it up. Instinctively, I know he's talking about Rowani. I hear her yell, a trumpet call, a siren; "Save my baby" is what is meant by her cry. I throw the towel to Isidro. He catches it like a heroic sportsman, except his frail long-limbed body is one of an endurance athlete's. He runs back towards the screams. I close my eyes against the sound, wishing the elephant was back here with me.

It's quiet now. It's been this way for a few hours. No more blood-curdling screams. Isidro hasn't returned, Ben hasn't either. Instinctively, I know what's happened, but I don't want to bring it to my full consciousness. I try to breathe into my toes, like mother taught me to, to bring myself out of my head.

"Did you see the head on that baby?" Ben pushes the door open, smiling, walking lop-sided like a crazed man.

He brings his hands into a triangle-like posture above his head. He looks like a yoga instructor gone mad.

"Its head was pointy; she must have been deformed," he continues.

Isidro coughs a laugh, diplomatically. "That's the first birth you've witnessed, Benjamin. They usually come out like that."

Ben looks offended, then sneers. "She sure was a loud bitch, good riddance to her." There is silence. Isidro brings me my dinner tray. His eyes avoid mine.

I can't stay quiet. "Did she die?"

Ben scoffs. "Of course she did. That's what mostly happens, you know. They croak when they're pushing the MicroScrepian baby out. We're a tough bunch."

The word "croak" leaves a bitter taste in my mouth. I gather saliva wanting to spit at his unbearable presence, his disgraceful speech. He seems to have forgotten that Surrogates were once considered MicroScrepians.

Isidro paces around my bed, making sure I'm all right. "She did her duty to MicroScrep. May she live happily in Shamok knowing she has contributed her life for the future of MicroScrep."

"What is Shamok?"

Isidro smiles. "Where all good servants of MicroScrep go after dying. Every faithful Surrogate and every brave Eunuch goes there after death. A place of peacefulness, happiness, and limitlessness." He gives me my food tray, his smile still plastered to his face.

Knowing now that Rowani is dead makes me want to cry, but I must remain strong. I can't let them see my weakness, not Ben at least.

"Thank you for the tray; I'm not hungry this evening."

Isidro opens his mouth to object, but Ben interjects. "Suit yourself." He pulls the tray out of my hands. "Go hungry."

Isidro gives me a piercing glance and then looks down. Ben leaves through the door before Isidro does. I really am not that hungry, but the baby inside is.

Chapter 15:

Zach's Assignments

A distinct sadness and vacant energy surrounds me. Ben killed her. She wasn't only a scientist; she was a mother. I'm not at fault. He went a little crazy when we arrived back at the tank. Ben grabbed the emergency kit and a self-cauterization swab. The sound of the hissing sickened me as he burnt his own brow, where the scientist had spat at him. The whole ride home, he shouted at the Eunuch in the driver's seat to drive faster, so we could be tested for viruses when we arrived back to the Eunuch center. I watched in silence thinking whatever chemical he applied to burn a deep hole into his brow was enough to take care of any virus or bacteria. A nagging suspicion fills me, could it be possible that the scientists aren't diseased at all? Is this another example of propaganda and fear tactics used by MicroScrep?

Shortly after both of us were deemed free of disease, we were initiated as Wardens and assigned to a center: Ben to Surrogacy Center One, and me to Surrogacy Center

Two. We started our initiation with a chant; that's how we always begin. Then the pills were passed around and everything became psychedelic and giddy. No more feelings, except one-minded wonder. I didn't like that feeling. Even in the village, somewhere in my subconscious, I knew it was a trick on my mind. I knew it when Ben was killing them, that it was wrong. I wasn't as brainwashed as Ben was. I still had control over my subjective thoughts.

Something is thudding; my fingers find their way to my temples, it's the pulse of my forehead. My mouth and nasal passages are sore and sour. Ben sits in the front row of the tank. He has a backpack strapped on; his eyes are closed. It's pitch-black outside. All I can hear is the soft scraping of tree branches as we pass through the bumpy road. I close my eyes for a moment, the darkness is comforting.

Is this a sham? Am I really supposed to be feeling so vacant? Ben seems to have reached the pinnacle of his aspirations, no sense of doubt, guilt, or shame in his eyes, or actions. A vacant body, a brainwashed mind. The only thing that keeps me moving forward is the goal of seeing Adriana and running away with her to our freedom. It's pointless otherwise, all these experiences, all this suffering.

Suddenly the tank stops. The door opens and the driver compels me to get out. We've reached Surrogacy Center Two.

Despite the darkness, my eyes adjust to the outline of a dark cement building. I sling a backpack that's been given to me over the orange cloak I'm wearing. There is sage burning; I can smell it. The entrance opens to a wall.

I can go left or right. I choose to go right. A terrible smell envelops me. It's of blood and pus. Fresh footprints of blood mark the ground. The pattern is one full footprint to one half footprint. The person must have had a limp. I survey the rest of the scene and notice bloody handprints on the wall too. My mind suddenly flashes to the terrifying possibility that the Surrogates are treated like dogs. Whipped and subdued into complacency. If only I had a camera, I could document the blood-stained scene.

"The most rebellious end up here. The ones who survive their first Surrogacy and must deliver their second."

I turn around and glance up at Numen Eunuch. He has steel grey eyes. His nose is bulbous, and the veins are stringy with blue burst vessels. He smiles smugly and I see a large gap in his front teeth.

"What have they done?" My eyes lock momentarily to his.

"They've survived the first Surrogacy Center, which means they are strong. Only the strong stand up against MicroScrep. As such, they must be exterminated for the good of MicroScrep."

His eyes squint and look again at me. "Your heroism during the initiation shows your loyalty. You are very lucky to be in the place that you are. We must be vigilant; the scientists are growing stronger. They've infiltrated and planted seeds of hate into our Surrogate sisters. We are the enforcers of MicroScrep's will. We are the only hope of instilling a sense of respect into these wayward, selfish women."

I can feel my temperature rise at his words. My face feels like a hot air balloon; any more pressure and it'll fly up to the ceiling. The sight of Numen warden's bulbous nose creates a sense of disgust in me. I can tell he is a foul, tyrannical leader. Completely bent on squelching resistance and using authoritarianism to get his way.

We meet two orange-cloaked Wardens, and they bow low to Numen Eunuch and me. Numen asks them to help me to my room. We enter an elevator that takes us up to the sixth floor. The elevator is surrounded by clear glass. I can see the ground floor with its blood-stained floors and splatter handprints on the wall.

The first floor looks like a hospital with sectioned-off rooms. The third floor is a garden where vegetables and fruits are grown indoors. The fourth has rooms with basic wooden doors. It looks sterile, like a hotel would. The fifth floor is more opulent, with Wardens eating and chatting on fancy furniture, playing chess or cards, laughing and drinking coffee. The sixth-floor rings a lovely chiming sound as the door opens. Marble floors and picture frames that have built-in water that flows and recycles. There are leather sofas and large bamboo shoots that decorate the hall. We arrive at a hand-carved mahogany door at the end of the corridor. There is a distinct smell of rosewood being burned.

I swallow back tears as I enter, remembering Adriana's promise to find me. She'll never be able to find me here. The two Wardens leave me in the room and close the door. I walk towards an opulent white bed large enough for four people. The canopy and curtains surrounding it are velvet and silk. Plush pillows lie at the head of the bed in accent colors. The bed smells fresh and clean. I pull back the covers. It's the softest material I've ever felt. I lie down and place my tired head on the feather pillow.

I think back to the ground floor and the dainty footprints on the ground. It's not the Surrogates who live a lavish life, it's the Wardens. I feel conflicted inside; the urgency of sleep and the rage against what might have befallen Adriana tears at my heart. She'll never find me here, but I might find her. She may even be here. My face flushes with the heat of hope. My eyes open and close rhythmically, getting heavier moment by moment.

Chapter 16:

The Second Birth

The water in the bathtub is full of Epsom salts. Isidro is spoiling me today. Maybe this is his way of apologizing for the misgivings he had about my escape. Adamant that I stay put to deliver the baby, he has hidden the wheelchairs and put them under lock and key. Without a wheelchair, I won't make it past the explosives outside.

The Surrogates that have been here a few months longer than me whispered to me the other day that when they arrived, one Surrogate tried to run away, only to be blown into tiny pieces in the courtyard. It took the Eunuchs days to wash off the pieces of her hair stuck to the windows. Isidro knows about the explosives, and the doctor probably gave Ester the wheelchair for her to run away with. Isidro didn't even know she was escaping. Isidro tells me there are no more explosives past the wall dividing the Center from the forest.

Isidro avoids my stares. The water trickles down my back as he presses the sponge to the back on my head. My stomach is swollen, but the baby hasn't dropped yet. Time is of the essence, and I'm getting anxious and have lost all hope of Isidro helping me escape. Despite Isidro hiding the wheelchair, I am frustrated that I won't be able to run away with his help. He knows I'll die either way. Wouldn't it be right to let me die by my will and not his? In fairness, he must be terribly conflicted, with what happened to his Ester and now the death of Rowani in room 111.

Isidro coughs and clears his throat. "You'll be having Ophelia soon, think of her..."

Wanting to speak, but knowing whatever I say will be rejected by Isidro, I remain quiet. He probably thinks I am being selfish by wanting to escape. He thinks he's buying me time, but I am the one who wants to take the chance. I loosen my jaw and breathe a deep sigh.

"Is this what you would say to Ester if she were alive?"

"Yes, I would. She'd still be alive if it wasn't for her stubbornness. I could have been here with her, but she didn't trust fate. That's the exact problem you have."

"I don't believe in this fate, and they wouldn't have to lie about the standards and treatment of Surrogates if those who created and run MicroScrep believed in it."

Isidro holds up my towel and wraps it around me. He dries me off, and I put on my clothes.

"I'll find my own way to my room. Don't bother bringing me food."

As I walk to the door, Isidro raises his voice. "It's not about who is in the right or wrong, Adriana, it is about your safety."

Isidro's words ring in my ears until I am back in my room, my rage cut with pity for Isidro. He's obviously brainwashed, as are most of the other Eunuchs I've encountered. The difference is he's retained at least some of his former self. I wonder if that's Ester's doing. I wonder if Zach is the same, or if he's like the other Eunuchs now? Somehow, I know he isn't. He's too good to be influenced by their darkness.

I fall on my bed and stare at the ceiling. Then suddenly, a flashback hits me. Blood, a terrible dog, it's eating a human jaw. A derelict shed, a little girl mauled by the dog. Laura—Laura and a camera in the pool. She is flashing it at me. She's talking on the phone with a man. *"She's a freak. I doubt the drugs are working on her."* The little girl is dead, eaten by the dog. Laura did it. She wanted her to die. She's on the phone with a man. She calls him Daddy. *"I'll get rid of her...and the Kevin problem."* My head hurts, and the flashback ends when I find myself beside the hole for a toilet in my room. I've vomited. I remember now. Laura is behind this. I need to find Zach. I need to tell him. If they kill me here, nobody will know the terrible deeds she's done and what she's capable of.

I sit, panting beside the toilet. I retch again. I need to find Zach. I need to tell him. This isn't about me anymore, or us, it's about uncovering the injustices that are happening, the injustices that are perpetrated in the name of Harmony.

Ben, he is my only recourse! I need to act fast. Perhaps he isn't as brainwashed as he appears. He's a new Eunuch; he doesn't have years of indoctrination. Besides, I need to find Zach and tell him what happened in MicroScrep, what I now remember, what I now need to tell him. How can I persuade Ben? What might he want? He seems bent on power. Money and power are always intermingled. I'll persuade him with the little I have; the watch Isidro gave me. Could he know of Zach's whereabouts? I'm getting desperate, and I know Isidro won't help me.

The door creaks open to Ben's pasty face. He's holding a tray.

"Look what I have for you today, fish and coleslaw."

The fish smells rank. It might be the coleslaw though; it looks withered and slimy. The fish falls apart before my fork can touch it. It looks like a gelatin dish that has been in the heat too long.

"I'm actually not that hungry, I'll just keep this slice of bread for later."

Ben acknowledges this by taking the tray and placing it at the front door.

He stops at my wardrobe and turns on his good heel in one swoop: "I have a question for you," Ben says. "Did you get that watch from Isidro?" He points to the watch that I've put on the wardrobe. I must have left it there before my bath. My jaw tightens and jitters. What can I do? I can lie, say I brought it with me from MicroScrep, but nobody owns these watches in MicroScrep. He'll eventually find out; I am sure there are ways he can find out; they must have some sort of internal surveillance.

"Yes, he's been very kind." I'll just brush it off as a mistake. "He didn't mean for me to have it for long though." I shut my mouth, in disbelief and my pathetic attempt to cover up. Anxiety is getting the better of me.

Ben nods his head. He turns to leave, but before he can reach for the doorknob, I say, "Now that you've had your question, I have one for you."

Ben turns around slowly this time; his eyebrows are furrowed.

"Do you know of any Eunuchs named Zach?"

Ben's face brightens, becoming jovial, as if he's all of a sudden decided he likes me due to association.

"Yes, I do. He was in the Eunuch Center with me."

I'm so surprised, I don't hide the absolute joy in my face.

"Is he a family member?"

"Yes, sort of. So you know him. You know where he is?"

For the first time, I see Ben contemplate, long and hard before he responds, "Yes, I do." He taps the scab on his forehead and scoffs.

This is my chance. I can't waste this; he'll give me some news about Zach. I must do something. Standing up, I fall at Ben's feet. "You must help me find him. You simply must help me. Please I'll do whatever you want."

A half-smile on his face makes one eye quiver and strain.

He walks over to the wardrobe and pulls the watch off. "We'll start with you giving me the watch you have."

"You can have it, but please tell me where he is." Rowani's dead anyways. I won't need it to help her. Absolute desperation takes over as I imagine this might be my last chance to find Zach. Then guilt. I've told him too much about Isidro. My face gets hot with uneasiness.

"My questions first, then you'll have your turn at questioning me."

I nod my head in agreement, desperate to know where Zach is and feeling completely pathetic about blowing Isidro's cover.

He holds up the watch. "So now I know that Isidro has been generous to you. Has he been feeding you with extra portions?" Ben eyes me shrewdly. "You are looking quite healthy."

I can't go back and undo what I've told Ben so far. I feel a blunt pain in my chest. *I am so pathetic,* I think to myself as I nod my head again. My eyes tear up. I've lost all dignity and hope in myself.

"Speak!"

"Yes, he has."

"And have you spoken to him about Zach?"

"Yes."

"So, you want to know where he is so you can reunite with him?"

"Yes." I bite my lower lip, which is trembling under my teeth. I can't cry, but what can I do but cry? I've completely jeopardized Isidro through my pathetic desperation.

"I see. How sweet." He grits his teeth when he says sweet, pronouncing the "t" with almost a spit.

"Very well, I can see what's happened. Now you can ask your questions."

A sinking feeling numbs my gut, making me feel ethereal. My mind is blank, and I want Ben to leave this room, leave me to my sinking, sickened feeling.

"Do you have a question?" Ben's mouth is in a twisted pout.

"No, I don't."

I should've kept my mouth shut from the very beginning when Ben came in. I should have known it was a dance with the devil to even entertain that he'd help me, and, in the process, I've hurt the only person who's shown me kindness here. If anything happens to him, it will now be completely my fault.

"Good." He limps to the door. "Sweet dreams," he says, an ominous grin on his face as he closes it shut.

I wake up to the smell of blood and a weakening feeling in the pit of my stomach. Raising myself up in bed, I see a pool of red streaming in from under my door, collecting into shallow potholes on the cement floor. Biting my lips to stop from screaming, I pinch myself, trying to wake from the nightmare, but it is no use. The red mark on my thigh is a dark reminder that I'm living the nightmare that is the Surrogacy Center. I try to get out of bed, but I'm frozen, afraid to confront reality. I hear chanting outside; it sounds wild and unhinged, in a strange language I've heard before. The Wardens speak it when they are whispering to each other in the halls.

"Mar! Mar! Mar." The sound is like a soulless, guttural, hateful slogan. There is a loud banging sound as if someone is hitting a nail to the wall. The stream of blood keeps on flowing. The pools expand in size. My legs are too weak to carry me, so I crawl out of bed and to the door. My knees and hands are wet with blood.

I try to open the door, but someone has locked it. Fear takes over, I start banging on the door, hollering for someone to open it. My head is spinning, and the smell is making me nauseous. Ben opens it. His hands are up to his elbows in blood and his eyes are cold and savage. Behind him is a crowd, chanting loudly, chanting obnoxiously. They move as a wave towards the wall. I look up past them. A decapitated head is hanging on the wall. At first, I don't recognize it. The ears are pinned to the wall with large rusty nails, making them look as if they've been stretched. But as I study the face, I become sick with understanding and turn my head to retch and vomit into the pool on the floor.

Isidro.

Hideous screams envelop me; they are my own sharp voice, shrill and uncontrolled. Uncontrollably, the screams come with sharp pain and then a rush of water between my legs. Have I pissed myself? I scream again, falling on my tummy. I am slipping on the blood as Ben drags me through the halls, every limp jostling me. The crowd behind him is still chanting, tearing Isidro's body to a million little pieces.

The world is colored red. The walls, the doctor, my screams, all are shrouded with a hue of red. My hands are caked with it. The smell is pungent. I am immersed in the red blood of Isidro. My hands are dirty. This is my fault.

"Push!"

The doctor commands me to push again. He pulls and I push. Then a release. As if a champagne bottle has exploded. It's done. I hear the cries.

"It's a girl."

My hands stretch towards her. "Please, let me hold her!"

The doctor doesn't hear, or is he ignoring me?

"Give me Ophelia!" I am crying, screaming. "Ophelia is mine, give her to me!"

The doctor cuts the umbilical cord. He wraps her and hands her to Ben.

"Stop, give her to me. You, you wretched beast, I hate you! You killed him, you scoundrel. You killed Isidro!" I don't care what they do to me anymore. I want Ophelia in my arms, and I don't stop screaming until the doctor injects me in the arm. Suddenly my eyes are heavy, and my voice feels far away. The last thing I see before the darkness takes me is Isidro's head, nailed to the wall, the cry of my Ophelia in the distance.

It's been two and a half days since they took Ophelia from me. I am an empty vessel, empty at the core of my being, like a body devoid of a gut. I'm gutted—gutless, I laugh maniacally and then the milk pours down my body. It's so strange, the female body. At first it feels like a twitching at the nipples, and then the milk is released, squirting, looking for a mouth, and then it streams down my body and into a puddle of milk on my bed sheets. My body won't move; I know it is mourning with me. My eyes don't cry anymore, but the tears are in my body, flowing out in the form of undrunk milk.

Sleep is fitful. The agony of losing all those close to me and the realization of the complete conspiracy of MicroScrep weighs heavily on my heart. The flashbacks have come too late. I've recalled too late. Maybe they have defeated me. I hate them. I hate them all—Laura, Ben, the system, their damned medicine, their algorithms, their Harmony, their perverted ways. When sleep comes to relieve me, I wake up with a sense of hollowness. The voidness is comforting in a way. There are moments between tears and agony, where there is a sense of elation, as if there is a paradigm where all this doesn't matter, a dramatic pause, one that is so void that it engulfs the pain too. I cannot hold on to these moments because they escape inevitably, and the rollercoaster ride of agony becomes sharply more striking.

It was on the second and a half day after they robbed Ophelia from me that someone familiar is wheeled into my room. An excess of Surrogates have survived their first birth and are being sent to the second Surrogacy Center.

"Do I know you?" My voice is strange to my own ears, faraway like I am underwater.

She tilts her head, studying my face. "I remember, you met me in Dr. Marks and Dr. Beata's waiting room. I was waiting to see the psychiatrist, and you were getting your eggs extracted."

A rush of memories floods back to me. Laura, the photos, the doctor and the psychiatrist, and Louise in the waiting room, waiting to see the psychiatrist because she couldn't sleep.

"Did you know then the horror—" The tears slide, and I can't go on.

She shakes her head. I notice her arms are bruised, and she's lost considerable weight. "Perhaps they knew I'd find out. I wasn't so easily brainwashed, you know, I had a big mouth, and a curious mind. I think they kill off those that know deep down inside that something doesn't add up in MicroScrep, the ones who question; they get rid of us by sending us here to die."

Collecting myself, I choke out, "It can't be only women who question."

"Maybe that's what Eunuchs are for."

"I refuse to think of Ben as anything other than pure evil," I respond.

Louise brings her hand up to her chin. "But Isidro was a kind Eunuch. I can't make sense of it."

Louise is right, Isidro was a kind and loyal friend. Why would they have made him become a Eunuch? Perhaps I'll never know. Then I think of Zach; has he changed? I doubt it. He had a rock-solid character, just as Isidro did.

"I wish I knew what a terrible heartless world we were born into. I'd have taken my life long ago," Louise says, brushing her hair out of her face. I see a gash on her wrists. She notices me staring and says, "I tried to take my life, but Isidro stopped me. He's the only reason I was able to survive so far. But I haven't seen him. I wish I knew where he went."

My face flushes and I swallow back tears, hardly squeaking out, "Me too."

The door opens abruptly.

"Lucky ladies, you get to go to the second Surrogacy Center." Ben has a sneer on his face. My teeth clench, and I have the urge to burst towards him and rip him to shreds with my own hands. Louise looks terrified. Her breath becomes loud, as if she's starved for oxygen, or having an anxiety attack. Ben staggers quickly towards her and grabs her by the neck. He squeezes, and I can hear her gargling, gagged screams. It takes considerable will to stop myself from pouncing on him and ripping his hair out. He lets go of Louise.

"You still have one child left to deliver, and then you can say goodbye to your wretched life."

Louise rubs her throat and gasps back tears, but they cascade down her cheeks anyways. I wish I had been kinder to her in the waiting room in MicroScrep.

Chapter 17:

Zach and Nohdan

Numen Warden stands on a flower strewn stage. He reads a meditation by Arthur Mills, the founding father of MicroScrep, claiming Mills created the secret language that the Wardens learn after castration. In the Warden caste system, the higher your rank, the better you learn to speak their language. Today, I am one of the orange cloaks among a sea of them.

"Shamok soooo, Shamok sooo." The chanting is like successive waves that hit my ears, a buzz that carries me away, and I am lost deep in space and time.

The word for Surrogate in the Eunuch language is "Nohdan," which means brainless. Adriana is not brainless, perhaps a bit naive, but not brainless. I wonder if maybe the smartest and ablest women of MicroScrep are picked to be Surrogates, so that they can eliminate all rebelliousness. It wouldn't surprise me if Harmony chose them specifically to kill off.

My hope is that she was able to survive and might be

here. If she was able to survive her first pregnancy, and has not run away, then she is here, close to me. My heart palpitates with fear and hope mingled inextricably. Everything is so heavily guarded and monitored; I'm not sure how I'll find her even if she is here.

Numen Warden has assigned me to a Surrogate in room 434. I get into the elevator and watch as it descends to a subterranean dungeon, reeling against the smell of blood and pus as the elevator door opens. I hold onto the door, steadying myself before retching. Everything is damp and infested. Rats scurry on the ground, disappearing out of view when I flash a light at them.

"Don't knock, just enter," Numen says to me.

A young red-haired girl comes into view. She is sitting on a rock placed in the middle of the room. There is no bed. Just a pillow on the rock next to her and a dirty rug as warmth. The smell is blinding. Rat feces and mold intermingle in the corners of the room. My worries are confirmed, Surrogates are treated poorly; we've been lied to all our lives.

The girl is curled up in the fetal position, rocking back and forth. She looks insane. This environment *would* drive one to insanity. The shock of knowing that you'll die a horrible death, and that all the fanfare was part of the propaganda machine in MicroScrep. The girl's eyes are wild, wide open as if she can't believe the reality of her cell. Numen walks up to her and kicks her several times. She rolls like an empty tin can every time he does, unanimated, mechanical, letting him kick her as she rolls in automated self-defense.

"You kick her now!" Numan instructs me.

I walk up to her, close my eyes, and kick, one swing, a

deadened thud, and then she rolls as I kick her again. Inside I am sickened and angry with myself. I've violated what it means to be human. Why doesn't she scream? I want her to scream so that I can manhandle her to the doctor's office, safely away from Numen.

"Grab the filthy Nohdan and take her to the doctor's office. Let's see if she'll survive the next nine months."

Numen leaves the room. She's shaking, alone with me now. Her legs are curled up to her chest. She squints her eyes, waiting for me to kick her again. Something in me breaks. It is a physical snap, a deep fiber in my being that tugs and lets go in relief. My body has lost its pretense, and I slump down next to her and sob like a child. Legs curled up to my chest. I heave with emotion until no tears are left.

Her mouth is agape. She doesn't know what to believe: the man who just kicked her on command, or the broken-down spectacle beside her. The silence is palpable, and I hope she can see the deep regret that enshrines me.

"I don't want to be here. I don't want to do this to you."

She nods her head, eyes wide open, a distant animal-like vulnerability showing in them.

"I have to take you to the doctor. I don't want to force you, but we'll have to make it look that way."

She nods her head again, and her head tilts from one side to the other, as if she's viewing a queer science specimen. Several times her mouth opens to form words, but as if she's forgotten them, she closes her mouth and turns her head obliquely. "My name is Louise", she whispers almost unintelligibly.

The steel handcuffs are almost too large for her petite hands. They are shockingly pale and shaky. She has bruises around her wrists, a gash where she's presumably tried to take her own life.

"Struggle against me as we leave the room and until I get you into the doctor's office."

We both perform all the way down the hall, I push her into the elevator, she makes it look like a hard push by falling against the clear glass. I coax her out of the elevator, and she falls on the swampy floor, where the doctor is waiting to receive us.

His hands shake, they get more agitated when he's holding the syringe, so I offer.

"Yes, and if you wouldn't mind." He motions to Louise's outspread legs propped up on the table stirrups.

"You want to guide me? I don't know what I'm doing."

The screen blinks and flashes. "That's where the embryo is." The doctor grins cheerfully.

He touches Louise's knees.

"You did a good job. Hopefully you'll be okay to deliver in nine months."

Louise doesn't say anything. She lies down, probably relieved to have at least something other than a damp and infested stone floor to lie on.

The doctor's back is to us. He's humming a tune as he sorts through his medical equipment. Does he have no clue what conditions the Surrogates live in?

I help Louise off the table and she's folded over. Her stomach growls.

"Oh dear, you'd better feed that tummy. Baby's already hungry." The doctor's comment falls flat. He laughs whimsically to himself and clatters away, sorting through syringes.

I handcuff Louise when we're outside, taking on a stern persona, pushing her into the elevator again.

The food tray at her door has ants crawling over it. She sighs and pushes it away with her feet. When we're inside, I tell her I'll be back to give her some food packages that I'll hide in my orange cloak.

Louise stares blankly at me and resumes her fetal position on the ground. Before I leave, she says, barely loud enough for me to hear. "Will you also feed Adriana?"

Chapter 18:

Green Eyes

Pushing me against the wall, Ben snaps handcuffs on me, laughing as he bites my ear and I yelp out in pain. He's been transferred here to the second Surrogate Center, effectively promoted for uncovering Isidro.

The hallway is damper than the first Surrogacy Center had been, and my feet are full of sludge by the time I'm dragged to the elevator. The handcuffs get in the way as I try to break my fall, and my gums start to bleed. Then we're moving up from the bottom floor to the hospital level.

"Ah, here we are, the second new Eunuch today, and the second new Surrogate as well!" The doctor's furry white eyebrows frame his wild fretting eyes. "And your good name?"

Ben looks at me and I look at him. "I'm Ben."

"Oh, lovely name. Goodness deary, look at those feet, full of mud! I hope you weren't playing on the lawn out there. It's terribly wet, awfully rainy for this time of year."

If it weren't for my conscious decision to look neutral, my mouth would have dropped open. I haven't seen or "played" outside in over nine months. I must think hard and calculate what season we're in, let alone the fact that I'd be blown up if I did venture outside.

"Very well, let's get started. Put this gown on and just like the last time you were given a child, spread your legs out on the table and your feet on the stirrups." He slaps my knee with encouragement as Ben leaves the room.

The doctor turns his back towards me and starts whistling the happy birthday song. When I've gotten into position, the doctor turns and faces me. His hands shake terribly, and I'm afraid he might drop the vial that has the embryo in it. He inserts the embryo, hollering in happiness when there's a burst of color on the monitor and a speck of flashing light.

As I look at the flash of the light on the screen, I realize that nobody leaves here and survives. This center is far worse than the first. One is either plunged into insanity, like the doctor who has turned his back to me again, methodically putting all the empty vials in a row, taking a ruler to measure the distance between them; or they die. I'm broken down. There is no hope left. I must follow the rules. Look what happened to Isidro when he didn't follow them! They found out and killed him. It was my fault for naively entertaining the thought that Ben might help me, and look what happened: he's dead.

"Don't just sit there in thought, you idiot!" Ben grabs my arm and puts me in handcuffs. He strides out of the room, dragging me along with him until I am back in my room. He leaves, and suddenly, there's a great bang. It's enough to shake all of us deep, down in our subterranean dungeon. I hear some sort of commotion, but the cement walls insulate all sound. I don't know if it's coming from the other Surrogates, or if it's coming from the floors above us. Then the sirens start. There are no sirens in our subterranean hell, so it must be coming from above. I try the door, it's locked. They don't trust us, even though they heavily outnumber us, and even though the lawn outside the Surrogacy Center is riddled with explosives.

Ben flings open the door, and it hits my forehead with such force that I fall down about a meter back, bottom first.

"You idiot, why the hell are you near the door?" He suddenly realizes why. "Get up!" He grabs my wrists and twists them, teeth clenched, hate spewing from his tight lips. He wrangles me into a corner and puts the handcuffs on. There is smoke coming from the end of the hall, which is already crowded with handcuffed Surrogates, held like prisoners by the Warden Eunuchs. Some are visibly pregnant, dwindled down into twigs. Their arms and legs waif-like, save their bulging bellies. They are hunched over, unable to hold themselves up without help of a Warden. The smoke starts off as a white mist and then gains density as we slog along up the staircase.

The smoke is getting thicker, and the Wardens and the Surrogates begin to cough. I look up briefly and recognize Louise's profile as she turns a corner. I get a glimpse of the orange-cloaked Warden trailing behind her, and I almost freeze. It's Zach. I just know it is. Oh goodness, can it be him! I must act soon, before they turn a corner and can't see me. Thinking of what happened to Isidro, I know I can't say his name—it would implicate him—so I scream out, "Louise, it's me, Adriana!" A heavy blow hits the back of my head, and then everything goes black.

My eyes open to whiteness, a translucent fog of white, but it doesn't smell of smoke. I know I'm safe. I turn on my side and see a row of Surrogates sleeping on the ground, spaced out before me. The white light cascades from the window onto my row. I sit up and see about a dozen Surrogates, each lying on cardboard mats, approximately a meter away from each other. I get up and tiptoe through the maze of cardboard beds until I feel a hand reach out and grab my ankle.

"What are you doing?" a familiar voice speaks. I look down to see Louise's squinting eyes.

I fall to the ground and hug her. "Louise, it's you," I whisper.

She smiles warmly back. "Shh, the others are sleeping." She looks healthy for a Surrogate here. I'm certain Zachary is keeping her alive, just as Isidro kept us alive.

"Louise, I've got to see where we are; they've moved us. I'll bring news back."

Louise frowns. "Be careful, they're ruthless."

I tiptoe to the door, careful not to wake any of the other sleeping Surrogates. Turning the knob, the door unlocks. Outside I see a dimly lit painted hall and several doors. There's an institutional voidness to the hallway, a plain grey carpet cushions the ground. Looking left and right, I hear humming from a room that I pass. The doors are closed as I scurry farther down the corridor. In the distance is the faint sound of a conversation. As I approach it, I notice that it's in the Warden language. Tuning my ear against the wall, I hear a familiar voice. I cup my hand to my ear, trying to get clearer recognition. Biting down hard on my lower lip, I recognize the voice as Laura's. She's speaking the Warden language. I close my eyes. There is a flash, then a memory. Laura is speaking in a derelict shed. She's on a weird looking phone. She calls the man on the other end Daddy. She says, "Yes, it is safe to speak in English." Then it hits me like a whip. Her goal all along was to join her daddy off grid! She knew about how they treated Surrogates all along. She is a ruthless, power-hungry devil!

"No, that's not the way to pronounce it." She raises her voice. "The word for death is mar, the 'a' is a long 'a' not a short sound. Get it right, or get the hell out of this Surrogacy Center!"

Suddenly, I hear a door open, and I stand up straight as an arrow. My heart is ready to jump out of my throat. I turn around slowly and see Louise furiously waving me back. She disappears back inside the Surrogate room, and I rush towards it, my face hot and my head light.

Chapter 19:

Zach and Espionage

The fire took out the surveillance system. What a wonderful stroke of luck, or was it? Could it have been the work of a mole? There have been instances of divided loyalties, for example, Kevin in MicroScrep. Perhaps it wasn't a coincidence. I can roam the hallways of the surrogacy dungeon and try to find Adriana at night when everyone is asleep. I peep my head into the rooms that are unlocked. They are sleeping, but once a few nights ago, a Surrogate rolled over in her sleep and my heart just about leaped out of my chest. But it wasn't Adriana. I am risking a lot, but Adriana's days are numbered, so why shouldn't mine be? Tonight, I can't find her either.

Guilt hits me every time I lay my head on the pillow, my bed is so fluffy and clean. My eyes become droopy, and I fall into a deep sleep. I've seen what the Surrogates sleep on, or rather what they sleep in—an inch of sludge. Their heads are held above it by a pillow on top of a rock. How could I have been fooled all these years in MicroScrep, thinking that the Surrogates lived lavish lives? What is so repulsive about the Surrogates that makes the system try to extinguish them so ruthlessly? How could the truth of this be hidden so effectively for so many years? My eyes become droopy, and I fall into a deep sleep. These thoughts haunt me in twisted dreams and in moments of silence in between wakings.

I wake up to the sound of rustling, someone is trying to scrunch something under the door to the entrance of my room. Sitting up, I notice a white envelope slip under the door. Scampering to the door, I pick up the envelope. "Zachary" is written in a familiar rushed and choppy printing. Ripping open the top of the envelope, I unfold a letter:

Dear Zach,

Meet me in room 224 on the right wing of the Eunuch Wards. Come after midnight. Come tonight, time is of the essence.

Your friend,
Cody

A deep relief floods my senses that Cody is here. It's like a weight has been lifted from my shoulders. I won't have to find Adriana alone. But as I fold the letter carefully and place it in my pocket, the relief is cancelled by a nagging suspicion: what is Cody doing here, off-grid? He isn't a Eunuch, and he doesn't work for MicroScrep or Harmony, as far as I know. How is this possible?

In my mind scenes of our friendship flash before my eyes. Swimming in the compound pool, soccer games with Kevin, now dead because of his tampering with Harmony. My mind flashes back to Cody's wedding, my sister, Laura;

they were the best of matches. Harmony was continually praised by him for giving him Laura. My teeth grit against each other—giving Laura to him but taking away sweet Adriana from me. Is his loyalty to Laura greater than his loyalty to Adriana and to me?

Anger boils through my veins as my imagination paints him out to be a collaborator of Adriana's misery and a cog in the wheel of the system. Perhaps he is a teacher in MicroScrep in the daytime, and a collaborator with Laura and the off-grid system of repression at nighttime? But then another scenario emerges: what if he wants to help and has come to give me information about Adriana's whereabouts? There are two scenarios for why he is here: he is either with the system or against it.

Sitting in the twilight darkness, my curiosity grows. What could he possibly want with me? Our lives have diverged; he is happily waiting for a baby to complete his Perfect Family Match. He definitely has something to tell me. Could it be a warning? Or could it be an offer? If I don't meet him, I might regret it for the rest of my life.

I don't knock. I stride into the room and see Cody on the bed, a broken piece of our surveillance system on his lap. He places it next to him and comes to me with open arms. His face is contorted with concern. I can see he is the eye in the storm, and has come to take me with him.

"Sit. We don't have time." He places a hand on my back and walks me to the bed. His eyes fret, scanning the wall and then my face. "Adriana is here, and she's not going to make it unless you save her."

"I know she's here, Cody."

Cody sighs gratefully; his shoulders hunch down.

"But the question is why are you here?" I shift my

weight away from Cody, staring at him with cautious suspicion.

"Do you think Kevin didn't know that MicroScrep was after him for the last year of his life? He knew he couldn't leave you, his biological son, unprotected and vulnerable. And he knew about the off-grid Surrogacy and Eunuch Centers, but more importantly, he knew about the off-grid scientists—intimately."

My face is clammy, and I can hear my heartbeat thump in my ears while Cody continues, "I know them too, and I also know the evil that is MicroScrep, emboldened by the power of Harmony."

My voice cracks as I ask, "Are you telling me you're a mole for the off-grid scientists?"

Cody nods his head. "You have proof of it right here." He points to the short-circuited motherboard of the surveillance system beside him.

"I started the fire to delay the surveillance here." He holds my shoulders as if trying to entrust me with faith in him. "We don't have time. They might be following me, just as they followed Kevin."

I look frantically in his eyes. "What about Laura? How much does she know about you—about this?"

Cody shakes his head in disappointment. "She works for MicroScrep, and her allegiances are to them only. Do not trust her under any circumstances. She is too far gone to even give a thought to you as her brother. She knows nothing of my real intentions."

My breath quivers as I think back to the little girl in the compound, eaten by the stray dog. Adriana tried to warn me; I should have known then. Swallowing the lump in my throat, I nod my head.

"Adriana is in the other wing of the Surrogacy Center here, in room 299. I was able to find where she was before starting the fire. Before they can fix the surveillance system, you must find her and escape."

I've been searching in all the wrong places. She's here but in the opposite wing. How foolish of me to concentrate my energies on this one wing.

"How am I supposed to smuggle her out of here with the explosives in the courtyard?"

Cody picks up the motherboard, raising it suggestively. "Tomorrow evening, I'm going to short-circuit the explosives and the west gate. You'll have from eight to ten o'clock to find Adriana and escape into the off-grid forests from that gate. From there, walk northeast until you find the off-grid scientist village."

Placing an antiquated compass in my hand and folding my fingers over it, Cody says, "When you find the village, enter the gates with your hands raised above your heads in a gesture of surrender. Ask for the Elder. He's the leader of the scientists. He'll help you."

After all that has changed in the last year between us, we sit together side by side, and a draft of cool air envelops us. The silence in the room is palpable. There is a dull sense of sadness and loss in the room for all that MicroScrep has taken from us: a father I hardly knew, parents who lovingly believed I was going to be in a better place, and worst of all, Adriana. For Cody, it's taken Adriana as well, a loving and loyal sister. But, the road to redemption, which is sketched so carefully and diligently before us is within reach. I breathe in the cool air and put my arm around Cody's shoulders. I do not have to speak words of appreciation because I know he senses it in the depths of the silence between us.

Room 299 is at the end of the corridor, beside the fire escape. This will take me and Adriana directly down to the west gate exit. I'm not sure if this is a stroke of luck or if it is providential fate. These days, I'm starting to believe in an Almighty force. It may be a way of coping with the uncertainty of death, or of coming to peace with the forces of evil in MicroScrep; a benevolent, merciful energy strictly opposed to the mechanical, inhumane, unfeeling data collection depot that is Harmony.

I tiptoed down the hallway last night after speaking with Cody. I couldn't resist. I couldn't wait to see her. She opened the door and broke down into tears. We held each other with only the moon shining through the window and our tears streaming down our faces. Even the sludge that drenched my shoes was no hindrance to the joy I felt being with her after all these months. She was barefoot, her feet swollen, wrinkly, and white after weeks of walking around in the turbid water that soaked the Surrogate quarters. As she held me, she whispered that it was the best feeling in the world to be held by loving, familiar hands. She told me the secrets that she's been keeping in her heart. How they killed Isidro, how they had killed Rowani, the treatment of the Surrogate and her deformed child. The insane doctor and his oblivion. We wept tears of deep sorrow as she told me of Ben's ruthlessness, his want of power and control, his sociopathic need to deliver pain.

I told her of the surgery that left me mangled and scarred. The drugs that were given to the Eunuchs to confuse and brainwash them. My descent into near madness, almost believing the lies that were perpetuated about MicroScrep and the Surrogates, until the initiation with Ben at the scientist village, Ben's delight and bloodthirstiness at killing the mother and her child there. I told her about the sinister power-mongering of the leaders of MicroScrep, and Numen Eunuch.

We decided late into the night that I'd come to her room, and we'd escape down the staircase at eight p.m. I would hold her in my arms and carry her out of the gates of the Surrogacy Center, just in case Cody isn't able to short-circuit the explosives surrounding the Surrogacy Center. I share that Cody is a mole for the off-grid scientists. That he was loyal to her all along. That he couldn't help our situation in MicroScrep, and the best he could do was follow us off-grid, play the system, until he was in a position to help.

"Adriana, but a terrible thought intrudes in my mind every so often. What if Cody is setting us up? What if this is all a ploy to create permanent distance between us?"

"The odds are not in our favor, but I trust my brother" Adriana says.

As I hold Adriana in my embrace, I worry that those who work for MicroScrep won't give up without a fight. They want to uproot those who are defiant to the system of control that MicroScrep has so carefully perpetuated for generations.

Chapter 20:

Dissent

The sun shone particularly bright this morning. The small window in each of our rooms, framed with bars and crusted in rust, didn't stand in the way of the miraculous, halo-like light that cascaded onto the opaque muck beneath our feet.

Since the fire, the Eunuchs have been busy elsewhere, probably trying to find the cause of it, and bring the dissenters, whoever they found to be guilty, to a terrible end. Thus, we were free to whisper to each other in the halls, or even to entertain each other for a few hurried minutes at the door to our rooms. Every so often, a Warden footstep could be heard coming down the stairs, and we'd all grow silent and recede into our rooms.

But as we sloshed through the roily water to perform our daily walks, or use the facilities, there was an ever so tiny glimmer of lightness that comforted our swollen bodies. In some Surrogates, I observed a lightness in the eyes, shining like a child's hopeful glance.

"They say the fire was started by a dissident Warden as a protest against Numen Eunuch's increasing power," a Surrogate with large owl-like brown eyes says as she passes me.

"Curse Ben, I hope he had his just desserts in the fire; perhaps he's dead," another responds, rubbing the whip marks on her forearm that he inflicted on her a week ago.

"I wonder if there is a war raging between the two groups in MicroScrep?" says a heavily pregnant Surrogate.

"Oh dear, don't think too much. You wouldn't want to give birth with no access to data or technology," replies another.

"Don't be daft. We're all meant to be exterminated. Perhaps the lack of technology will help keep us alive for a little longer." The heavily pregnant Surrogate rubs her tummy. I notice the veins on her calves protrude like bluish-green worms.

We hear a Warden's distinctive boot-clad footsteps descend the stairs. Raising my arm above my head to alert everyone, the Surrogates make haste and find their rooms, or bow their heads in silence as they wade through the ankle-deep, turbid waters.

When he patrols the halls and then ascends the stairs again, we emerge like blooming sea anemones. Whispers start again, and the sobering light of the day shines resplendent on our faces. We do not squint, but soak in the sun like lotus flowers on tenuous muddy waters.

There is a sense of vastness that comes along with the slight freedom we have. My thoughts continually spin away in fantasy. Since seeing Zach alive last night, deep gratitude combined with moments of great anxiety weigh on my mind. I am preoccupied with remembrance, more contemplative than usual, and this is something that the other Surrogates notice.

"Hey, freaky-eyes, what are you so preoccupied with?" The heavily pregnant Surrogate with wormy veins ridicules just loud enough so a few others stop and chuckle.

A half-smile cracks my lips, the first time I've smiled in a long time. The feeling is numbing, as if my lips had been sitting in cement and now the smile comes to break the hardening sediment. I like the heavily pregnant Surrogate. There is something very innocent and motherly about her, but at the same time a childish curiosity that provokes a humor, even in this darkened underworld. I laugh along but hold my tongue. Without words to confirm their projections, I fall away into yet another mystery that keeps our little hopes alive.

I welcome the sound of the sirens as I sit with whatever I've been able to bundle in the waist of my pants and in my pockets. The doors open and all the Surrogates, except for me, move up the stairs into the holding pen on the first floor, their barefoot footsteps distinctly different from the Wardens, who have heavy steel-toe boots under their orange cloaks. The Surrogates are murmuring to each other above me, and I can hear the Wardens stomping through the halls of the upper floors. They are trying to figure out whether it's a real fire or if it is again a breach of security.

After several minutes of silence, I hear a set of boots bounding down the stairs. The door bursts open to

Zachary. It takes me a moment to register it. My breath momentarily stops. I bite the inside of my lip, afraid to blink, afraid he'll disappear if I do. Oh, it's Zachary, beautiful, sweet Zachary! He is wearing his orange cloak, a hump on his back where his backpack is. Panting, his brow slightly sweaty, he grabs my hand and takes me to the staircase. We ascend several flights of stairs and spiral through a few corridors until we reach a door that is flashing a red caution sign. He opens it and the cool evening air hits my face. For the first time in weeks, I'm breathing fresh air. He bends and whisks me in his arms, then runs with me in a lover's leap, across the courtyard and to the west gate. The iron-barred gate is open. The lock has malfunctioned because of the security breach. When he finally lets me down on the forest floor, I have to pinch myself to believe that I'm not dreaming. I choke back cries of relief, sinking to the ground and holding onto his legs.

"Get up, Adriana. Now's not the time!" He takes my hand, and I run head down behind him, gasping for air.

"Come on Adriana, just a kilometer more."

"I can't, my legs are giving in on me!"

We stop and he pulls me over his shoulder. I bounce around for a few moments before squeaking, "You're going to hurt the baby!"

Zach sets me down and looks at me sternly. I realize that it would probably be in my best interest to miscarry. We carry on for another two or three kilometers, sometimes I'm riding on his shoulder and sometimes I hold his hand, running and tripping over tree roots and camber.

The forest is getting dark; only a hint of light shines

through the canopy of trees above us. Zachary sets me down and gathers tree branches. He has several tent poles in his backpack and wraps me in his orange cloak. He works swiftly, and I drift off to sleep.

The next morning, I awake to an orange tent. The cloth of several cloaks is stitched together to create a dome over the tree branches that are nailed and fitted together. A stabbing pain knocks the air out of me. My stomach muscles tighten as I unwind the cloaks around me.

Zach sleeps in a fetal position near the entrance slit of the tent. I rub my hands together to warm them up and place them on my stomach where the spasm of pain is coming from. I get up quietly and tiptoe around Zach to the slit opening of the tent. The ground is dewy, and its coolness distracts me from the cramping pain in my abdomen. I find a tree stump and squat down, feeling my bowels release with a tinge of blood that trickles down onto the forest floor. A bubble-like feeling passes between my legs. I grasp at some moss and wipe myself before noticing a small sac of blood. I prod it with my finger and am just about turn it over when I hear the sound rustling in the distance. I crawl to a thick, overgrown tree stump and hide myself behind it.

The sound of the forest mulch being crushed under feet advances closer to me before a loud holler is heard in the distance and then the quickening sound of running disappears slowly. My fingers are tingling with fear as I gain composure of myself and climb the tree. It is my first time climbing a real tree. In MicroScrep we learn how to climb on self-sanitizing walls. The bark is uneven and rough, but oddly crumbles under pressure. From this vantage point, I see a group of Wardens, headed by Ben slashing through the thick forest. They are holding a gruesome body, slashed and bruised. Though squinting, I can't make out who it is. I can only recognize a light labored breathing escaping its mouth. Its identity is covered by dried blood and gashes that bleed fresh blood.

Looking around, I spot our tent and breathe a sigh of relief. It's in the opposite direction and is camouflaged with tree twigs, only bits of orange show through the brown. I scamper down the tree and run towards the tent.

"Zachary, get up! They're looking for us."

Zachary shoots up like an arrow and starts to quickly push our possessions into a backpack.

"Come on, help me!" He throws his backpack to me and runs outside to disassemble the twigs and branches he's pinned together to create a camouflage.

"Grab the cloaks," he whispers harshly through the cracks of the branches.

After a few minutes, he comes to the entrance. "Forget it, let's go. We don't have time. Which direction were they going?"

I rummage through the backpack and find the compass. "They were going south."

To this, Zachary lets out a deep sigh.

"Thank goodness. Did you recognize anybody?"

"Yes, Ben." My eyes tear up, and Zach stops and straightens his back at the mention of Ben.

"And...and there was a body, half alive, that they were carrying with them..." I pause by a tree to catch my breath and cannot stop the tears from flowing.

"Was it Cody?" A stoic look overcomes Zach's face.

I hadn't thought of that earlier. In the throes of panic and fear I had only seen a tortured body; I couldn't process that it might be my dear brother. The thought of it sickens me and I double over in pain... "I don't know who else it could be." Tears fall off my cheeks and onto the forest ground.

"He's leading them away from us."

⃠

Night falls again in the forest. We've been walking for hours, following the compass and the directions that Cody gave. Zach hasn't said a word in hours, his face has the same deadpan expression it did in the morning. His cheeks are hollow with dehydration, and his stare is vapid and open-eyed. He walks with an urgent hopelessness, slightly limping, like a wounded animal trying to find water in a vast wasteland.

"I can't go on, Zach. I need some water. You need some too."

With a distant, preoccupied glance, he nods his head and swings the backpack off his shoulder. His hands quiver as he holds the water canister out to me. The water tastes metallic and bitter, as if tinged with the tears of near-dead Surrogates, but it quenches my scaly and dry tongue. Zach places the lid on and brings his face to the ground, running his hand on the grass and licking his hardly wet palm.

"No, drink this." I push the canister to him.

"I don't want us to run out," he mumbles as I hold the canister up to his lips. He takes a few reluctant sips before setting it down and fastening the lid tight.

A howling sound brings us to attention. We scramble towards a tall tree in fear of being found, and Zach helps me up. I reach a strong branch and sit there, urging Zach up the tree. The sound of howling is closer, and I frantically look towards it. On the other side of the clearing is a muscular dog. It has a spiked collar tightly gripping its neck and is sniffing in our direction. I scream out subconsciously, and it races towards the tree.

"Quick, Zach, climb. Please!"

Zach throws up the backpack and I catch it. He tries to climb the tree with one hand, the other holding the water canister. The dog is fast approaching, and I yell out a warning. Taking a look behind him at the snarling dog a few meters away, Zach drops the canister and climbs up just in time. The dog scratches at the trunk and jumps towards us, his bark making me jump. I feel Zach's arms go around me; he's almost shaking as much as I am.

We watch the dog get distracted sniffing the water canister and there's something familiar about it. Before I can figure out why, Zach whispers, "Quiet, Adriana. The dog will lose interest in a while and leave."

My hands quiver with such fear that I lose control of my bladder, a yellow trickle of urine flows down the trunk like oil on canvas. The dog snarls at us, exposing his teeth. I notice blood on his jowls and wonder if he's already had his dinner.

"I feel like I've seen that dog before, but I can't remember when or where."

Zach holds me closer, bringing my head to his heart. His pulse is racing, and I can hear a few sobs escape his throat. What he says next brings me back to a foggy memory. "You told me about Laura giving a dog to a little girl in your compound who was later mauled and killed by it. I should have believed you. Instead, we took you to the hospital. The doctor gave you selective amnesia."

The scene is vivid now. The little girl, whose mauled remains were being chewed by the terrible dog scratching at the trunk below us. I must be strong; I must give Zach hope.

"Zach, it's going to leave, we just have to wait it out."

The dog scratches the trunk a few more times, pisses on it, and lays down.

"I can't get my head around why Laura would allow for this to happen to the little girl, to us, to me and you, her brother and her sister-in-law," Zach croaks out in exasperation.

"If that was Cody I saw last night, tortured so terribly, then I don't understand how Laura could allow for that to happen to her own husband. That's the question that bothers me so deeply," I say.

Zach shakes his head. "Her loyalty is to MicroScrep first; that's what Cody told me. Those are the kind of people who they want in the government."

I'm not sure how long we stay in the tree. I drift in and out of sleep. Zach holds me, eyes wild and wide open. At times, I'd hear him mumble words that made no apparent meaning, as if in a trance. When I'd look up at him, he'd stop.

"Are you speaking the Warden language?"

"Huh?" He snaps out of his imaginary thoughts with a shake of his head. "I need water."

As Zach manages to peel a small piece of bark and chew on it to satiate his thirst, I look down to the dog, awake and laying at the base of the tree.

"We have no choice but to kill it with our own hands," Zach says dully, spitting out the bark.

"What do you mean?" I look at Zach, shocked at his response.

Zach's eyes grow foggy, and his eyes open and close mechanically as if he's fighting off sleep.

"Zach, wake up!" I put my hands on his arms and tussle him.

"There's something in the bark, it's making me want to sl—"

His eyes roll back, and he slumps between the branch and the trunk. A few minutes later I hear his rhythmic snoring. I hold on to him, my eyes searching the surroundings. The dog has awoken and is scratching and barking at the trunk. My mouth is parched and my mind races. I need to stay calm until Zach wakes up. The dog's jowls are stretched into a sinister sneer, he notices my observation and barks in retaliation.

A half-hour or so passes. My arms are tired from keeping Zach propped up against the trunk. Suddenly, Zach's eyes open wide, and he sighs as if he's awoken from an eternity of sleep.

"I feel so fresh."

"That's nice to hear. I wish I could say the same."

Laughter breaks the tension of the last half-hour, and I can't help but chuckle along. The dog cocks his head up at us and barks loudly, jumping up against the trunk. He runs back a few meters and then sprints towards the tree, flinging himself as far up as he can.

"He needs some sleep, he's quite cranky," I say as my final laugh ebbs.

Zach's eyes grow wild with excitement. "That's it! You're a genius, Adriana. We'll bait him with the bark, and once he chews it, he'll fall asleep!"

Minutes later, Zach has managed to climb to a higher branch and snap a long twig. He comes back to where I am sitting.

"Here, hold this." He gives me the branch and starts to bite his nail down.

"Ouch." Blood emerges from his nail bed. "This will make sure that he bites this branch." He smears blood onto the end of the twig. "Now follow me down to that branch there, I reckon I can hold it down and have him bite it." He places the branch into his hands and motions with his head that I go first.

I carefully climb down while the dog is jumping, whipping around in circles, and then jumping again. I reach the branch and test it with an extended leg. It seems safe enough, and I sit down.

Zach slips down faster and puts one leg on the branch where I'm sitting and folds over. The dog jumps, but the branch isn't close enough.

Seeing Zach struggle to get the branch within reach, I say, "Give it to me, I think I can hang it down closer!"

I bend down and wave the twig at the dog. It sneers and barks, runs a few meters before returning, and jumps, cleanly stealing the twig from me. Immediately it starts to lick the caked blood and chew on the twig. A few moments later, he curls up into a ball and loses consciousness.

We both look at each other in amazement.

"Come on, Adriana. We don't have time."

We climb down the tree, my mind buzzing with relief. Zach picks up the canister and pours water down my throat and neck and then takes a victorious gulp himself. It doesn't even matter that it is hot and terribly metallic. He takes a knife out of his backpack.

“We’re going to have to kill it.” He looks imploringly into my eyes. “It will follow us and surely kill us if we don’t.”

He raises the knife high above its head and I look away just as he brings it down. There’s a blunt sound, and then I hear the spilling of blood. Zach wipes the blade on the grass and takes my hand as we descend deeper into the forest.

Chapter 21:

Torn

It's hard to see the sky through the trees. Zach is quiet in the darkness. We both twitch at the hoots and cries of nocturnal animals. Grass and brush rustle with our footsteps, and our breathing swiftens, surrounded by reflective darting pupils dispersed between the tree trunks and in the branches.

"I think we should stop and sleep in a tree. I have a terrible feeling that we're too vulnerable on the forest floor."

Holding his hand, I squeeze it, too depleted to use words.

He climbs up the tree first and sits on a thick branch halfway up the tree.

"We'll take turns to sleep. You sleep first and I'll stand guard and hold you tightly, so that you don't fall."

Once I settle into him, he pulls out a flashlight and searches our surroundings. The brush is heavy and the leaves are a fibrous dark green. It feels safer up here enveloped by the darkness and the fingers and skin of trees.

Worried about Zach's ability to stay awake, my sleep is fitful. This might cause both of us to meet an unfriendly forest floor and risk injury on the giant roots that burst from the hardened earth.

"It's your turn, Zach, I'm rested enough."

He hands me the flashlight. It flickers a few times before going dark.

"Shoot, it's not working anymore." I flick the switch several times before I give up and throw the flashlight onto the forest floor.

"It was going to happen sooner or later," Zach says before he holds me around my waist. "I think we're close to the scientist village."

He tilts his head and places it against mine. I'm not sure if he's trying to be positive or if he's just so steeped in denial that he has become careless.

"I'm so tired; I just need to sleep for a few hours. Are you going to be able to hold me that long?"

"Of course I will, Zach."

He yawns and before long is snoring softly against me.

It's just before dawn and my eyes are getting heavy, the impermeable darkness fighting my resistance to sleep, when I see a flare and smoke rise several hundred meters away from us.

"Zach, wake up. I see something in the distance!" Zach jumps from his sleep and inspects the horizon.

"It looks like someone has set up camp." After a moment of silence, he says, "I'll go see what it is."

Grabbing onto his arm, I say, "No, you can't leave me. You promised we'd be together."

He sighs and remains silent as I insist.

"All right."

We descend the tree, and our feet hit the dewy forest floor below.

"We need to stay as quiet as possible." He holds my hand in his as we gingerly walk towards the camp. As we get closer, Zach gets onto the forest floor and moves like a snake, using his elbow and hips to weave in and out. He urges me to do the same. He stops at the trunk of a thick and well-shaded tree.

"We can see the camp well from that vantage point." He points to a branch above us, covered well with leaves and other branches. Following him up the tree, we end up on the strong branch, and he peers ahead as I put my head against his shoulder. The sun has risen enough for us to see more than the forms and figures of the group in the clearing. The same group of Wardens stand in the center of the clearing, huddled around a body. But instead of Ben, Laura is there. She is leading this whole gang against us. I always knew she was cruel, but how can she be so heartless? She's trying to destroy her own brother. How could she be so calculating? She is closer to Numen Warden than I thought, otherwise someone else would be leading this group. Suddenly Ben stumbles out of the opposite side of the forest. He looks like a sickened dog, barking unintelligibly. The Wardens part to give him room, and I see the same purple and bruised victim lying on the ground. As I focus better, I see pus oozing from several wounds on his body. Like a battering ram, Ben shuffles towards the body and kicks it in the head.

"The bloody bastard lied to us," he shouts at the top of his lungs. "The dog's been killed!" He looks at Laura with maniacal rage.

She walks circles around the body and spits on it. "What a waste of the months I lived with this filth!"

Blood rushes to my head in a mixture of rage and horror. The body on the ground is Cody. A flashback hits me. Laura in the shed, speaking on the phone to daddy, "Father, I don't want this match. I don't want to be with him. I can't stand the guy." Laura couldn't stand Cody. That's who she was talking about in the shed. She hated him all along. My dear brother, thrown to the wolves of MicroScrep. I hate everything MicroScrep stands for as I watch Cody protect us to his horrific death. Hate bubbles up and fills my jaws as I tremble. I hate every single compliant MicroScrepian tool in that circle. It takes deep resolve not to rush forth and rip Laura to pieces with my own hands. I look at Zach's face, a deep shade of red, his fists clenched.

"Let's leave him for dead. A wild beast will surely eat him," Laura taunts as she kicks Cody in the ribs. "He's slowing us down anyway." She points at Ben and two other orange-cloaked Wardens. "You three go south."

Laura grabs the shoulders of the two Wardens on either side of her. "We'll go north." She points at four others. "You two to the east and to the west." Her eyes bulge when no one moves, and she shouts, "Come on! No time to waste! We'll find the bastards and get rid of them once and for all."

Zach turns to me and whispers, "Look, she's wearing the amulet, the real one!"

My eyes search Zach's. He can see me wincing from the rage that has built in my bloodstream.

"We'll get that amulet and once we do, we'll destroy Harmony once and for all. We'll topple down the system that's repressed us for generations. I won't stop until I have it."

"Listen, Adriana, we'll need to get to the scientist village for the time being. There we'll be safe."

"I'm tired of hiding. I want to pursue and confront her to get the amulet." My voice breaks with indignation.

"We can't. There are two others with her, they outnumber us. For now, we have to survive; we're the only hope of the Surrogates, let alone MicroScrep."

With that, he urges me to climb down, and we crawl through the forest, following the compass needle a few meters until I grab onto Zach's foot. "Wait, we can't leave Cody behind!"

Zach stops crawling forward and sighs. "What if one of them is standing guard away from sight?"

I crawl closer to Zach, almost face to face, and whisper, "He's saved both our lives. We owe it to him."

Zach stands up, his clenched fists to his side. He's speaking to himself, working himself up. "I'm going to run and get him. You wait here." Without waiting for a response, he sprints into the clearing. The sounds of hooting cries overhead make me huddle at the base of the trunk. The sound passes and I'm left with the creeping worms that weave in and out of the brush. My heart starts racing, and I'm up in a moment and run towards Zach.

I arrive to see Zach holding Cody close to his chest and weeping bitterly. Cody's lacerated and bruised face turns towards me. His face is so swollen that his two slits for eyes barely open. As he breathes, blood pumps out of clumps of meat that have been chewed of his limbs.

"Help me move him to the forest." Zach instructs me to hold his arms.

We drag Cody's body to the forest amid his grunts of pain and the continuing cries from the birds overhead until we are under a well-shaded tree. Zach slings the backpack off his back and brings the water canister to Cody's blue lips. Cody shakes his head no and grunts. His breathing is fitful and he's shaking, his face taking on a plastic white hue.

"Come on, Cody, take some water!" Zach brings the canister again to his lips and pours out some water that soaks his cheeks and neck. Cody's eyes close and he shakes violently. He moves his hand to his pocket but doesn't have the power to take whatever he wants out of it.

"I think he wants us to check his pocket, Adriana."

My hand touches his blood-soaked pocket while Cody grunts. My fingers touch a ridged oblong ball. I pull it out and stare for a few minutes at it.

"It's a tiny grenade!" Zach exclaims. "He's giving us his last weapon."

Cody smiles broadly and then hiccups with pain before closing his eyes.

"Cody, fight! We're going to find the scientists. They'll help you, please!" Zach's eyes will Cody to go on. Cody sighs and he flutters his eyelids. His mouth opens, but no words come out.

"Don't leave us, Cody. Please, please don't go," I beg him, smoothing the hair off his face, wiping the tears from his eyes, until I realize my own tears are falling on his. He opens his eyes and chokes, "Go...go without me...I'll...slow you down...fight...a winning fight." His eyes roll back into his head. His shaking stops. Zach and I are silent for several minutes, in utter disbelief at the cruelty he's had to endure.

Zach moves to touch his brow, his lips quiver and tears stream successively down his face and onto Cody, and then he sweeps his eyelids closed with one decisive motion. The darkness lifts with the dawn and with that I see a patch of wildflowers a few meters away. I stand up and walk over to them, picking them carefully from the soil, roots intact. I lay down the flowers one by one onto Cody's chest as Zach bows his head in silence punctuated by sobs.

Chapter 22:

Zach's Destiny

We traipse through the thicket for several miles before finding a small pond. I dip my fingers in the water, raise it above my mouth, and let a drop fall into my parched mouth.

"It's freshwater, Adriana, but you drink what's in the canister. Time will tell if it's tinged with something else." I've become paranoid that Laura and the Wardens have laced the water with something sinister, so I won't let Adriana drink it for another few hours.

She's depleted, seeing Cody in such a terrible state has worn on her. I can see it in her walking. She's hunched over, like an old woman. Her face has lost its youthful glow and is tinted a greyish green. Under her eyes are sunken and the greyish hue takes on a darker tone.

Finally, a footpath becomes clear in the forest. The rocks have been pounded by feet, and the roots of trees have become exposed.

Looking at my compass I murmur, "Let's follow this.

It's pointing in the correct direction." We walk for a mile or so, and the path becomes more foot-worn as we advance.

"Does it look like someone has used it recently?" Adriana asks in a hushed whisper.

"I can't tell." Inside I'm hoping that she doesn't mean Laura and the Wardens.

Adriana stops and rests against a tree, bending over to remove her shoe and shake the dust and rocks out.

"You stay here. I'm just going to go off the path and see if I can spot something. Just climb the tree, so you can see where I am."

Adriana doesn't respond. Her limbs look frail and jelly-like as she climbs the tree and perches herself on a branch. She waves her hand at me, and I turn and run off into the woods. The green gets thicker, and the tree trunks and branches become more wizened and solid. Dispersed through the tree trunks are bougainvillea bushes; sharp thorny branches scratch my arms and ankles. Someone must have planted them here, and it must have been the scientists. I haven't seen bougainvillea anywhere off-grid yet. I decide to turn around and make my way back to where Adriana is, but I hear some footsteps close by and hide myself behind a thick bougainvillea bush. Thorns scratch at my head and body, but I endure them quietly as I notice a large gangly-limbed Warden walking with Laura in the opposite direction to where I sit.

"Numen Warden promised me that any Warden that brings back the Surrogate and that traitor's head will be given three hundred scrobles."

They are soon too far for me to hear them. They plod slowly down the path, becoming smaller and smaller until they're specks in the distance. All of a sudden, a cold, searing thought strikes: what if they find Adriana? I must get back to her as soon as possible. I peer left and right and then scurry off into the direction of the tree where I left Adriana. I meet her as she's descending the tree trunk, her face white and bloodless.

"Oh, thank goodness you're back! Laura and a Warden were walking over there. Quick." Her voice is desperate. "We must get to the scientist village before they do. It isn't too far. I spotted it past this bougainvillea. We'll have to scrape through. If we get near the village, they won't follow us inside. They're too afraid of their diseases."

The urgency in her voice reminds me of the time in MicroScrep when she discovered that Laura had been flashing pictures of her. I didn't listen to her then. I am not playing with fire twice.

She takes the lead, using the backpack as a shield against the bougainvillea. The thorns catch on our clothes, arms, and ankles, a reminder of the enormity of what we are fighting.

After a few hundred meters, we finally emerge from the forest to a familiar wall.

I stop, almost unable to believe my eyes, and Adriana turns to me. "We've made it; we've found the village," I say, hugging her close. Tears flow freely down my face in relief. I can't believe that we've succeeded.

Adriana is bursting with happiness as she covers me in kisses. She grabs my hand and looks at me, a radiant smile on her face. And suddenly we're sprinting hand in hand toward the gate. They won't hurt us, or give us their diseases. They'll help us. We'll fight alongside them. If Adriana can trust them so can I. The world is a blur of green clearing, blue sky, and brown fortress wall. The wind hisses past our ears, and I can hear Adriana's rhythmic breathing, until it all stops, and we are tumbling to the ground.

When I finally stop rolling, I look across from me at Adriana, her face grimacing in pain. Sticking out of her shoulder is an arrow. The circle of blood on her t-shirt gradually becomes bigger. Behind her is Laura and an ugly ogre-like Warden.

Gritting my teeth together, I jump to my feet and run at the enemy, jumping clear of Adriana and ramming head-first into the oversize-headed Warden's stomach. My hands and fingernails are tearing at his terrible bald head as he pushes me to the ground. Making a war-like cry, Adriana tumbles on the ground beside me, her hands pulling at Laura's hair, while Laura has Adriana in a chokehold.

"I am finally reunited with my father off-grid, but your curious, little mind had to get in the way." Laura's eyes are stone-cold, defiant as ever. I leave the Warden and tackle Laura from the side.

"You disloyal swine! I am disgraced to be your sister," Laura sneers through her teeth, jumping up and attacking me. Holding onto my arms, she pushes me to the ground and bites my shoulder. I yowl in pain, but she doesn't distract me with her hateful words. "You fool. You really think love is real, don't you? How pathetic!" I grab onto her amulet and rip it off, flinging it to the ground and hoping that Adriana is near to pick it up. Our fight will not be in vain. We'll be able to change Harmony for the good of all MicroScrepians. Laura screeches, letting me go so she can crawl towards it. But before she can reach it, the

Warden snatches it off the ground.

"It's mine now!" the Warden bellows before storming off towards the bougainvillea forest. Kicking her feet free of me, Laura stands and runs after the Warden. I look frantically to Adriana, my mind warring between not wanting to leave her and wanting to go after the amulet. Adriana hollers, "Get the amulet. Whatever you do, get it!" I take off immediately as she trails behind me, favoring her shoulder with her hand and limping with pain.

Catching up to the Warden, Laura jumps on his back and knocks him down with a loud thud. He holds fast to the amulet, even when she starts choking the ugly ogre, screaming words in the Warden language, spitting on his face. "When I return to Numen Warden, I'll see to it that you're killed just like Cody was." Her arms constrict tighter as he gasps for air.

I look to see Adriana approach, slowing down to catch her breath. The Warden's struggles become less animated, his gasps wheezing until there is no breath left in him. Suddenly, Adriana's face twists, and with a burst, she sprints and hits Laura, both tumbling to the ground. Running forward, I claim the amulet from the Warden's lifeless fist.

"Run!" Adriana screams at me. "To the gate. It's open!" she says before Laura smacks her to the ground. They tumble and roll. Laura's face is red with blood, as she spews out her insane hate for us. "Moles—terrible, disloyal blasphemers! Damn those imposter scientists that wait for you! Just wait until I have you two. What a horrific death I have planned!"

Gathering all the will I have, I turn to the gate and run as fast as my feet can carry me. The gate is open, and there's a congregation of people urging me towards them.

I stop and look back, not wanting to leave Adriana behind. Laura is running towards me, Adriana just behind her. The world becomes blurry, and the words "Don't leave her" are reverberating from me. I don't know if they are my own consciousness or whether they are the words of the scientists urging me on. Laura's face is sickeningly triumphant as I near her. Dodging her, I grab Adriana's outstretched hand, and we run towards the bougainvillea forest away from her and the crowd.

"Give me your grenade, Adriana." With an open palm, we exchange amulet for the grenade. I rip the pin out.

"You want the amulet, Laura?" She's sprinting towards us.

"Here, catch!" I throw the grenade, and we turn and duck behind the large ogre on the ground, hearing only the harsh crashing and falling of shrapnel around us.

When the dust clears, Laura's dismembered body lays strewn across the clearing. There is a faint applause that grows louder and louder as the scientists approach us.

Chapter 23:

Zach's Promise

Adriana is met with cheers and tears of jubilance; she is scooped up by the scientists and moments later is crowd-surfing on their shoulders to the middle of the village. I trail behind, my heart full for Adriana's instant popularity. They place her back on the ground, and she looks behind at me, smiling. She walks against the crowd, extending her arms out to me. There is a loud honk of a conch as she hugs me, and the crowd disperses into a circle around us. An old, grey bearded man walks to the center of the circle, a severe look furrowing his already wizened face. He snaps his fingers and four large men pull Adriana and me apart. One confiscates my backpack as the other two restrain me with handcuffs.

"He's a Eunuch", the man who takes my backpack says as he pulls out the jar containing my severed manhood.

"I'll bet he'll need that if he plans to hug her any closer", a ginger bearded, barrel-chested man to my right says. The crowd laughs at my utter mortification as the

Elder silences them. Adriana crumples to the ground and weeps.

"Hush!" the old man says. "Dear girl, what do you want from this Eunuch? He's responsible for one of our scientist's deaths."

Adriana looks up to me. Confusion and worry shroud her face.

My heart pounds loudly in my ears. I must say something, "I didn't kill the scientists, Ben did it—I, I was complicit in it because I wanted to find Adriana. I, I, love her, and in MicroScrep we wouldn't have been able to love."

There are oohs and aahs from the crowd. Tears stream down Adriana's face.

"Please—don't hurt him." Adriana's mouth contorts into a frown as she pleads.

Just then I hear a holler in the distance. A thin, emaciated man runs towards the circle, waving what looks like a letter in his hand.

"Anthony!" The old man bellows. "What did you find on your mission?"

He enters the circle, bends over, holding onto his knees as he catches his breath. "This is Kevin Mills's biological son." He points to me.

The crowd breaks out into a frenzy of chatter.

"What? But he has blood on his hands!" the old man booms.

The murmurs of the crowd grow progressively louder as if they are a colony of bees who have had their nest turned over. Anthony tilts his head back and forth as if weighing this new information. "But, with all due respect, dear Elder—he's destined to be our next messenger."

I shoot a look to Adriana. I wasn't expecting to hear I had any other destiny than being paired with her.

"I love him. I know he'd never do anything evil." Adriana says, as if what she says holds any weight whatsoever.

A restless murmur of sounds come from the crowd as if they are deliberating over my innocence or guilt. The Elder sighs deeply and winces his eyes. "Silence!" he booms, and instantly, there is such silence that I can hear the wind whistle through tree branches in the distance.

Pulling his beard, the Elder speaks. "I have a proposition for you. We can have her marry you, and then fix your severed part, if you promise to fulfil your destiny as our next messenger."

A baffling silence is broken by Anthony's clapping. Then the cacophony of claps envelops me like a great wave. Adriana looks towards me, her eyes flashing sympathetic and hopeful at the same time.

The events of the day pass before me like a disjointed nightmare. Cody's hacked body, the fear of illness, Adriana narrowly escaping death, the grenade, the moment the dust settled, the humiliation of my severed manhood on display for all these strangers to see. But I want Adriana more than anything; I long for her to be mine. I want to be able to consummate our love, now I know it isn't wrong anymore. I look around at the faces in the crowd, some anticipating, some amused at my perplexity, the Elder pulling the straggly bits of his grey beard, Anthony still breathless from his sprint. I then look at Adriana, her unique eyes, two different colors, always, always promising me happiness and fulfillment. I must take this opportunity; she'd want me to.

"I'll be whatever you want me to be!" I proclaim loudly before Adriana runs towards me and holds me closer than she ever has before.

Chapter 24:

Family

"Now, remember Zachary, your promise to us—to be our next messenger?"

"Yes."

"Just making sure before the vows are said." The Elder pulls at his beard, sizing me up.

"Very well, do you, Zachary, take Adriana to be your lawfully wedded wife?"

Zachary is wearing an emerald bow tie the same color as his eyes. As he answers, his eyes sparkle in the natural light that spills into the hall.

The Elder asks me the same, but I barely hear him. Taking a deep breath in and squinting away the sudden mist in my eyes I whisper, "I do." I can barely believe that we are here. That this is happening.

Claps rise and reverberate loudly from the scientists who have given us a second chance. Two weeks ago, we didn't know of a place that would accept our love for each other, a place that wouldn't shame the possibility of consummating of our love, a place where we could choose each other. Everything about our lives has changed.

"You can now kiss your chosen bride." The Elder formalizes our union and joins us together in an embrace.

"We hope that you may consummate your love for one another once Zach is back from his journey," he whispers to us as he gathers us together. "Forget the dogma of MicroScrep; this is how nature intended for us to join together." He pulls away and smooths his long grey beard, his face pensive and serious.

The reception afterwards is informal. No one scans obsessively for microbes. No pills to feign love. No starch dry patriotic speeches. The music isn't the horrible, hypnotic, electronic drone of MicroScrepian music. Instead, a beautiful, little girl sings an angelic song of love. She is accompanied by a string instrument; I believe the one that is being played is called a harp. I look at her, captivated by the sound and the sad remembrance of the little girl in MicroScrep, killed by ruthless Laura. I resolve then and there to return to MicroScrep after Zach's journey and use the amulet to change Harmony for the better.

I walk down the carpet that has been unfurled for us. Villagers are dancing, swaying in time to the music in the square that has been made festive for our wedding. A white canopy has been raised at the village square, and the breeze is intoxicating as I take in the view around me: small children chasing each other and hiding under the large oak tables that the community have filled with juices, desserts, and hors d'œuvres. The wildflowers blowing in the distance, past the canopy. But still my heart hurts with anxiety. Zach's life is endangered again, but the consequences of his mission, if he succeeds, will be stupendous.

Zachary joins me and presses my hand firmly as if he knows that I am not fully joyous on what should be the happiest day of my life. We make our way around the tent, people striking up conversations as we go.

"Ah, a Warden becomes a sympathizer! Only the child of Kevin Mills could be known to do such a thing." Anthony winks, his curly red hair bouncing with the wind and the gap between his teeth prominent, as he places a hand on Zach's shoulder.

Anthony was informed of Zachary and me through Kevin the day before he was killed in MicroScrep. We've learned in the last two weeks that Kevin and Cody were moles in MicroScrep and had loyal Wardens and doctors off-grid who would help send mail to the off-grid scientists. Kevin knew he was in imminent danger. He knew that I'd be sent off as a Surrogate. He also prophesied that because of my strong will, I'd find a way out of the Surrogate Center. Telling by the algorithms in Harmony, he knew that Zachary was hopelessly in love with me. Love is such a strong force; that was why Arthur Mills wanted to eradicate it, so that his future progeny could rule with the help of the ultimate scapegoat, Harmony.

Zach responds to Anthony. "Yeah, and I'm not the only sympathizer."

"You don't think I know that?" Anthony quips before taking a sip of his beverage.

"You just wait, the sympathizers have already infiltrated the Warden caste; it's just a matter of time until we take down Numen Warden." Numen Warden, we learned, was Kevin's Perfect Family Father, Milton Mills, who abused Kevin throughout his childhood.

Zach nods his head approvingly. "I wish I knew who the sympathizers were. Definitely not Ben."

"Ah, you'll find out soon enough, Zach. But what are we talking about! It's your wedding. Time to enjoy."

As if on cue, the music takes an upbeat pace and Anthony pulls me and Zach by the hands. "Come on, I know that our destiny is great."

⃠

The evening carries on, and the moon rises high in the sky. Most of the families have bundled their children in blankets and have gone home to their humble huts.

Zach and I hold hands and walk side by side, barefoot on the grass. "I love you, Adriana."

Turning to him, I peer into his eyes, wet with tears, conflicted by the happiness of our union, but pained by the fear that he'll have to fight the powers that be soon.

"I love you too, Zach."

We walk quietly back to our hut, which has been decorated with garlands of flowers. I grasp the amulet around my neck before taking it off and placing it on the bedside table.

"I don't want this life to end, but I fear that if we don't use the amulet, the poor people of MicroScrep, the Surrogates, and Eunuchs will suffer needlessly."

Zach sits down on the bed, his eyebrows weaving together the way they do when he's sorting through his emotions. "I one hundred percent agree with you, Adriana." He pauses for a few moments. "I'll fight with everything in me to come back to you, and then together we'll end the tyranny in MicroScrep. Then we'll be able to have children. The Scientists have promised me that."

I agree, "I have nightmares of what the Surrogates must be enduring now."

And with nothing else to say, we embrace each other without shame or fear, filled only with our love and our hope for a new world. We'll fight the good fight to stop the tyranny in MicroScrep, but not today.

About Atmosphere Press

Atmosphere Press is an independent, full-service publisher for excellent books in all genres and for all audiences. Learn more about what we do at atmospherepress.com.

We encourage you to check out some of Atmosphere's latest releases, which are available at Amazon.com and via order from your local bookstore:

Twisted Silver Spoons, a novel by Karen M. Wicks

Queen of Crows, a novel by S.L. Wilton

The Summer Festival is Murder, a novel by Jill M. Lyon

The Past We Step Into, stories by Richard Scharine

The Museum of an Extinct Race, a novel by Jonathan Hale Rosen

Swimming with the Angels, a novel by Colin Kersey

Island of Dead Gods, a novel by Verena Mahlow

Cloakers, a novel by Alexandra Lapointe

Twins Daze, a novel by Jerry Petersen

Embargo on Hope, a novel by Justin Doyle

Abaddon Illusion, a novel by Lindsey Bakken

Blackland: A Utopian Novel, by Richard A. Jones

The Jesus Nut, a novel by John Prather

The Embers of Tradition, a novel by Chukwudum Okeke

Saints and Martyrs: A Novel, by Aaron Roe

When I Am Ashes, a novel by Amber Rose

About the Author

Boshra Rasti-Ghalati is an Iranian-Canadian expatriate, writer and educator. She currently lives in Qatar as a teacher.

She is the author of several published poems, "Connection in the City", a poem about the city of Surrey,

BC, Canada, as well as the author of "In the Chrysalis," a poem about the COVID-19 pandemic, published in *Together...Apart*, an anthology of creative works by HBKU Press. Her short stories have been published by Grattan Street Press, Literally Stories, and South Florida Poetry Journal.

Boshra draws inspiration from the teenage mind, one she may not have fully outgrown. She also is an avid runner who enjoys the self-torture of running in Qatar. She has other eclectic interests such as making vegan ice-cream.

She may or may not use a pen name in the future to prevent a life-long tendency that people have of butchering her name. She hopes to someday make her home somewhere that doesn't include burning up due to the consequences of global warming. You can find her works on her website: https://boshrawrites.com/